Praise for
THE SALMON OF DOUBT

"Fortunately . . . we get one last look at Adams's wonderfully mad universe."
—*San Francisco Chronicle*

"A bittersweet reminder of what the master could have contributed if only the ride had lasted a few light years longer."
—*Pittsburgh Tribune-Review*

"For devoted fans, this is more than a taste of lost pleasures: it's a rich, diverse feast, albeit a sadly final one."
—Scifi.com

"You are on the verge of entering the wise, provoking, benevolent, hilarious, and addictive world of Douglas Adams. Don't bolt it all whole—as with Douglas's beloved Japanese food, what seems light and easy to assimilate is subtler and more nutritious by far than it might at first appear."
—STEPHEN FRY, author of *The Liar* and *Making History: A Novel*

"The pieces here bounce with charm. . . . Fans will dig the paranormal but incomplete *The Salmon of Doubt* itself. . . . A beautiful sendoff, Douglas, wherever you are."
—*Kirkus Reviews*

"Contains items of rare originality . . . At times, reading Douglas Adams is like watching Isaac Asimov meet P. G. Wodehouse, a twentieth-century humorist Adams venerated. For me, his essay on 'Sunset at Blandings' is one of the special pleasures of this volume."
—London *Observer*

THE
SALMON
OF DOUBT

*Hitchhiking the Galaxy
One Last Time*

DOUGLAS ADAMS

BALLANTINE BOOKS · NEW YORK

The Salmon of Doubt is a work of fiction. Names, characters, places, and incidents are products of the author's imagination. Any resemblance to actual events, locales, or persons, living or dead, is entirely coincidental.

2005 Del Rey Books Mass Market Edition

Published in the United States by Del Rey Books, an imprint of The Random House Publishing Group, a division of Random House, Inc., New York.

Del Rey is a registered trademark and the Del Rey colophon is a trademark of Random House, Inc.

This edition published by arrangement with Harmony Books, a member of The Crown Publishing Group, a division of Random House, Inc.

Grateful acknowledgment is made to the following for permission to reprint previously published material: **American Atheist Press:** "Interview with Douglas Adams" *American Atheist*, vol. 40, no. 1(Winter 2001-2002). Reprinted by permission of the American Atheist Press. **Byron Press Visual Publications:** "Introduction" from *The Hitchhikers Guide to the Galaxy (Collected Edition)* DC Comics, volume 1 (May 1997). Reprinted by permission of Byron Press Visual Publications. **Daily Nexus:** "Interview with Daily Nexus" by Brendan Buhler, of the University of California Santa Barbara Daily Nexus, *Artsweek*, (April 5, 2001). Reprinted by permission of Daily Nexus. **Richard Dawkins:** "A Lament for Douglas Adams" by Richard Dawkins, *The Guardian* (May 14, 2001). Reprinted by permission of the author. **The Graham Chapman Estate:** "The Private Life of Genghis Khan" Based in part on an original sketch by Graham Chapman and written by Graham Chapman and Douglas Adams for the Graham Chapman Television Show, "Out of the Trees," 1975. Reprinted by permission of the Graham Chapman Estate. **Matt Newsome:** "Douglas Adams Interview" by Matt Newsome. Copyright © 1998, 2002 by Matt Newsome. Reprinted by permission of the author. **The Onion A.V. Club:** "Douglas Adams Interview" by Keith Phipps, from *The Onion A.V. Club* (January 1998). Reprinted by permission of The Onion A.V. Club. **Random House, Inc.:** Excerpts from the *Original Hitchiker Radio Scripts* by Douglas Adams. Copyright © 1995 by Serious Productions Ltd. Reprinted by permission of Harmony Books, a division of Random House, Inc. **Robson Books:** "Maggie and Trudie" from *Animal Passions* edited by Alan Coven. Reprinted by permission of Robson Books. **Virgin Net Limited:** "Interview with Virgin.net, Ltd." conducted by Claire Smith (September 22, 1999). Reprinted by permission of Virgin Net Limited. **Nicholas Wroe:** "The Biography of Douglas Adams" by Nicholas Wroe, *The Guardian* (June 3, 2000). Reprinted by permission of the author.

ISBN 0-345-45529-0

Printed in the United States of America

www.delreybooks.com

OPM 9 8 7 6 5 4 3 2

For Polly

An Introduction
to the Introduction
to the New Edition

This Introduction to the Introduction to the New Edition is a highly significant one in the history of Introductions. Its presence on these pages means that this book has achieved the World Record for the Number of Introductions in a Book of This Nature. With the addition of this Introduction to the Introduction to the New Edition, *The Salmon of Doubt* can now claim to have no less than three Introductions, one Prologue, and one Editor's Note. That is two Introductions more than Joseph Conrad's *Heart of Darkness* and one Introduction, one Prologue, and one Editor's Note more than *The Cambridge History of Medieval English Literature*. Even the *Oxford English Dictionary* can only boast one Preface, one Historical Introduction, one General Explanations, and a List of Abbreviations—that's two Introductions short of *The Salmon of Doubt*.

You are, without doubt, holding in your hands one of the best-introduced books in the English language. We hope you enjoy the Introduction to the New Edition that follows this Introduction to it and continue to read on even into the book itself.

—Terry Jones
FEBRUARY 2, 2003

Introduction to the New Edition

Hi! I hope you enjoyed that Introduction to this Introduction to the New Edition. I know that some of you may think it unimportant that Douglas's final volume should have the distinction of a World Record of this sort. But, as a friend, I often felt that Douglas was sadly shortchanged in the matter of Introductions. I could never pick up Charles Dickens's *Bleak House*, with its Note on Dickens by Angus Calder, its handsome twenty-three-page Introduction, its Note on the Text, and, finally, its Suggested Further Reading, without recalling sadly Douglas's *The Hitchhiker's Guide to the Galaxy*, which could boast neither Preface, Foreword, nor Introduction. It was the same with *The Restaurant at the End of the Universe*, *Life, the Universe and Everything*, and *Mostly Harmless*. It is true that *So Long, and Thanks for All the Fish* has a Prologue, but on inspection that turns out to be all part of the book and not an Introduction at all. Even *Dirk Gently's Holistic Detective Agency* aspires to only an Author's Note, and even that, I believe, Douglas had to write himself! Indeed the overall lack of Introductions has reduced the majority of Douglas's work to the level of such poorly introduced books as T. S. Eliot's *Collected Poems*, Iris Murdoch's *The Bell*, and *The Gospel According to St. Matthew*—none of which have any preamble of any kind whatsoever.

But with this handsome volume, I hope that Douglas's work

has finally achieved the full complement of Introductions that it deserves. Perhaps future editions might even boast a Foreword and a Foreword to the Foreword, so as to keep Douglas's wonderful writing to the forefront of properly prefaced literature.

Please enjoy this book and, when you have finished it, do not leave it on the train.

—Terry Jones
FEBRUARY 1, 2003

Editor's Note

I first met Douglas Adams in 1990. Newly appointed his editor at Harmony Books, I had flown to London in search of Douglas's long-overdue fifth Hitchhiker novel, *Mostly Harmless.* No sooner was I buzzed in the door to the Adams residence in Islington than a large, ebullient man bounded down the long staircase, greeted me warmly, and thrust a handful of pages at me. "See what you think of these," he said over his shoulder as he bounded back up the stairs. An hour later he was back, new pages in hand, eager to hear my opinion of the first batch. And so the afternoon passed, quiet stretches of reading alternating with more bounding, more conversation, and fresh pages. This, it turned out, was Douglas's favorite way of working.

In September 2001, four months after Douglas's tragic, unexpected death, I received a phone call from his agent, Ed Victor. A good friend had preserved the contents of Douglas's many beloved Macintosh computers; would I be interested in combing through the files to see if they contained the makings of a book? A few days later a package arrived, and, curiosity whetted, I tore it open.

My first thought was that Douglas's friend, Chris Ogle, had undertaken a Herculean task—which, as it turned out, he had. The CD-ROM onto which Douglas's writing had been collected contained 2,579 items, ranging from huge files that stored the complete text of Douglas's books to letters on behalf of "Save the Rhino," a favorite charity. Here, too, were fascinating glimpses into dozens of half-brewed ideas for books, films, and television programs, some as brief as a sentence or two, others running to half-a-dozen pages. Alongside these were drafts of speeches, pieces Douglas had written for his website, introductions to various books and events, and musings on subjects near to Douglas's heart: music, technology, science, endangered species, travel, and single-malt whisky (to name just a few). Finally, I found dozens of versions of the new novel Douglas had been wrestling with for the better part of the past decade. Sorting these out to arrive at the work-in-progress you'll find in the third section of this book would prove my greatest challenge, although that makes it sound difficult. It was not. As quickly as questions arose they seemed to answer themselves.

Conceived as a third Dirk Gently novel, Douglas's novel-in-progress began life as *A Spoon Too Short*, and was described as such in his files until August 1993. From this point forward, folders refer to the novel as *The Salmon of Doubt*, and fall into three categories. From oldest to most recent, they are: "The Old Salmon," "The Salmon of Doubt," and "LA/Rhino/Ranting Manor." Reading through these various versions, I decided that for the purposes of this book, Douglas would be best served if I stitched together the strongest material, regardless of when it was written, much as I might have proposed doing were he still alive. So from "The Old Salmon" I reinstated what is now the first chapter, on DaveLand. The following six chapters come intact from the second, and longest, continuous version, "The Salmon of Doubt." Then, with an eye to keeping the story line clear, I dropped in two of his three most recent chapters from "LA/Rhino/Ranting Manor" (which became Chapters Eight and Nine). For Chapter Ten I went back to the last chapter from

"The Salmon of Doubt," then concluded with the final chapter from Douglas's most recent work from "LA/Rhino/Ranting Manor." To give the reader a sense of what Douglas planned for the rest of the novel, I preceded all this with a fax from Douglas to his London editor, Sue Freestone, who worked closely with Douglas on his books from the very first.

Inspired by reading these various Adams treasures on the CD-ROM, I enlisted the invaluable aid of Douglas's personal assistant, Sophie Astin, to cast the net wider. Were there other jewels we might include in a book tribute to Douglas's life? As it turned out, during fallow periods between books or multimedia mega-projects, Douglas had written articles for newspapers and magazines. These, together with the text on the CD-ROM, provided the magnificent pool of writings that gave life to this book.

The next task was selection, which involved not the slightest shred of objectivity. Sophie Astin, Ed Victor, and Douglas's wife, Jane Belson, suggested their favorite bits, beyond which I simply chose pieces I liked best. When Douglas's friend and business partner Robbie Stamp suggested the book follow the structure of Douglas's website ("life, the universe, and everything"), it all fell into place. To my delight, the arc of the collected work took on the distinct trajectory of Douglas Adams's too brief, but remarkably rich, creative life.

My most recent visit with Douglas took place in California, our afternoon stroll along Santa Barbara's wintry beach punctuated by running races with his then six-year-old daughter, Polly. I had never seen Douglas so happy, and I had no inkling that this time together would be our last. Since Douglas died he has come to mind with astonishing frequency, which seems to be the experience of many who were close to him. His presence is still remarkably powerful nearly a year after his death, and I can't help thinking he had a hand in the amazing ease with which this book came together. I know he would have keenly wanted you to enjoy it, and I hope you will.

—Peter Guzzardi
Chapel Hill, North Carolina
FEBRUARY 12, 2002

Contents

Prologue

Nicholas Wroe, in *The Guardian*
SATURDAY, JUNE 3, 2000

IN 1979, SOON AFTER *The Hitchhiker's Guide to the Galaxy* was published, Douglas Adams was invited to sign copies at a small science-fiction bookshop in Soho. As he drove there, some sort of demonstration slowed his progress. "There was a traffic jam and crowds of people were everywhere," he recalls. It wasn't until he had pushed his way inside that Adams realised the crowds were there for him. Next day his publisher called to say he was number one in the London Sunday *Times* best-seller list and his life changed forever. "It was like being helicoptered to the top of Mount Everest," he says, "or having an orgasm without the foreplay."

Hitchhiker had already been a cult radio show, and was made in both television and stage versions. It expanded into four more books that sold over 14 million copies worldwide. There were records and computer games and now, after twenty years of Hollywood prevarication, it is as close as it's ever been to becoming a movie.

The story itself begins on earth with mild-mannered suburbanite Arthur Dent trying to stop the local council demolishing his house to build a bypass. It moves into space when his friend, Ford Prefect—some have seen him as Virgil to Dent's Dante—reveals himself as a representative of a planet near Betelgeuse and informs Arthur that the Earth itself is about to be demolished to make way for a hyperspace express route. They hitch a ride on a Vogon spaceship and begin to use the *Hitchhiker's Guide* itself—a usually reliable repository of all knowledge about life, the universe and everything.

Adams's creativity and idiosyncratic intergalactic humour have had a pervasive cultural influence. The phrase "hitchhiker's guide to . . ." quickly became common parlance, and there have been numerous copycat spoof sci-fi books and TV series. His Babel fish—a small fish you can place in your ear to translate any speech into your own language—has been adopted as the name of a translation device on an Internet search engine. He followed up his success with several other novels as well as a television programme, and a book and CD-ROM on endangered species. He has founded a dot-com company, H2G2, that has recently taken the idea of the guide full circle by launching a service that promises real information on life, the universe, and everything via your mobile phone.

Much of his wealth seems to have been spent fuelling his passion for technology, but he has never really been the nerdy science-fiction type. He is relaxed, gregarious, and a solidly built two meters tall. In fact, he has more the air of those English public-school boys who became rock stars in the 1970s; he once did play guitar on stage at Earls Court with his mates Pink Floyd. In a nicely flash touch, instead of producing a passport-size photo of his daughter out of his wallet, he opens up his impressively powerful laptop, where, after a bit of fiddling about, Polly Adams, aged five, appears in a pop video spoof featuring a cameo appearance by another mate, John Cleese.

So this is what his life turned into; money, A-list friends, and nice toys. Looking at the bare facts of his CV—boarding school, Cambridge Footlights, and the BBC—it seems at first sight no surprise. But his has not been an entirely straightforward journey along well-worn establishment tracks.

Douglas Noel Adams was born in Cambridge in 1952. One of his many stock gags is that he was DNA in Cambridge nine months before Crick and Watson made their discovery. His mother, Janet, was a nurse at Addenbrooke's Hospital, and his father, Christopher, had been a teacher who went on to become a postgraduate theology student, a probation officer, and finally a management consultant, which was "a very, very peculiar move," claims Adams. "Anyone who knew my father will tell you that management was not something he knew very much about."

The family were "fairly hard up" and left Cambridge six months after Douglas was born to live in various homes on the fringes of East London. When Adams was five, his parents divorced. "It's amazing the degree to which children treat their own lives as normal," he says. "But of course it was difficult. My parents divorced when it wasn't remotely as common as it is now, and to be honest I have scant memory of anything before I was five. I don't think it was a great time, one way or another."

After the breakup, Douglas and his younger sister went with their mother to Brentwood in Essex, where she ran a hostel for sick animals. He saw his by now comparatively wealthy father at weekends, and these visits became a source of confusion and tension. To add to the complications, several step-siblings emerged as his parents remarried. Adams has said that while he accepted all this as normal on one level, he did "behave oddly as a result," and remembers himself as a twitchy and somewhat strange child. For a time his teachers thought he was educationally subnormal, but by the time he went to the direct-grant Brentwood Prep School, he was regarded as extremely bright.

The school boasts a remarkably diverse list of postwar alumni: clothing designer Hardy Amies; the disgraced historian David Irving; TV presenter Noel Edmonds; Home Secretary Jack Straw; and London *Times* editor Peter Stothard were all there before Adams, while comedians Griff Rhys Jones and Keith Allen were a few years behind him. There are four alumni—two Labour and two Conservative—in the current House of Commons. In a scene that now seems rather incongruous in the light of Keith Allen's hard-living image, it was Adams who helped the seven-year-old Allen with his piano lessons.

When Adams was thirteen, his mother remarried and moved to Dorset, and Adams changed from being a "day boy" at the school to a boarder. It appears to have been an entirely beneficial experience. "Whenever I left school at four in the afternoon, I always used to look at what the boarders were doing rather wistfully," he says. "They seemed to be having a good time, and in fact I thoroughly enjoyed boarding. There is a piece of me that likes to fondly imagine my maverick and rebellious nature. But more accurately I like to have a nice and cosy institution that I can rub up against a little bit. There is nothing better than a few constraints you can comfortably kick against."

Adams ascribes the quality of his education to being taught by some "very good, committed, obsessed and charismatic people." At a recent party in London he confronted Jack Straw on New Labour's apparent antipathy to direct-grant schools, on the basis that it had done neither of them much harm.

Frank Halford was a master at the school and remembers Adams as "very tall even then, and popular. He wrote an end-of-term play when *Doctor Who* had just started on television. He called it 'Doctor Which.'" Many years later, Adams did write scripts for *Doctor Who*. He describes Halford as an inspirational teacher who is still a support. "He once gave me ten out of ten for a story, which was the only time he did throughout his long school career. And even now, when I have a dark night of the soul as a writer and think that I can't do this anymore, the thing that I reach for is not the fact that I have had best-sellers or huge advances. It is the fact that Frank Halford once gave me ten out of ten, and at some fundamental level I must be able to do it."

It seems that from the beginning Adams had a facility for turning his writing into cash. He sold some short, "almost haiku-length," stories to the *Eagle* comic and received ten shillings. "You could practically buy a yacht for ten shillings then," he laughs. But his real interest was music. He learned to play the guitar by copying note for note the intricate finger-picking patterns on an early Paul Simon album. He now has a huge collection of left-handed electric guitars, but admits that he's "really a folkie at heart. Even with Pink Floyd on stage, I played a very simple guitar figure from 'Brain Damage' which was in a finger-picking style."

Adams grew up in the sixties, and the Beatles "planted a seed in my head that made it explode. Every nine months there'd be a new album which would be an earth-shattering development from where they were before. We were so obsessed by them that when 'Penny Lane' came out and we hadn't heard it on the radio, we beat up this boy who had heard it until he hummed the tune to us. People now ask if Oasis are as good as the Beatles. I don't think they are as good as the Rutles."

The other key influence was Monty Python. Having listened to mainstream British radio comedy of the fifties he describes it as an "epiphanous" moment when he discovered that being funny could be a way in which intelligent people expressed themselves—"and be very, very silly at the same time."

The logical next step was to go to Cambridge University, "because I wanted to join Footlights," he says. "I wanted to be a writer-performer like the Pythons. In fact I wanted to be John Cleese and it took me some time to realise that the job was in fact taken."

At university he quickly abandoned performing—"I just wasn't reliable"—and began to write self-confessed Pythonesque sketches. He recalls one about a railway worker who was reprimanded for leaving all the switches open on the southern region to prove a point about existentialism; and another about the difficulties in staging the Crawley Paranoid Society annual general meeting.

The arts administrator Mary Allen, formerly of the Arts Council and the Royal Opera, was a contemporary at Cambridge and has remained a friend ever since. She performed his material and remembers him as "always noticed even amongst a very talented group of people. Douglas's material was very quirky and individualistic. You had to suit it, and it had to suit you. Even in short sketches he created a weird world."

Adams says, "I did have something of a guilt thing about reading English. I thought I should have done something useful and challenging. But while I was whingeing, I also relished the chance not to do very much." Even his essays were full of jokes. "If I had known then what I know now, I would have done biology or zoology. At the time I had no idea that was an interesting subject, but now I think it is the most interesting subject in the world."

Other contemporaries included the lawyer and TV presenter Clive Anderson. The culture secretary Chris Smith was president of the union. Adams used to do warm-up routines for debates, but not because of any political interest: "I was just looking for anywhere I could do gags. It is very strange seeing these people dotted around the public landscape now. My contemporaries are starting to win lifetime achievement awards, which obviously makes one feel nervous."

After university, Adams got the chance to work with one of his heroes. Python member Graham Chapman had been impressed by some Footlights sketches and had made contact. When Adams went to see him, he was asked, much to his delight, to help out with a script Chapman had to finish that afternoon. "We ended up working together for about a year. Mostly on a prospective TV series which never made it beyond the pilot." Chapman at this time was "sucking down a couple of bottles of gin every day, which obviously gets in the way a bit." But Adams believes he was enormously talented. "He was naturally part of a team and needed other people's discipline to enable his brilliance to work. His strength was flinging something into the mix that would turn it all upside down."

After he split up with Chapman, Adams's career stalled badly. He continued to write sketches but was not making anything like a living. "It turned out I wasn't terribly good at writing sketches. I could never write to order, and couldn't really do topical stuff. But occasionally I'd come out with something terrific from left field."

Geoffrey Perkins, head of comedy at BBC television, was the producer of the radio version of *Hitchhiker*. He remembers first coming across Adams when he directed a Footlights show. "He was being heckled by a cast member, and then he fell into a chair. I next came across him when he was trying to write sketches for the radio show *Weekending,* then regarded as the big training ground for writers. Douglas was one of those writers who honourably failed to get anywhere with *Weekending*. It put a premium on people who could write things that lasted thirty seconds, and Douglas was incapable of writing a single sentence that lasted less than thirty seconds."

With his dreams of being a writer crumbling around him, Adams took a series of bizarre jobs, including working as a chicken-shed cleaner and as a bodyguard to the ruling family of Qatar. "I think the security firm must have been desperate. I got the job from an ad in the *Evening Standard.*" Griff Rhys Jones did the same job for a while on Adams's recommendation. Adams recalls becoming increasingly depressed as he endured night shifts of sitting outside hotel bedrooms: "I kept thinking this wasn't how it was supposed to have worked out." At Christmas he went to visit his mother and stayed there for the next year.

He recalls a lot of family worry about what he was going to do, and while he still sent in the occasional sketch to radio shows, he acknowledges that his confidence was extremely low. Despite his subsequent success and wealth, this propensity for a lack of confidence has continued. "I have terrible periods of lack of confidence," he explains. "I just don't believe I can do it and no evidence to the contrary will sway me from that view. I briefly did therapy, but after a while I realised it is just like a farmer complaining about the weather. You can't fix the weather—you just have to get on with it." So has that approach helped him? "Not necessarily," he shrugs.

Hitchhiker was the last throw of the dice, but in retrospect the timing was absolutely right. *Star Wars* had made science fiction voguish, and the aftermath of Monty Python meant that while a sketch show was out of the question, there was scope to appeal to the same comic sensibility.

Python Terry Jones heard the tapes before transmission and

remembers being struck by Adams's "intellectual approach and strong conceptual ideas. You feel the stuff he is writing has come from a criticism of life, as Matthew Arnold might say. It has a moral basis and a critical basis that has a strong mind behind it. For instance, John Cleese has a powerful mind, but he is more logical and analytical. Douglas is more quirky and analytical." Geoffrey Perkins agrees, but remembers there was little grand plan behind the project.

"Douglas went into it with a whole load of ideas but very little notion of what the story would be. He was writing it in an almost Dickensian mode of episodic weekly installments without quite knowing how it would end."

By the time the series aired in 1978, Adams says, he had put about nine months' solid work into it and had been paid one thousand pounds. "There seemed to be quite a long way to go before I broke even," so he accepted a producer's job at the BBC but quit six months later when he found himself simultaneously writing a second radio series, the novel, the television series, and episodes of *Doctor Who*. Despite this remarkable workload, he was already building a legendary reputation for not writing. "I love deadlines," he has said. "I love the whooshing noise they make as they go by."

Success only added to his ability to prevaricate. His publishing editor, Sue Freestone, quickly realised that he treated writing as performance art, and so she set up her office in his dining room. "He needs an instant audience to bounce things off, but sometimes this can weirdly backfire.

"There was a scene early in one book when he talked about some plates with, very definitely, one banana on each. This was obviously significant, so I asked him to explain. But he liked to tease his audience and he said he'd tell me later. We eventually got to the end of the book and I asked him again, 'Okay,

Douglas, what's with the bananas?' He looked at me completely blankly. He had forgotten all about the bananas. I still occasionally ask him if he has remembered yet, but apparently he hasn't."

Writer and producer John Lloyd has been a friend and collaborator with Adams since before *Hitchhiker*. He remembers the "agonies of indecision and panic" Adams got into when writing. "We were on holiday in Corfu with three friends when he was finishing a book, and he ended up taking over the whole house. He had a room to write in, a room to sleep in, a room to go to when he couldn't sleep, and so on. It didn't occur to him that other people might want a good night's sleep as well. He goes through life with a brain the size of a planet, and often seems to be living on a different one. He is absolutely not a malicious person, but when he is in the throes of panic and terror and unable to finish a book, everything else pales into insignificance."

However the work was dragged out, it was extremely popular. The books all became bestsellers, and Adams was given an advance of over $2 million by his American publishers. He wrote a hilarious spoof dictionary with John Lloyd, *The Meaning of Liff*, in which easily recognised concepts, such as the feeling you get at four in the afternoon when you haven't got enough done, were given the names of towns—Farnham being the perfect choice for this low-grade depression. In the late eighties he completed two spoof detective novels featuring Dirk Gently.

For all his facility with humour, Freestone says she has been touched by how profoundly Adams's work has connected with some readers. "In *Hitchhiker*, all you have to do to be safe is have your towel with you," she explains. "I heard about this woman who was dying in a hospice who felt she would be fine because she had her towel with her. She had taken Douglas's universe and incorporated it into her own. It embarrassed the hell out of Douglas when he heard about it. But for her it was literally a symbol of safety when embarking on an unknown journey."

There are serious themes within his work. The second Dirk Gently novel can easily be read as being about people who are homeless, displaced, and alienated from society. "His imagination goes much deeper than just cleverness," says Freestone. "The social criticism is usually buried by the comedy, but it's there if you want to find it."

Having been through such a lean period, Adams worked constantly until the mid-nineties, when he very deliberately applied the brakes. "I had got absolutely stuck in the middle of a novel, and although it sounds ungrateful, having to do huge book signings would drive me to angry depressions."

He says that he still thought of himself as a scriptwriter and only inadvertently found himself as a novelist. "It sounds absurd, but a bit of me felt cheated and it also felt as if I had cheated. And then there is the money cycle. You're paid a lot and you're not happy, so the first thing you do is buy stuff that you don't want or need—for which you need more money."

His financial affairs got into a mess in the 1980s, he says. He won't discuss the details, but says that the knock-on effect was considerable, so that everyone assumed he was wealthier than he actually was. It is possible to track the movement of Adams's life even between the first and second series of the radio show. In the first there were a lot of jokes about pubs and being without any money. The second had more jokes about expensive restaurants and accountants.

"I felt like a mouse in a wheel," he says. "There was no pleasure coming into the cycle at any point. When you write your first book aged twenty-five or so, you have twenty-five years of experience, albeit much of it juvenile experience. The second book comes after an extra year sitting in bookshops. Pretty soon you begin to run on empty."

His response to running out of fuel was to attempt some "creative crop rotation." In particular, his interest in technology took off, as did a burgeoning passion for environmental issues. In 1990 he wrote *Last Chance to See.* "As is the way of these things, it was my least successful book, but is still the thing I am most proud of."

The book began when he was sent to Madagascar by a magazine to find a rare type of lemur. He thought this would be quite interesting, but it turned into a complete revelation. His fascination with ecology led to an interest in evolution. "I'd been given a thread to pull, and following that lead began to open up issues to me that became the object of the greatest fascination." A link at the bottom of his e-mails now directs people to the Dian Fossey Trust, which works to protect gorillas, and Save the Rhino. Adams was also a signatory to the Great Ape Project, which argued for a change of moral status for great apes, recognising their rights to "life, liberty, and freedom from torture."

He was a founding member of the team that launched Comic Relief, but he has never been a hairshirt sort of activist. The parties he held at his Islington home would feature music by various legendary rock stars—Gary Brooker of Procol Harum once sang the whole of "A Whiter Shade of Pale," including all the abandoned verses—and were peopled by media aristocracy and high-tech billionaires. Slightly less orthodoxly—for an enthusiastic, almost evangelical atheist—he would also host carol services every Christmas.

"As a child I was an active Christian. I used to love the

school choir and remember the carol service as always such an emotional thing." He adds Bach to the Beatles and the Pythons in his pantheon of influences, but how does this square with his passionate atheism? "Life is full of things that move or affect you in one way or another," he explains. "The fact that I think Bach was mistaken doesn't alter the fact that I think the B-minor Mass is one of the great pinnacles of human achievement. It still absolutely moves me to tears to hear it. I find the whole business of religion profoundly interesting. But it does mystify me that otherwise intelligent people take it seriously."

This attachment to traditional structures, if not traditional beliefs, is carried over in the fact that his daughter, Polly, who was born in 1994, has four non-godparents. Mary Allen is one of them, and it was she who introduced Adams to his wife, the barrister Jane Belson. Allen says, "In the early eighties Douglas was going through some writing crisis and was ringing me every day. I eventually asked him whether he was lonely. It seemed that he was, so we decided he needed someone to share his huge flat. Jane moved in." After several false starts, they married in 1991 and lived in Islington until last year, when the family moved to Santa Barbara.

Adams says the initial move was harder than he expected. "I've only recently understood how opposed to the move my wife was." He now says he would recommend it to anyone "in the depths of middle age just upping sticks and going somewhere else. You reinvent your life and start again. It is invigorating."

His role in his dot-com business fits into this sense of invigoration. His job title is chief fantasist. "I've never thought of myself in the role of a predictive science-fiction writer, I was never an Arthur C. Clarke wannabe. The *Guide* was a narrative device for absorbing all those ideas that spark off the flywheel, but it has turned out to be a very good idea. But it's early days," he warns. "We're still in a swimming pool and there is an ocean out there."

Other new ventures are a novel—eight years late and counting—talk of a Dirk Gently film, the H2G2 Web site and an e-novel. "I've been talking about how electronic books will come, and how important they will be, and all of a sudden Stephen King publishes one. I feel a complete idiot, as it should have been me."

The film project has been "twenty years of constipation," and he likens the Hollywood process to "trying to grill a steak by having a succession of people coming into the room and breathing on it." He is surprisingly enthusiastic about this apparently antique art form.

"With new, more-immature technologies there is a danger in getting excited about all the ways you can push them forward at the expense of what you want to say. It is therefore rewarding to work in a medium where you don't have to solve those problems because it is a mature medium."

After such a long fallow period he wisely notes that many of these new projects and ideas will fall by the wayside. "But I've been out of the mainstream of novel writing for several years and I really needed to take that break. I've been thinking hard and thinking creatively about a whole load of stuff that is not novel writing. As opposed to running on empty, it now feels like the tank is full again."

LIFE AT A GLANCE: *Douglas Noel Adams*

BORN: *March 11, 1952, Cambridge.*

EDUCATION: *Brentwood School, Essex; St. John's College, Cambridge.*

MARRIED: *1991 Jane Belson (one daughter, Polly, born 1994).*

CAREER: *1974–78 radio and television writer; 1978 BBC radio producer.*

SOME SCRIPTS: The Hitchhiker's Guide to the Galaxy, *1978 and 1980 (radio), 1981 (television).*

GAMES: The Hitchhiker's Guide to the Galaxy, *1984;* Bureaucracy, *1987;* Starship Titanic, *1997.*

BOOKS: The Hitchhiker's Guide to the Galaxy, *1979;* The Restaurant at the End of the Universe, *1980;* Life, the Universe and Everything, *1982;* The Meaning of Liff *(with John Lloyd), 1983;* So Long, and Thanks for All the Fish, *1984;* Dirk Gently's Holistic Detective Agency, *1987;* The Long Dark Tea-Time of the Soul, *1988;* Last Chance to See, *1990;* The Deeper Meaning of Liff *(with John Lloyd), 1990;* Mostly Harmless, *1992.*

Introduction

Douglas Adams was—in every sense of the word—larger than life. To begin with he was prodigious in stature, towering over the world at six feet five inches or more. (Indeed, even as a child on school trips, Douglas writes, his teachers "wouldn't say 'meet under the clock tower,' or 'meet under the War Memorial,' but 'meet under Adams.'")

He was larger than life as a personality, too: expansive and joyous and perpetually curious, always intrigued by new opportunities, and eager to pursue them with a single-mindedness and charm that usually proved irresistible. I had the good fortune to have lunch with him in Islington a few hours after he had received a formal invitation—as a result of his recent embrace of the "Save the Rhino International" movement—offering him the opportunity to get dressed up as a rhinoceros and, despite being weighed down by the cumbersome costume, climb Mount Kilimanjaro, the highest peak in Africa. The event was, apparently, imminent, and, of course, the proposed date for the climb coincided with several important writing deadlines. (Douglas was also peerless in his ability to procrastinate—but more about that later.) "Are you going to do it?" I asked. "Of course," he replied, "Why wouldn't I?" (And he did—an adventure recounted in "The Rhino Climb," which appears, for the first time in book form, in this volume.)

One of Douglas's most endearing attributes was the incessant delight he took in sharing his wide-ranging, and always evolving, ideas and enthusiasms with virtually anyone who seemed to appreciate them. Indeed, it was this quality, along with his unparalleled humor, kindness, and generosity, that made him such a unique and wonderful friend. I first met him at an American Bookseller's Association convention in the early 1980s. We were introduced by our mutual colleague (and literary agent) Ed Victor, who knew that I was an unabashed *Hitchhiker* fanatic and that Douglas had become intrigued with a medium that *I* had been busy learning about—the computer text adventure, a genre of interactive fiction that, as Douglas himself has characterized it, allows the storyteller to "respond to the audience, rather than just having the audience respond to the storyteller."

Douglas and I, it turned out, were both fascinated by the prospect of trying to anticipate what readers might type into their computers under various circumstances and coming up with witty—and, hopefully, surprising—prepackaged rejoinders. Luckily, I had met Marc Blank, co-creator of Infocom's groundbreaking *Zork* adventure game, and was able to introduce him to Douglas—a meeting that, I'm proud to say, helped pave the way for Infocom's eventual publication of Douglas's marvelous *Hitchhiker's Guide to the Galaxy* game (which he wrote in collaboration with Steve Zeretsky), and set the stage, many years later, for his award-winning resurrection of the text-adventure format with *Starship Titanic*.

It wasn't long before Douglas and I discovered several more common passions: the Pythons, *Beyond the Fringe*, and *The Goon Show;* the then newly-released Macintosh computer; the *Weekly World News* (the funniest tabloid on the planet); and the remarkably eclectic music of Procol Harum and their pianist-lead singer, Gary Brooker, whose work, we instantly agreed, had—with the exception of "A Whiter Shade of Pale"— never really gotten the attention it deserved. (I was amazed to learn that the group's "Grand Hotel"—one of my favorite songs of all time—had been the inspiration for Douglas's second *Hitchhiker* book, *The Restaurant at the End of the Universe*.)

The reference to Procol Harum brings to mind an incident that demonstrates what many of Douglas's friends regard as perhaps his most seductive quality: his unflagging ability to get us to do things that we were secretly dying to do, but somehow thought were indefensibly silly or irresponsible. I was sitting in my New York apartment one afternoon in the early 1990s—just a day or two before I was to fly across the Pacific to Japan to meet Douglas (and a few hundred others) at an international conference sponsored by Apple Computer—when I received a breathless call from him: "If I can persuade Gary Brooker to have dinner with me in London the day after our meetings are done with, will you promise to fly back to New York via the U.K and join us?"

"Have you actually ever *met* Gary Brooker?" I asked.

"Not yet," he confessed. "In fact, I'm not even exactly sure how to find him. But England *is* a small country. . . . So then, will you promise?"

I did, and the next thing I knew—having traveled three-quarters of the way around the world in less than a week—I found myself sitting with Douglas, his wife Jane, and a somewhat puzzled Gary Brooker at the Adams's dinner table in Islington. We happily peppered Brooker with questions about his career and work, and it turned out (why should it have been a surprise?) that Douglas—there was apparently nothing he couldn't do well—actually remembered some of Gary's songs better that Gary did, and sat down at the piano to remind him how to play them.

Above all, of course, Douglas Adams was a transcendent, multi-faceted, comic genius. What made Douglas's work unique,

I think, were the wildly contradictory attributes he displayed in his writing. He seamlessly blended world-class intelligence—and a daunting knowledge about an impossible variety of subjects (literature, computers, evolution, pop culture, genetics, and music, to name but a few)—with cosmic silliness; technophobia with a lust for, and fascination with, every high-tech toy imaginable; deep cynicism about virtually everything with an effusively joyful spirit; and one of the quickest wits I've ever encountered with a relentless perfectionism in pursuing his craft.

Mix in a bit of impish mischief (if, indeed, anyone who weighed over 260 pounds could ever be accused of being "impish"), an unrivaled sense of irony, and a peculiar knack for making absurd—yet logical—connections, and you get such one-of-a-kind creations as the line of electromechanical security robots who repeatedly shout "Resistance is useless!" even as they're destroyed by their attackers; or the guidebook publisher who, after carefully reviewing every aspect of life on earth, decides that all the useful information a space traveler could ever want about the human race can be summed up in the phrase "Mostly harmless"; or—to choose an example from the tantalizing fragment of Douglas's unfinished (and oft-postponed) next novel that appears in this volume—the cab driver who, having noted that no one has ever jumped into his taxi and shouted the much ballyhooed phrase "Follow that cab!", reaches the obvious conclusion that his must be the cab that all the other cabs are following.

The writings collected in the volume you're holding in your hand were retrieved posthumously from the disk drive of Douglas's Mac and masterfully assembled by Peter Guzzardi—assisted heroically by Jane Belson, Douglas's widow, and his long-time assistant, Sophie Astin. The pieces anthologized here not only show off, as do all his books, the remarkable breadth of Douglas's interests and talent, but also reveal—unlike his novels—the constant, irresistible invitation to share something new and exciting that opened those of us fortunate enough to know him personally to so many rewarding pursuits and pleasures. If you're at all like me, before you've finished reading these pages you'll have taken Douglas's advice and picked up a copy of Richard Dawkins's *The Selfish Gene*, or listened once again (perhaps more closely than ever) to the Beatles' "Drive My Car" or Bach's *Fifth Brandenburg Concerto*, or taken it upon yourself to learn more about the Dagenham Girl Pipers, or brewed—for the first time in your life—a truly proper British cup of tea.

And now—at last—it's time to address Douglas's extraordinary ability to procrastinate. It has become legendary that at least three of Douglas's publishers—Sue Freestone, Sonny Mehta, and Shaye Areheart—have found it necessary to lock themselves up in the same room with him for days at a time in order to get him to complete a scandalously overdue book. (I've often wondered if they would have resorted to such rash measures if he weren't such delightful company!) Douglas's excuses for his books being late in the first place (covering up what was actually a daunting blend of perfectionism and a terror of failing in his quest to put, as he liked to phrase it, "a hundred thousand words in a cunning order") are even more extraordinary; the rhino climb referenced above must certainly have startled the editor whose deadline Douglas missed because of it, as, I'm sure, did the unexpected news of his hastily-arranged trip to Australia to attempt a "comparative test drive" between a "sub bug"—a sort of underwater jet ski designed to propel scuba divers—and a manta ray, an excursion which caused him to miss yet another crucial due date (see "Riding the Rays," also reprinted in this book).

Unfortunately—incomprehensibly!—a heart attack that no one could have predicted has prevented Douglas from postponing the completion of his long-awaited, and many-times delayed next book, *The Salmon of Doubt*, which interviews just before his death indicate he was still many, many months—if not years!—away from finishing. Would it have remained a Dirk Gently book, or would he instead have transformed it—as he hinted he might—into the sixth and final volume in the *Hitchhiker* trilogy? Why—I find myself wondering—didn't he find an excuse to procrastinate during his fateful trip to the gym last spring?

Television viewers who tune into *Between the Lions*, the daily children's literacy education program that Michael Frith—another of Douglas's American friends—and I helped create for PBS, will note that one of the lead lion characters, Lionel, habitually wears a rugby shirt featuring the number 42. This small testament may not be the answer to "life, the universe, and everything" (as the famed "Deep Thought" computer from the *Hitchhiker* trilogy determined "42" to be), but if it serves to remind people what a brilliant, unique, irreplaceable force Douglas Adams was in the lives of virtually everyone who knew or read him—well, at least it's a step in the right direction.

Douglas, I loved you dearly and I'll miss you terribly. And I'm grateful you left that hard disk behind so we can all share this one last conversation with you . . .

Christopher Cerf
New York
FEBRUARY 2002

LIFE

Dear Editor,

The sweat was dripping down my face and into my lap, making my clothes very wet and sticky. I sat there, walking, watching. I was trembling violently as I sat, looking at the small slot, waiting—ever waiting. My nails dug into my flesh as I clenched my hands. I passed my arm over my hot, wet face, down which sweat was pouring. The suspense was unbearable. I bit my lip in an attempt to stop trembling with the terrible burden of anxiety. Suddenly, the slot opened and in dropped the mail. I grabbed at my Eagle *and ripped off the wrapping paper.*

My ordeal was over for another week!

> D. N. Adams (12), Brentwood, Essex,
> JANUARY 23, 1965,
> Eagle *and Boys' World Magazine*

*   *   *

[Editor's Note: In the sixties The Eagle *was an enormously popular English science-fiction magazine. This letter is the first known published work of Douglas Adams, then age twelve.]*

*

The Voices of All Our Yesterdays

I vaguely remember my schooldays. They were what was going on in the background while I was trying to listen to the Beatles.

When "Can't Buy Me Love" came out, I was twelve. I sneaked out of school during morning milk break, bought the record, and broke into matron's room because she had a record player. Then I played it, not loud enough to get caught, but just loud enough to hear with my ear pressed up against the speaker. Then I played it again for the other ear. Then I turned the record over and did the same for "You Can't Do That." That was when the housemaster found me and put me into detention, which is what I had expected. It seemed a small price to pay for what I now realize was art.

I didn't know it was art then, of course. I only knew that the Beatles were the most exciting thing in the universe. It wasn't always an easy view to live with. First you had to fight the Stones fans, which was tricky because they fought dirty and had their knuckles nearer the ground. Then you had to fight the grownups, parents and teachers who said that you were wasting your time and pocket money on rubbish that you would have forgotten by next week.

I found it hard to understand why they were telling me this. I sang in the school choir and knew how to listen for harmony and counterpoint, and it was clear to me that the Beatles were something extraordinarily clever. It bewildered me that no one else could hear it: impossible harmonies and part playing you had never *heard* in pop songs before. The Beatles were obviously just putting all this stuff in for some secret fun of their own, and it seemed exciting to me that people could have fun in that way.

The next exciting thing was that they kept on losing me. They would bring out a new album and for a few listenings it would leave me cold and confused. Then gradually it would begin to unravel itself in my mind. I would realize that the reason I was confused was that I was listening to Something that was simply unlike anything that anybody had done before.

"Another Girl," "Good Day Sunshine," and the extraordinary "Drive My Car." These tracks are so familiar now that it takes a special effort of will to remember how alien they seemed at first to me. The Beatles were now not just writing songs, they were inventing the very medium in which they were working.

I never got to see them. Difficult to believe, I know. I was alive at the time the Beatles were performing and never got to see them. I tend to go on about this rather a lot. Do not go to San Francisco with me, or I will insist on pointing out Candlestick Park to you and bleating on about the fact that in 1966 the Beatles played their last concert there, just shortly before I'd woken up to the fact that rock concerts were things you could actually go to, even if you lived in Brentwood.

A friend of mine at school once had some studio tickets to see David Frost's show being recorded, but we ended up not going. I watched the show that night, and the Beatles were on it playing "Hey Jude." I was ill for about a year. Another day that I happened not to go to London after all was the day they played their rooftop concert in Savile Row. I can't—ever—speak about that.

Well, the years passed. The Beatles passed. But Paul McCartney has gone on and on. A few months ago the guitarist Robbie McIntosh phoned me and said, "We're playing at the Mean Fiddler in a few days, do you want to come along?"

Now this is one of the daftest questions I've ever been asked, and I think it took me a few moments even to work out what he meant. The Mean Fiddler, for those who don't know, is a pub in an unlovely part of northwest London with a room at the back where bands play. You can probably get about two hundred people in.

It was the word *we* that temporarily confused me, because I knew that the band that Robbie was currently playing in was

Paul McCartney's, and I didn't think that Paul McCartney played in pubs. If Paul McCartney *did* play in pubs, then it would be daft to think that I would not saw my own leg off in order to go. I went.

In front of two hundred people in a pub, Paul McCartney stood up and played songs he'd never, I think, played in public before. "Here, There and Everywhere" and "Blackbird," to name but two. *I've* played "Blackbird" in pubs, for heaven's sake. I spent weeks learning the guitar part when I was supposed to be revising for A-levels. I almost wondered if I was hallucinating.

There were two moments of complete astonishment. One was the last encore, which was an immaculate, thunderous performance of, believe it or not, "Sgt. Pepper's Lonely Hearts Club Band." (Remember, this was in a *pub*.) And the other was one of the world's greatest rock 'n' roll songs, "Can't Buy Me Love," which I had first heard crouching with my ear cupped to the Dansette record player in the school matron's room.

There is a game people like to play that goes, "When would you most like to have lived and why?" The Italian Renaissance? Mozart's Vienna? Shakespeare's England? Personally, I would like to have been around Bach. But I have a real difficulty with the game, which is that living at any other period of history would have meant missing the Beatles, and I honestly don't think I could do that. Mozart and Bach and Shakespeare are always with us, but I grew up with the Beatles and I'm not sure what else has affected me as much as that.

So Paul McCartney is fifty tomorrow. Happy birthday, Paul. I wouldn't have missed it for the world.

The [London] *Sunday Times,*
JUNE 17, 1992

Brentwood School

I was at Brentwood School for twelve whole years. And they were, by and large, in an up and downy kind of way, pretty good years: fairly happy, reasonably leafy, a bit sportier than I was in the mood for at the time, but full of good (and sometimes highly eccentric) teaching. In fact, it was only later that I gradually came to realise how well I had been taught at Brentwood—particularly in English, and particularly in Physics. (Odd, that.) However, the whole twelve-year experience is, for me, completely overshadowed by the memory of one terrible, mind-scarring experience. I am referring to the episode of The Trousers. Let me explain.

I have always been absurdly, ridiculously tall. To give you an idea—when we went on school expeditions to Interesting and Improving Places, the form-master wouldn't say "Meet under the clock tower," or "Meet under the War Memorial," but "Meet under Adams." I was at least as visible as anything else on the horizon, and could be repositioned at will. When, in Physics, we were asked to repeat Galileo's demonstration that two bodies of different weight fall to the ground at the same speed, I was the one who was given the task of dropping the cricket ball and the pea, because it was quicker than going to an upstairs window. I always towered over everybody. Right back at the very beginning of my school career, aged seven, I introduced myself to another new boy (Robert Neary) by coming up behind him and, in a spirit of experiment, dropping a cricket ball on his head and saying, "Hello, my name's Adams, what's yours?" This, for Robert Neary, I'm sure was his one terrible, mind-scarring memory.

In the Prep School, where I was for five years out of my twelve, we all wore short trousers: grey shorts with blazers in the summer, and in the winter those pepper-and-salt tweed suits with short trousers. There is of course an extremely good reason for wearing shorts when you're young, even in the depths of an English winter (and they were colder then, weren't they?). According to *Wired* magazine, we can't expect to see self-repairing fabrics until about the year 2020, but ever since we emerged from whatever trees or swamps we lived in five million years ago, we have had self-repairing knees.

So, shorts made sense. Even though we all had to wear them, it did begin to get a bit ridiculous in my case. It wasn't towering over the other boys I minded so much, it was towering over the masters. Wearing shorts. My mother pleaded with the principal on one occasion to please make an exception in my case and let me wear long trousers. But Jack Higgs, ever fair but firm, said no: I was only six months away from going up to the main school, whereupon I, along with everybody else, would be able to wear long trousers. I would have to wait.

At last I left the Prep School. And two weeks before the beginning of the Michaelmas term, my mother took me along to the school shop to buy—at last—a long-trousered school suit. And guess what? They didn't make them in a size long enough for me. Let me just repeat that, so that the full horror of the situation can settle on you reading this as it did on me that day in the summer of 1964, standing in the school shop. They didn't *have* any school trousers long enough for me. They would have to make them specially. That would take six weeks. *Six* weeks. Six minus two was, as we had been so carefully and painstakingly taught, four. Which meant that for four whole weeks of the next term I was going to be the *only* boy in school wearing shorts. For the next two weeks I took up playing in the traffic, being careless with kitchen knives, and neglecting to stand clear of the doors on station platforms, but, sadly, I led a charmed life, and I had to go through with it: four weeks of the greatest humiliation and embarrassment known to man or, rather, to that most easily humiliated and embarrassed of all creatures, the overgrown twelve-year-old boy. We've all experienced those painful dreams in which we suddenly discover we are stark naked in the middle of the high street. Believe me, this was worse, and it wasn't a dream.

The story rather fizzles out there because a month later, of course, I got my long trousers and was readmitted into polite society. But, believe me, I still carry the scars inside, and though I try my best to bestride the world like a Colossus, writing bestselling books and . . . (well, that's about it, really, I suppose), if I ever come across as a maladjusted, socially isolated, sad, hunched emotional cripple (I'm thinking mainly of Sunday mornings in February, here), then it's those four weeks of having to wear short trousers in September 1964 that are to blame.

✳

Y

"Why" is the only question that bothers people enough to have an entire letter of the alphabet named after it.

The alphabet does not go "A B C D What? When? How?" but it does go "V W X Why? Z."

"Why?" is always the most difficult question to answer. You know where you are when someone asks you "What's the time?" or "When was the battle of 1066?" or "How do these seatbelts work that go tight when you slam the brakes on, Daddy?" The answers are easy and are, respectively, "Seven-thirty-five in the evening," "Ten-fifteen in the morning," and "Don't ask stupid questions."

But when you hear the word "Why?," you know you've got one of the biggest unanswerables on your hands, such as "Why are we born?" or "Why do we die?" and "Why do we spend so much of the intervening time receiving junk mail?"

Or this one:

"Will you go to bed with me?"

"Why?"

There's only ever been one good answer to that question "Why?" and perhaps we should have that in the alphabet as well. There's room for it. "Why?" doesn't have to be the last word, it isn't even the last letter. How would it be if the alphabet ended, "V W X Why? Z," but "V W X Why not?"

Don't ask stupid questions.

—From *Hockney's Alphabet*
(Faber & Faber)

*

The Meaning of Liff* started life as an English exercise I had to do at school, which then got turned into a game fifteen

---

**The Meaning of Liff* and its successor, *The Deeper Meaning of Liff*, are books coauthored by Douglas Adams and John Lloyd.

years later by John Lloyd and myself. We were sitting with a few friends in a Greek taverna playing charades and drinking retsina all afternoon until we needed to find a game that didn't require so much standing up.

It was simply this (it needed to be simple; the afternoon was too far advanced for complicated rules): someone would say the name of a town and somebody else would say what the word meant. You had to be there.

We rapidly discovered that there were an awful lot of experiences, ideas, and situations that everybody knew and recognized, but that never got properly identified simply because there wasn't a word for them. They were all of the "Do you ever have the situation where . . . ," or "You know what feeling you get when . . . ," or "You know, I always thought it was just me . . ." kind. All it needs is a word, and the thing is identified.

So, the vaguely uncomfortable feeling you got from sitting on a seat which is warm from somebody else's bottom is just as real a feeling as the one you get when a rogue giant elephant charges out of the bush at you, but hitherto only the latter has actually had a word for it. Now they both have words. The first one is "shoeburyness," and the second, of course, is "fear."

We started to collect more and more of these words and concepts, and began to realize what an arbitrarily selective work the *Oxford English Dictionary* is. It simply doesn't recognize huge wodges of human experience. Like, for instance, standing in the kitchen wondering what you went in there for. Everybody does it, but because there isn't—or wasn't—a word for it, everyone thinks it's something that only they do and that they are therefore more stupid than other people. It is reassuring to realize that everybody is as stupid as you are and that all we are doing when we are standing in the kitchen wondering what we came in here for is "woking."

Gradually, little stacks of index cards with these words on them started to grow in John Lloyd's bottom drawer, and anybody who heard about them would add concepts of their own.

They first saw the light of day when John Lloyd was putting together the *Not 1982* calendar, and was stuck for things to put on the bottoms of the pages (and also the tops and quite a few middles). He turned out the drawer, chose a dozen or so of the best new words, and inserted them in the book under the name *Oxtail English Dictionary*. This quickly turned out to be one of the most popular bits of *Not 1982*, and the success of the idea in this small scale suggested the possibility of a book devoted to it—and here it is: *The Meaning of Liff*, the product of a hard lifetime's work studying and chronicling the behaviour of man.

From Pan Promotion News 54,
OCTOBER 1983

*

My Nose

My mother has a long nose and my father had a wide one, and I got both of them combined. It's large. The only person I ever knew with a nose substantially larger than mine was a master at my prep school who also had tiny little eyes and hardly any chin and was ludicrously thin. He resembled a cross between a flamingo and an old-fashioned farming implement and walked rather unsteadily in crosswinds. He also hid a great deal.

I wanted to hide, too. As a boy, I was teased unmercifully about my nose for years until one day I happened to catch sight of my profile in a pair of angled mirrors and had to admit that it was actually pretty funny. From that moment, people stopped teasing me about my nose and instead started to tease me unmercifully about the fact that I said words like "actually," which is something that has never let up to this day.

One of the more curious features of my nose is that it doesn't admit any air. This is hard to understand or even believe. The problem goes back a very long way to when I was a small boy living in my grandmother's house. My grandmother was the local representative of the RSPCA, which meant the house was always full of badly damaged dogs and cats, and even the occasional badger, stoat, or pigeon.

Some of them were damaged physically, some psychologically, but the effect they had on me was to seriously damage my attention span. Because the air was thick with animal hair and dust, my nose was continually inflamed and runny, and every fifteen seconds I would sneeze. Any thought I could not explore, develop, and bring to some logical conclusion within fifteen seconds would therefore be forcibly expelled from my head, along with a great deal of mucus.

There are those who say that I tend to think and write in one-liners, and if there is any truth to this criticism, then it was almost certainly while I lived with my grandmother that the habit developed.

I escaped from my grandmother's house by going to boarding school, where, for the first time in my life, I was able to breathe. This new-found blissful freedom continued for a good two weeks, until I had to learn to play rugby. In about the first five minutes of the first match I ever played, I managed to break my nose on my own knee, which, although it was clearly an extraordinary achievement, had the same effect on me that those geological upheavals had on whole civilizations in Rider Haggard novels—it effectively sealed me off from the outside world forever.

Various ENT specialists have, at different times, embarked on major speleological expeditions into my nasal passages, but most of them have come back baffled. The ones who didn't come back baffled didn't come back at all, and are therefore now part of the problem rather than part of the solution.

The only thing that ever tempted me to try taking cocaine was the dire warning that the stuff eats away at your septum. If I thought cocaine could actually find a way through my septum, I would happily shove it up there by the bucketful and let it eat away as much as it liked. I have been put off, however, by the observation that friends who do shove it up their noses by the bucketful have even shorter attention spans than mine.

So, by now I am pretty well resigned to the fact that my nose is decorative rather than functional. Like the Hubble Space Telescope, it represents a massive feat of engineering, but is not actually any good for anything, except perhaps a few cheap laughs.

Esquire, SUMMER 1991

The Book That Changed Me

1. Title:
   The Blind Watchmaker.

2. Author:
   Richard Dawkins.

3. When did you first read it?
   Whenever it was published. About 1990, I think.

4. Why did it strike you so much?
   It's like throwing open the doors and windows in a dark and stuffy room. You realise what a jumble of half-digested ideas we normally live with, particularly those of us with an arts education. We "sort of" understand evolution, though we secretly think there's probably a bit more to it than that. Some of us even think that there's some "sort of" god, which takes care of the bits that sound a little bit improbable. Dawkins brings a flood of light and fresh air, and shows us that there is a dazzling clarity to the structure of evolution that is breathtaking when we suddenly see it. And if we don't see it, then, quite literally, we don't know the first thing about who we are and where we come from.

5. Have you reread it? If so, how many times?
   Yes, once or twice. But I also dip into it a lot.

6. Does it feel the same as when you first read it?
   Yes. The workings of evolution run so contrary to our normal intuitive assumptions about the world that there's always a fresh shock of understanding.

7. Do you recommend it, or is it a private passion?
   I'd recommend it to anybody and everybody.

Maggie and Trudie

I am not, I should say at once, in any formal relationship with a dog. I don't feed a dog, give it a bed, groom it, find kennels for it when I'm away, delouse it, or suddenly arrange for any of its internal organs to be removed when they displease me. I do not, in short, own a dog.

On the other hand, I do have a kind of furtive, illicit relationship with a dog, or rather two dogs. And in consequence I think I know a little of what it must be like to be a mistress.

The dogs do not live next door. They don't even live in the same—well, I was going to say street and tease it out a bit, but let's cut straight to the truth. They live in Santa Fe, New Mexico, which is a hell of a place for a dog, or indeed anyone else, to live. If you've never visited or spent time in Santa Fe, New Mexico, then let me say this: you're a complete idiot. I was myself a complete idiot till about a year ago when a combination of circumstances that I can't be bothered to explain led me to borrow somebody's house way out in the desert just north of Santa Fe to write a screenplay in. To give you an idea of the sort of place that Santa Fe is, I could bang on about the desert and the altitude and the light and the silver and turquoise jewelry, but the best thing is just to mention a traffic sign on the freeway from Albuquerque. It says, in large letters, GUSTY WINDS, and in smaller letters MAY EXIST.

I never met my neighbours. They lived half a mile away on top of the next sand ridge, but as soon as I started going out for my morning run, jog, gentle stroll, I met their dogs, who were so instantly and deliriously pleased to see me that I wondered if they thought we'd met in a previous life (Shirley MacLaine lived nearby and they might have picked up all kinds of weird ideas from just being near her).

Their names were Maggie and Trudie. Trudie was an exceptionally silly-looking dog, a large, black French poodle who moved exactly as if she had been animated by Walt Disney: a kind of lollop that was emphasised by her large floppy ears at the front end and a short stubby tail with a bit of topiary-work on the end. Her coat consisted of a matting of tight black curls, which added to the general Disney effect by making it seem that she was completely devoid of naughty bits. The way in which she signified, every morning, that she was deliriously pleased to see me was to do a thing that I always thought was called "prinking" but is in fact called "stotting." (I've only just discovered my error, and I'm going to have to replay whole sections of my life through my mind to see what confusions I may have caused or fallen afoul of.) "Stotting" is jumping upward with all four legs simultaneously. My advice: do not die until you've seen a large black poodle stotting in the snow.

The way in which Maggie would signify, every morning, that she was deliriously pleased to see me was to bite Trudie on the neck. This was also her way of signifying that she was deliriously excited at the prospect of going for a walk, it was her way of signifying that she was having a walk and really enjoying it, it was her way of signifying she wanted to be let into the house, it was her way of signifying she wanted to be let out of the house. Continuously and playfully biting Trudie on the neck was, in short, her way of life.

Maggie was a handsome dog. She was not a poodle, and in fact the sort of breed of dog she was was continuously on the tip of my tongue. I'm not very good with dog breeds, but Maggie was one of the real classic, obvious ones: a sleek, black and tan, vaguely retrieverish sort of big beagle sort of thing. What are they called. Labradors? Spaniels? Elkhounds? Samoyeds? I asked my friend Michael, the film producer, once I felt I knew him well enough to admit that I couldn't quite put my finger on the sort of breed of dog Maggie was, despite the fact that it was so obvious.

"Maggie," he said, in his slow, serious Texan drawl, "is a mutt."

So every morning the three of us would set out: me, the large English writer, Trudie the poodle, and Maggie the mutt. I would run-jog-stroll along the wide dirt track that ran through the dry red dunes, Trudie would gambol friskily along, this way and that, ears flapping, and Maggie would bowl along cheerily biting her neck. Trudie was extraordinarily good-natured and long-suffering about this, but every now and then she would suddenly get monumentally fed up. At that moment she would execute a sudden midair about-turn, land squarely on her feet facing Maggie, and give her an extremely pointed look, whereupon Maggie would suddenly sit and start gently gnawing her own rear right foot as if she were bored with Trudie anyway.

Then they'd start up again and go running and rolling and tumbling, chasing and biting, out through the dunes, through the scrubby grass and undergrowth, and then every now and then would suddenly and inexplicably come to a halt as if they had both, simultaneously, run out of moves. They would then stare into the middle distance in embarrassment for a bit before starting up again.

So what part did I play in all this? Well, none really. They completely ignored me for the whole twenty or thirty minutes.

Which was perfectly fine, of course, I didn't mind. But it did puzzle me, because early every morning they would come yelping and scratching around the doors and windows of my house until I got up and took them for their walk. If anything disturbed the daily ritual, like I had to drive into town, or have a meeting, or fly to England or something, they would get thoroughly miserable and simply not know what to do. Despite the fact that they would always completely ignore me whenever we went on our walks together, they couldn't just go and have a walk without me. This revealed a profoundly philosophical bent in these dogs that were not mine, because they had worked out that I had to be there in order for them to be able to ignore me properly. You can't ignore someone who isn't there, because that's not what "ignore" means.

Further depths to their thinking were revealed when Michael's girlfriend Victoria told me that once, when coming to visit me, she had tried to throw a ball for Maggie and Trudie to chase. The dogs had sat and watched stony-faced as the ball climbed up into the sky, dropped, and at last dribbled along the ground to a halt. She said that the message she was picking up from them was "We don't do that. We hang out with writers."

Which was true. They hung out with me all day, every day. But, exactly like writers, dogs who hang out with writers don't like the actual writing bit. So they would moon around at my feet all day and keep nudging my elbow out of the way while I was typing so that they could rest their chins on my lap and gaze mournfully up at me in the hope that I would see reason and go for a walk so that they could ignore me properly.

And then in the evening they would trot off to their real home to be fed, watered, and put to bed for the night. Which seemed to me like a fine arrangement, because I got all the pleasure of their company, which was considerable, without having any responsibility for them. And it continued to be a fine arrangement till the day when Maggie turned up bright and early in the morning ready and eager to ignore me on her own. No Trudie. Trudie was not with her. I was stunned. I didn't know what had happened to Trudie and had no way of finding out, because she wasn't mine. Had she been run over by a truck? Was she lying somewhere, bleeding by the roadside? Maggie seemed restless and worried. She would know where Trudie was, I thought, and what had happened to her. I'd better follow her, like Lassie. I put on my walking shoes and hurried out. We walked for miles, roaming around the desert looking for Trudie, following the most circuitous route. Eventually I realised that Maggie wasn't looking for Trudie at all, she was just ignoring me, a strategy I was complicating by trying to follow her the whole time rather than just pursuing my normal morning walk route. So eventually I returned to the house, and Maggie sat at my feet and moped. There was nothing I could do, no one I could phone about it, because Trudie didn't belong to me. All I could do, like a mistress, was sit and worry in silence. I was off my food. After Maggie sloped off home that night, I slept badly.

And in the morning they were back. Both of them. Only something terrible had happened. Trudie had been to the groomers. Most of her coat had been cropped down to about two millimeters, with a few topiary tufts on her head, ears, and tail. I was outraged. She looked preposterous. We went out for a walk, and I was embarrassed, frankly. She wouldn't have looked like that if she was my dog.

A few days later I had to go back to England. I tried to explain this to the dogs, to prepare them for it, but they were in denial. On the morning I left, they saw me putting my cases in back of the 4WD, and kept their distance, became tremendously interested in another dog instead. Really ignored me. I flew home, feeling odd about it.

Six weeks later I came back to work on a second draft. I couldn't just call round and get the dogs. I had to walk around in the backyard, looking terribly obvious and making all sorts of high-pitched noises such as dogs are wont to notice. Suddenly they got the message and raced across the snow-covered desert to see me (this was mid-January now). Once they had arrived, they continually hurled themselves at the walls in excitement, but then there wasn't much else we could do but go out for a brisk, healthy Ignore in the snow. Trudie stotted, Maggie bit her on the neck, and so we went on. And three weeks later I left again. I'll be back again to see them sometime this year, but I realise that I'm the Other Human. Sooner or later I'm going to have to commit to a dog of my own.

—*Animal Passions* (ed. Alan Coren; Robson Books; SEPTEMBER 1994).

✳

The Rules

In the old Soviet Union they used to say that anything that wasn't forbidden was compulsory; the trick was to remember which was which. In the West we've always congratulated ourselves on taking a slightly more relaxed, commonsense view of things, and forget that common sense is often just as arbitrary. You've got to know the rules. Especially if you travel.

A few years ago—well, I can tell you exactly, in fact, it was early 1994—I had a little run-in with the police. I was driving along Westway into central London with my wife, who was six months pregnant, and I overtook on the inside lane. Not a piece of wild and reckless driving in the circumstances, honestly, it was just the way the traffic was flowing; but anyway I suddenly found myself being flagged down by a police car. The policemen signalled me to follow them down off the motorway and—astonishingly—to stop behind them *on a bend in the slip road*, where we could all get out and have a little chat about my heinous crime. I was aghast. Cars, trucks, and, worst of all, white vans were careering down the slip road, none of them, I'm sure, expecting to find a couple of cars actually *parked* there, right on the bend. Any one of them could easily have rear-ended my car—with my pregnant wife inside. The situation was frightening and insane. I made this point to the police officer, who, as is so often the case with the police, took a different view.

The officer's point was that overtaking on an inside lane was inherently dangerous. Why? Because the law said it was. But being parked on a blind bend on a slip road was not dangerous because I was there on police instructions, which made it legal and hence (and this was the tricky bit to follow) safe.

My point was that I accepted I had (quite safely) made a manoeuvre that was illegal under the laws of England, but that our current situation, parked on a blind bend in the path of fast-moving traffic, was life-threatening by reason of the actual physical laws of the universe.

The officer's next point was that I wasn't in the universe, I was in England, a point that has been made to me before. I gave up trying to win an argument and agreed to everything so that we could just get out of there.

As it happened, the reason I had rather overcasually overtaken on the inside lane was that I am very used to driving in the United States where everybody routinely exercises their constitutional right to drive in whatever damn lane they please. Under American law, overtaking on the inside lane (where traffic conditions allow) is perfectly legal, perfectly normal, and, hence, perfectly safe.

But I'll tell you what isn't.

I was once in San Francisco, and I parked in the only available space, which happened to be on the other side of the street. The law descended on me.

Was I aware of how dangerous the manoeuvre I'd just made was? I looked at the law a bit blankly. What had I done wrong?

I had, said the law, parked against the flow of traffic.

Puzzled, I looked up and down the street. What traffic? I asked.

The traffic that would be there, said the law, if there was any traffic.

This was a bit metaphysical, even for me, so I explained, a bit lamely, that in England we just park wherever we can find a parking space available, and weren't that fussy about which side of the street it was on. He looked at me aghast, as if I was lucky to have got out of a country of such wild and crazy car parkers alive, and promptly gave me a ticket. Clearly he would rather have deported me before my subversive ideas brought chaos and anarchy to streets that normally had to cope with nothing more alarming than a few simple assault rifles. Which, as we know, in the States are perfectly legal, and without which they would be overrun by herds of deer, overbearing government officers, and lawless British tea importers.

My late friend Graham Chapman, an idiosyncratic driver at the best of times, used to exploit the mutual incomprehension of British and U.S. driving habits by always carrying both British and California driver's licences. Whenever he was stopped in the States, he would flash his British licence, and vice versa. He would also mention that he was just on his way to the airport to leave the country, which he always found to be such welcome news that the police would breathe a sigh of relief and wave him on.

But though there are frequent misunderstandings between the Europeans and the Americans, at least we've had decades of shared movies and TV to help us get used to each other. Outside those bounds you can't make any assumptions at all. In China, for instance, the poet James Fenton was once stopped for having a light on his bicycle. "How would it be," the police officer asked him severely, "if everybody did that?"

However, the most extreme example I've come across of something being absolutely forbidden in one country and normal practice in another is one I can't quite bring myself to believe, though my cousin swears it's true. She lived for several years in Tokyo, and tells of a court case in which a driver who was being prosecuted for driving up onto the pavement, crashing into a shop window and killing a couple of pedestrians was allowed to enter the fact that he was blind drunk at the time as a plea in mitigation.

What are the rules you need to know if you are moving from one country to another? What are the things that are compulsory in one country and forbidden in another? Common sense won't tell you. We have to tell each other.

The Independent on Sunday, JANUARY 2000

✳

Introductory Remarks, Procol Harum at the Barbican

Ladies and gentlemen:

Anybody who knows me will know what a big thrill it is for me to be here to introduce this band tonight. I've been a very great fan of Gary Brooker and Procol Harum ever since thirty years ago when they suddenly surprised the world by leaping absolutely out of nowhere with one of the biggest hit records ever done by anybody at all ever under any circumstances. They then surprised the world even more by turning out to be from Southend and not from Detroit as everybody thought. They then surprised the world even more by their complete failure to bring out an album within four months of the single, on the grounds that they hadn't written it yet. And then, in a move of unparalleled marketing shrewdness and ingenuity, they also actually left "A Whiter Shade of Pale" off the album. They never did anything straightforwardly at all, as anyone who's ever tried to follow the chords of "A Rum Tale" will know.

Now, they had one very very particular effect on my life. It was a song they did, which I expect some of you here will know, called "Grand Hotel." Whenever I'm writing, I tend to have music on in the background, and on this particular occasions I had "Grand Hotel" on the record player. This song always used to interest me because while Keith Reid's lyrics were all about this sort of beautiful hotel—the silver, the chandeliers, all those kinds of things—but then suddenly in the middle of the song there was this huge orchestral climax that came out of nowhere and didn't seem to be about anything. I kept wondering what was this huge thing happening in the background? And I eventually thought, "It sounds as if there ought to be some sort of floor show going on. Something huge and extraordinary, like, well, like the end of the universe." And so that was where the idea for *The Restaurant at the End of the Universe* came from—from "Grand Hotel."

Anyway, enough from me. We're in for a great night tonight. There's no band quite like them. And tonight I'm glad to say the London Symphony Orchestra is going to sit in with them. So I'd like for you to welcome please—the London Symphony Orchestra; the Chameleon Arts Chorus; Procol Harum; the conductor, the great Nicholas Dodd; and Gentleman-Scholar-Musician, and I believe now also Rear Admiral—Gary Brooker. Thank you very much.

—From the Procol Harum and London
Symphony Orchestra concert,
FEBRUARY 9, 1996

*

Hangover Cures

What is it we are all going to be trying to make next Saturday? Not New Year's Resolutions, if we're halfway sane. They all fail so embarrassingly early into the New Year that few of us are going to want to compound our sense of futility by making New Millennium Resolutions and have them fail, relatively speaking, a thousand times earlier than usual.

In fact—if I may digress for a moment (and if you don't want me to digress, then you may find that you are reading the wrong column)—it turns out that there may be a very good reason why we fail to keep our New Year's Resolutions other than the obvious abject feebleness of will. It's this. We can't remember what they are. Simple. And if we actually wrote them down, then we probably can't remember where we put the piece of paper, either. Oddly enough, the piece of paper has sometimes been known to turn up again exactly a year later when you're casting around for something on which to write the next year's abortive attempts to pull your life into some kind of shape. This is not, it turns out, a coincidence.

Incidentally, am I alone in finding the expression "it turns out" to be incredibly useful? It allows you to make swift, succinct, and authoritative connections between otherwise randomly unconnected statements without the trouble of explaining what your source or authority actually is. It's great. It's hugely better than its predecessors "I read somewhere that . . ." or the craven "they say that . . ." because it suggests not only that whatever flimsy bit of urban mythology you are passing on is actually based on brand new, ground breaking research, but that it is research in which you yourself were intimately involved. But again, with no *actual* authority anywhere in sight. Anyway, where was I?

It seems that the brain is affected by alcohol. Well, we know that, of course, and those who don't yet are about to find out. But there are different gradations to the effect, and herein lies the crux. The brain organises its memories like a kind of hologram (it turns out). To retrieve an image, you have to re-create the exact conditions in which it was captured. In the case of a hologram, it's the lighting, in the case of the brain it is, or can be (it turns out), the amount of alcohol sloshing around in it. Things that happen to you or, frighteningly enough, that you yourself say or do while under the influence of alcohol will only be recalled to your memory when you are under the influence of that exact same quantity of alcohol again. These memories are completely beyond the reach of your normal, sober mind. Which is why, after some ill-advised evening out, you will be the only person who is completely unaware of some barkingly stupid remark you made to someone whose feelings you care about deeply, or even just a bit. It is only weeks, months, or, in the case of New Year's Eve, exactly a year later that the occasion suddenly returns to your consciousness with a sickening whump and you realise why people have been avoiding you or meeting your eyes with a glassy stare for so long. This can often result in your saying "Jesus God" to yourself in a loud voice and reaching for a stiff drink, which leads you up to the next point of inebriation, where of course fresh shocks await your pleasure.

And the same is true on the way back down. There are certain memories that will only be retriggered by revisiting exactly the same state of dehydration as the one in which the original events occurred. Hence the New Year's Resolution problem, which is that you never actually remember the resolutions you made, or even where you wrote them down, until the exact same moment the following year, when you are horribly reminded of your complete failure to stick by them for more than about seven minutes.

So what is the answer to this terrible, self-perpetuating problem? Well, obviously, rigorous self-discipline. A monastic adherence to a regime of steamed vegetables, plain water, long walks, regular workouts, early nights, early mornings, and probably some kind of fragrant oils or something. But seriously, the thing we are most going to want on New Year's Day, and be desperately trying to remember how to make, is a good hangover cure, and especially one that doesn't involve diving through the ice on the Serpentine. The trouble is, we can never remember them when we want them, or even know where to find them. And the reason we can never remember them when we want them is that we heard about them when we didn't actually need them, which isn't any help, for the reasons outlined above. Nauseating images involving egg yolks and Tabasco sauce swill through your brain, but you are not really in any fit state to organise your thoughts. Which is why we need, urgently, to organise them now while there is still time. So this is an appeal for good, effective methods of freshening up the brain on New Year's Day that don't involve actual cranial surgery. Hangover cures, please, therefore, to www.h2g2.com. And may the next thousand years be especially good ones for you and your descendants.

The Independent on Sunday,
DECEMBER 1999

✷

My Favourite Tipples

I love whisky in every way. I love the way it looks in the bottle, that rich golden colour. I love the labels arranged on the shelf—the kilts and claymores and slightly out-of-focus sheep. I love the sense that it's a drink that—unlike, for instance, vodka from Warrington—is rich in the culture and history of the place where it is distilled. I love particularly the smoky, peaty aromas of the single malts. In fact the only thing I don't like about whisky is that if I take the merest sip of the stuff it sends a sharp pain from the back of my left eyeball down to the tip of my right elbow, and I begin to walk in a very special way, bumping into people and snarling at the furniture. I have therefore learnt to turn my attention to other tipples.

Margaritas I'm very fond of, but they make me buy very stupid things. Whenever I've had a few margaritas I always wake up in the morning with a sense of dread as to what I will find downstairs. The worst was a six-foot-long pencil and a two-foot-wide India eraser that I had shipped over from New York as a result of one injudicious binge. The confusing thing was that they arrived home several weeks after I did, so I found them downstairs one morning after having had just one glass of Chianti with my evening pizza.

I therefore now drink Stolichnaya vodka martinis if I go to New York, because they're very smart and sophisticated and New Yorky, but, most important, they render me incapable of doing anything stupid, or indeed anything at all, though I occasionally converse very knowledgeably about quantum chromodynamics and pig farming when under their influence.

I like Bloody Marys, but only ever have them in airports. I have no explanation for this. It never occurs to me to have a Bloody Mary in the normal course of events, but put me in an airport lounge and I make for the Stoli and the tomato juice like a rat from a sinking ship, and arrive a few hours later at my destination throbbing with jet lag.

At home I tend to drink whatever is lying around in the fridge, which is usually very little. My fridge has a peculiar feature: you put a bottle of good champagne in it, and when you come to look for it you find a bottle of noxious cheap white wine in its place. I still have not worked out how this happens, but I usually console myself with a glass of the world's most boring drink, the only one I can drink with no ill effects whatsoever: a gin and tonic.

The Independent on Sunday,
DECEMBER 1990

Radio Scripts Intro

I do enjoy having these little chats at the front of books. This is a complete lie, in fact. What actually happens is that you are battling away trying to finish, or at least start, a book you promised to deliver seven months ago, and faxes start arriving asking you if you could possibly write yet another short little introduction to a book that you clearly remember writing "The End" to in about 1981. It won't, promises the fax, take you two minutes. Damn right it won't take you two minutes. It actually takes about thirteen hours and you miss another dinner party and your wife won't speak to you, and the book gets so late that you start missing entire camping holidays in the Pyrenees and your wife won't talk to you, particularly since the camping holiday was your idea and not hers and she was only going on it because you wanted to and now she has to go and do it by herself when you know perfectly well that she hates camping. (So do I, incidentally. I am making this bit up.)

And then more faxes come in demanding more introductions, this time for omnibus editions of books, each of which I have already written individual introductions to. After a while I find I have written so many introductions that someone collects them all together and puts them in a book and asks me to write an introduction to it. So I miss another dinner party and also a scuba-diving trip to the Azores and I discover that the reason my wife isn't talking to me is that she is now in fact married to someone else. (I am making this bit up as well, as far as I know.)

In the days when I used to be able to go to parties, in other words, in the days when I had only written a couple of books and the business of writing introductions to them had yet to become a full-time activity, it used to save a lot of time when I discovered that two of my friends didn't know each other, just to say to them, "This is Peter, this is Paula, why don't you introduce yourselves?" This usually worked fantastically well, and before you knew it Peter and Paula would be a happy couple going off on joint skiing holidays in the French Alps with your wife and her second husband.

So. Dear reader. This is the anniversary reissue of the *Hitchhiker's Guide to the Galaxy* radio scripts. Why don't you introduce yourselves?

I have enjoyed this little chat.

—Introduction to *The Original Hitchhiker Scripts,* 10th Anniversary Edition (Harmony Books, MAY 1995)

* * *

How should a prospective writer go about becoming an author?

First of all, realise that it's very hard, and that writing is a grueling and lonely business and, unless you are extremely lucky, badly paid as well. You had better really, really, really want to do it. Next, you have to write something. Unless you are committed to novel writing exclusively, I suggest that you start out writing for radio. It's still a *relatively* easy medium to get into because it pays so badly. But it is a great medium for writers because it relies so much on the imagination.

✳

Unfinished Business of the Century

Just a few more days to go. I think it's important not to leave a century, let alone a millennium, without cleaning up behind you, and there is clearly unfinished business to attend to. I suggest that the Net community try to identify this unfinished business and see if, between us, we can't get it squared away so that we can all enjoy the New Year celebrations with the sense of a century well done.

But first, a word to the pedants.

Yes, I know you all think that the millennium doesn't change till a year later, and very tedious you are about it, too. In fact, you are so keen to have something you can wag your fingers at the rest of the world about, that you are completely missing the point. IT HAS NO SIGNIFICANCE WHATSOEVER! It is merely an excuse to go "Whoa! Look at that! There they go!" as all the digits change.

What other significance can it *possibly* have? Ten (along with its multiples) is an arbitrary number. January 1 is an arbitrary date. And if you happen to think that the birth of Jesus Christ is a significant moment, then all we can say with any certainty is that 1 A.D. isn't when it happened. Or 0 A.D., if the previous year had been called that (which, as we all know because the pedants keep banging on about it, it wasn't).

Then, as the historians (a *much* more interesting bunch than the pedants) tell us, the calendar has been played around with so many times in the intervening years anyway that the whole thing is doubly meaningless.

Consider this: we've only relatively recently got our time- and date-keeping precisely defined and standardised, with the aid of atomic clocks and suchlike. And on January 1, 2000 (if the doomsayers are to believed) all of our computer systems will go haywire and plunge us back in the stone age (or not, as the case may be). So it seems to me that midnight on December 31 is the only solid and reliable point we have in the entire sorry mess, and so perhaps we should be celebrating that just a little bit. And instead of saying that we have got the end of the millennium (or bi-millennium) wrong, we should say that our ancestors got the *beginning* of it wrong, and that we've only just sorted the mess out before starting a new mess of our own. What the hell does it matter anyway? It's just an excuse for a party.

But first, to unfinished business.

One particularly niggling piece of Unfinished Business, it occurred to me the other day in the middle of a singing session with my five-year-old daughter, is the lyrics to "Do-Re-Mi," from *The Sound of Music*. It doesn't exactly rank as a global crisis, but nevertheless it brings me up short anytime I hear it, and *it shouldn't be that difficult to sort it out.*

But it is.

Consider.

Each line of the lyric takes the name of a note from the sol-fa scale, and gives its meaning: "*Do* (doe), a deer, a female deer; *Re* (ray), a drop of golden sun," etc. All well and good so far. "*Mi* (me), a name I call myself; *Fa* (far), a long, long way to run." Fine. I'm not saying this is Keats, exactly, but it's a perfectly good conceit and it's working consistently. And here we go into the home stretch. "*So* (sew), a needle pulling thread."

Yes, good. *"La,* a note to follow *so . . ."* What? Excuse me? *"La,* a note to follow *so . . ."* What kind of lame excuse for a line is that?

Well, it's obvious what kind of line it is. It's a placeholder. A placeholder is what a writer puts in when he can't think of the right line or idea just at the moment, but he'd better put in something and come back and fix it later. So, I imagine that Oscar Hammerstein just bunged in "a note to follow *so*" and thought he'd have another look at it in the morning.

Only, when he came to have another look at it in the morning, he couldn't come up with anything better. Or the next morning. Come on, he must have thought, this is simple. Isn't it? *"La . . . a* something, something . . . what?"

One can imagine rehearsals looming. Recording dates. Maybe he'd be able to fix it on the day. Maybe one of the cast would come up with the answer. But no. No one manages to fix it. And gradually a lame placeholder of a line became locked in place and is now formally part of the song, part of the movie, and so on.

How difficult can it be? How about this for a suggestion? "La, a . . . , a . . ."—well, I can't think of one at the moment, but I think that if the whole world pulls together on this, we can crack it. And I think we shouldn't let the century end with such a major popular song in such an embarrassing state of disarray.

What else? Well, what do *you* think? What are the things we really owe it to ourselves to sort out in the next few months, before the digits roll over and we all have a set of brand-new shiny twenty-first-century problems to deal with? World hunger? Lord Lucan? Jimmy Hoffa? Where to put old eight-track tapes so that no one in the twenty-first century will ever have to see one ever again? Suggestions, please, and answers, to www.h2g2.com.

The Independent on Sunday,
NOVEMBER 1999

*

The Dream Team

DREAM FILM CAST: Sean Connery as God, John Cleese as the Angel Gabriel, and Goldie Hawn as Mother Theresa's younger sister, Trudie. With a guest appearance by Bob Hoskins as Detective Inspector Phil Makepiece.

DREAM ROCK BAND: My absolute dream rock band no longer exists because their rhythm guitarist was shot. But I'd have their bass player because he is unquestionably the best. There may be more pyrotechnical players, but for sheer musicality, invention, and drive, there's no one better than McCartney. He'd share vocals with Gary Brooker, the greatest soul voice of British rock and roll and a hell of a piano player. Two lead guitarists (they can take turns to play rhythm): Dave Gilmour, whom I've always wanted to hear play with Gary Brooker because they share a taste for huge drama and soaring melody lines; and Robbie McIntosh, who is both a great blues rocker and an exquisite acoustic guitar picker. Drummer—Steve Gadd (remember "50 Ways"?). By the time you've got a band this size, you more or less have to have maestro Ray Cooper in it as well, on percussion, though it would also be very tempting to include the incredible woman percussionist whose name I don't know from Van Morrison's band. Strings? Brass section? Royal Philharmonic? A New Orleans jazz band? For all that, you'd need synth wizard Paul "Wix" Wickens. And a large truck.

DREAM LOVER: The Dagenham Girl Pipers. With all due respect and love to my dear wife, there are some things that, however loving or tender your wife may be, only a large pipe band can give you.

DREAM PROJECT: Given unlimited financial resources, I would love to fund a major research project into human origins, the transition from ape to man. A couple of years ago I became fascinated by the Aquatic Ape Hypothesis, the notion that our transitional ancestors spent a period in a semiaquatic environment. I've heard the idea ridiculed many times but never convincingly refuted, and I would love to discover the truth, one way or the other.

DREAM ALTERNATIVE CAREERS: Zoologist, rock musician, system software designer.

DREAM HOLIDAY: Intense scuba diving in Australia, out beyond the Great Barrier Reef to the wonderful clarity of the Coral Sea—Cod Hole, shark diving, wreck diving; then to Western Australia to dive with enormous whale sharks, and finally to Shark Bay to dive with dolphins. Then I'd stop off for dinner in Hong Kong on the way home.

DREAM HOME: Something large and rambling on the beach somewhere, probably Far North Queensland, with lots of wildlife around and high-bandwidth computer connections to the rest of the world. Also a boat and a pickup truck.

DREAM CUISINE: If I was told I had to choose the cuisine of one country and eat only that for the rest of my life, I'd choose Japanese.

DREAM DAY OUT: I've already had this, in fact. It was 1968— a friend of mine and I took a day off school, went up to London, and saw *2001* in Cinerama in the afternoon and Simon and Garfunkel live at the Albert Hall in the evening.

The Observer, MARCH 10, 1995

✳   ✳   ✳

Where do you get the inspiration for your books?

I tell myself I can't have another cup of coffee till I've thought of an idea.

✳

Intro for Comic Books #1

People often ask me where I get my ideas from, sometimes as often as eighty-seven times a day. This is a well-known hazard for writers, and the correct response to the question is first to breathe deeply, steady your heartbeat, fill your mind with peaceful, calming images of birdsong and buttercups in spring meadows, and then try to say, "Well, it's very interesting you ask that . . ." before breaking down and starting to whimper uncontrollably.

The fact is that I don't know where ideas come from, or even where to look for them. Nor does any writer. This is not quite true, in fact. If you were writing a book on the mating habits of pigs, you'd probably pick up a few goodish ideas by hanging around a barnyard in a plastic mac, but if fiction is your line, then the only real answer is to drink way too much coffee and buy yourself a desk that doesn't collapse when you beat your head against it.

I exaggerate, of course. That's my job. There are some specific ideas for which I can remember exactly where they came from. At least, I think I can; I may just be making it up. That also is my job. When I've got a big writing job to do, I will often listen to the same piece of music over and over again. Not while I'm doing the actually writing, of course, you need things to be pretty quiet for that, but while I'm fetching another cup of coffee or making toast or polishing my spectacles or trying to find more toner for the printer or changing my guitar strings or clearing away the coffee cups and toast crumbs from my desk or retiring to the bathroom to sit and think for half an hour— in other words, most of the day. The result is that a lot of my ideas come from songs. Well, one or two at least. To be absolutely accurate, there is just one idea that came from a song, but I keep the habit up just in case it works again which it won't, but never mind.

So now you know how it's done. Simple, isn't it?

—From *The Hitchhiker's Guide to the Galaxy* (collected edition), DC Comics, MAY 1997

*

Interview with Virgin.net

If there's one man who should know a thing or two about travel, it has to be the guy who's eaten burgers and fries in the restaurant at the end of the universe. We tracked down author Douglas Adams at his new home in the States, where he recently relocated for the filming of The Hitchhiker's Guide to the Galaxy.

What's your best childhood holiday memory?

My childhood holidays were pretty modest—the highlight was a fortnight in the Isle of Wight when I was about six. I remember catching what I was convinced was a plaice, though it was only the size of a postage stamp and promptly died when I tried to keep it as a pet.

Have you been back there since you were a child?

I've been back to the Isle of Wight about once. I stayed at a hotel where the evening's entertainment was to turn off the lights in the restaurant and watch as a family of badgers played on the lawn.

Where did you go the first time you went on holiday without your parents?

I hitchhiked round Europe when I was eighteen.

What did you get up to?

I went to Austria, Italy, Yugoslavia, and Turkey, staying in youth hostels and campsites, and supplemented my diet by going on free tours' round breweries. Istanbul was particularly wonderful, but I ended up with terrible food poisoning and had to return to England by train, sleeping in the corridor just next to the loo. Ah, magical times . . .

Have you been back there since?

I returned to Istanbul once. I was flying back from Australia and arbitrarily decided to stop off in Istanbul on the way back. But getting a taxi in from the airport and staying in a nice hotel instead of getting a ride on the back of a truck and sleeping in the back room of a cheap boardinghouse somehow robbed it of its magic. I wandered around for a couple of days trying to avoid carpet sellers and then gave up.

Where is the most remote or bizarre place you have ended up?

Easter Island is, of course, the most remote place on earth, famous for being farther from anywhere than anywhere else is. Which is why it is odd that I ended up there completely by accident and only for about an hour. I learned a very important lesson from this, which was—read your ticket.

When were you there and why?

I was flying from Santiago to Sydney and was a bit tired, having spent the previous two weeks looking for fur seals, and didn't wake up to what the plane's itinerary was until the pilot mentioned that we were just coming in for our one-hour stopover on Easter Island.

There was a little fleet of minibuses at the airport, which whisk you away for a quick peek at the nearest statue while the plane refuels. It was incredibly frustrating because if I had been paying attention the day before, I could easily have changed my ticket and stayed over for a couple of days.

What's your favourite city? What fascinates you most about it?

In my imagination, it's Florence, but that's only because of memories of traveling there as a student and spending days on end blissed out on sun, cheap wine, and art. Recent visits have overlaid those earlier memories with traffic jams and smog.

Now I think I'd say that my favourite city is just a small town—Santa Fe, New Mexico. I love the high desert air, the margaritas and guacamole, the silver belt buckles and the sense that people sitting at the next table to you in the cafe are probably Nobel laureates.

When was the last time you hitchhiked?

About ten years ago, on the island of Rodrigues in the Indian Ocean. Hitchhiking was the only method of getting around the island. There was no public transport, but a couple of people owned Land Rovers, so you just had to hope they'd be passing. I ended up in a forest at dusk wearing shorts, but having left my mosquito repellent behind. As a result I endured the most agonising night of my life.

Where was your favourite place when you were on the road of Last Chance to See?

Madagascar—though in fact that was a kind of prelude to *Last Chance to See.* I loved the forest and the lemurs and the warmth of the people.

What do you consider the most interesting man-made structure in the galaxy?

The dam they are building at the Three Gorges on the Yangtse. Though perhaps "baffling" would be a better word. Dams almost never do what they were intended to do, but create devastation beyond belief. And yet we keep on building them, and I can't help but wonder why. I'm convinced that if we go back far enough in the history of the human species, we will find some beaver genes creeping in there somewhere. It's the only explanation that makes sense.

Have you ever been there?

I haven't been to the Yangtse since construction started. I never want to see the thing.

And the most interesting natural structure?

A giant, two-thousand-mile-long fish in orbit around Jupiter, according to a reliable report in the *Weekly World News*. The photograph was very convincing, and I'm only surprised that more-reputable journals like *New Scientist,* or even just *The Sun,* haven't followed up with more details. We should be told.

If you were to name a place that "looks like it's just been dropped from outer space," where would you think of?

Fjordland in South Island, New Zealand. An impossible jumble of mountains, waterfalls, lakes, and ice—the most extraordinary place I think I've ever seen.

If you could go anywhere in the universe right now, where would you go, how would you get there, and who and what would you take with you?

Locally, I think Europa, one of the sixteen moons of Jupiter. It's one of the most mysterious bodies in the solar system, much beloved of science-fiction writers because it's one of the few places that could possibly sustain life of some kind, and there are certain oddities in its structure which have led to wild speculations about its being artificial. Plus, on nights when the orbital alignments are right, you must get a great view of the fish.

—Interview conducted by Claire Smith,
Virgin Net Limited, SEPTEMBER 22, 1999

✱

Riding the Rays

Every country is like a particular type of person. America is like a belligerent adolescent boy, Canada is like an intelligent thirty-five-year-old woman. Australia is like Jack Nicholson. It comes right up to you and laughs very hard in your face in a highly threatening and engaging manner. In fact it's not so much a country as such, more a sort of thin crust of semi-demented civilisation caked around the edge of a vast, raw wilderness, full of heat and dust and hopping things.

Tell most Australians that you like their country and they will give a dry laugh and say, "Well, it's the last place left now, isn't it?" which is the sort of worrying thing that Australians say. You don't *quite* know what they mean but it worries you in case they're right.

Just knowing that the place is lurking there on the other side of the world where we can't see it is oddly unsettling, and I'm always looking for excuses to go even if only to keep an eye on it. I also happen to love it. Most of it I haven't even seen yet, but there's one place that I've long wanted to revisit, because I had some frustratingly unfinished business there.

And just a few weeks ago I suddenly found the excuse I'd been looking for.

I was in England at the time. I could tell I was in England because I was sitting in the rain under a wet blanket in a muddy field listening to some fucking orchestra in a kind of red tent playing hits from American movie soundtracks. Is there *any-*

where else in the world where people would do such a thing? Anywhere? Would they do it in Italy? Would they do it in Tierra del Fuego? Would they do it on Baffin Island? No. Even in Japan, where national pastimes include ripping out your own intestines with a knife, I think they would draw the line.

In between the squalls of rain and trumpets I fell into conversation with an engaging fellow who turned out to be my sister's next-door neighbour up there in Warwickshire, which was where the sodden field was. His name was Martin Pemberton, and he was an inventor and designer. Among the things he had invented or designed, he told me, were various crucial bits of tube trains, a wonderful new form of thinking toaster, and also a Sub Bug.

What, I asked politely, was a Sub Bug?

A Sub Bug, he explained, was a jet-propelled underwater buggy sort of thing. A bit like the front half of a dolphin. You hold on to the rear and it pulls you through the sea at depths of up to thirty feet. Remember that bit in the movie of *Thunderball*? A bit like those things. Great for exploring coral reefs.

I'm not sure if that's exactly what he said. He may have said "azure sea" or "limpid depths." Probably not, but that was the picture in my brain as I sat in the blustery rain watching an escaped umbrella totter past the bandstand.

I had to try one. I said so to Martin. I may even have wrestled him to the ground and knelt on his windpipe, everything was a bit of a blur to be honest, but anyway he said he would be delighted to let me try one. The question was where? I could *try* it anywhere, even just in the local swimming pool. No. The trick was to get to try it in Australia, on the Great Barrier Reef. I needed an angle, though, if I was going to get some hapless magazine to stump up a trip for me to try it which, believe me, is the only way to travel.

Then I remembered my unfinished business in Australia.

There's an island I had visited briefly once ten years ago in the Whitsundays, at the southern end of the reef. It was a pretty dreadful place, called Hayman Island. The island itself was beautiful, but the resort that had been built on it was not, and I had ended up there by mistake, exhausted, at the end of an author tour. I hated it. The brochure was splattered with words like "international" and "superb" and "sophisticated," and what this meant was that they had Muzak pumped out of the palm trees and themed fancy-dress parties every night. By day I would sit at a table by the pool getting slowly sozzled on Tequila Sunrises and listening to the conversations at nearby tables which seemed mostly to be about road accidents involving heavy-goods vehicles. In the evening I would retire woozily to my room in order to avoid the sight of maddened drunk Australians rampaging through the night in grass skirts or cowboy hats or whatever the theme of the evening was, while I watched Mad Max movies on the hotel video. These also featured a lot of road accidents, several of which involved heavy-goods vehicles. I couldn't even find anything to read. The hotel shop only had two decent books, and I'd written both of them.

On one occasion I talked to an Australian couple on the beach. I said, "Hello, my name is Douglas, don't you hate the Muzak?" They said they didn't, as a matter of fact. They thought it was very nice and international and sophisticated. They lived on a sheep farm some 850 miles west of Brisbane, where all they ever heard, they said, was nothing. I said that must be very nice and they said that it got rather boring after a while, and that a little light Muzak was balm to them. They refused to go along with my assertion that it was like having Spam stuffed in your ears all day, and after a while the conversation petered out.

I made my escape from Hayman Island and ended up on a scuba-diving boat on Hook Reef, where I had the best week of my life, exploring the coral, diving with a wild variety of fish, dolphins, sharks, and even a minke whale.

It was only after I had left Hayman Island that I heard of something really major that I had missed there.

There was a bay tucked round on the other side, called Manta Ray Bay, that was full, as you might expect, of manta rays: huge, graceful, underwater flying carpets, one of the most beautiful animals in the world. The man who told me about it said that they were such placid and benign creatures that they would even allow people to ride on their backs underwater.

And I had missed it. For ten years I fretted about this.

Meanwhile I had also heard that Hayman Island itself had changed out of all recognition. It had been bought up by the Australian airline Ansett, who had spent a squillion dollars on ripping the Muzak out of the palm trees and transforming the resort into something that was not only international and superb and sophisticated and so on, but also breathtakingly expensive and, by all accounts, actually pretty good.

So here, I thought, was the angle. I would write an article about taking a Sub Bug all the way to Hayman Island, finding a friendly manta ray, and doing, effectively, a comparative test drive.

Now any sane, rational person might say that that was a thoroughly stupid idea, and indeed a lot of them did. However, this is that article: a comparative test drive between an underwater propeller-driven, blue and yellow one-person Sub Bug, and a giant manta ray.

Did it work out?

Guess.

The sheer fatuous unreality of the idea struck me forcibly as we watched the huge forty-kilogram silver box containing the Sub Bug being wheeled across the tarmac at Hamilton Island airport. There was, I realised, a huge difference between telling people in England that I was *going* to Australia to do a comparative test drive between a Sub Bug and a manta ray, and telling people in Australia that I had *come* to do a comparative test drive, etc. I suddenly felt like an extremely idiotic Englishman whom everyone would hate and despise and point at and snigger about and make fun of.

My wife, Jane, calmly explained to me that I always became completely paranoid when I had jet lag, and why didn't I just have a drink and relax.

Hamilton Island looks like a pretty good example of what not to do to a beautiful subtropical island on the edge of one of the great wonders of the natural world, which is to cover it with hideous high-rise junk architecture, and sell beer and T-shirts and also picture postcards of how beautiful it used to be before all the postcard shops arrived. However, we would only be there for a few minutes. Sitting waiting for us at the jetty by the small airport was the *Sun Goddess*, which was the sort of glamorous gleaming white boat that James Bond always seemed to spend an inordinate amount of time on, considering he was actually supposed to be a civil servant. It had been sent to meet guests going on to Hayman Island, and was the first indication of how much the place had changed.

We were ushered graciously aboard. One attendant offered us glasses of champagne while another stood guard by the sliding glass doors that led into the air-conditioned interior.

His job was to push them open for us. He explained that this had become necessary because unfortunately the doors didn't open automatically when you approached them, and some of their Japanese visitors would often just stand in front of them for whole minutes getting increasingly bewildered and panic-stricken until someone slid them open by hand.

The journey took about an hour, streaking effortlessly over the dark and gleaming sea under a brilliant sun. Smaller lush green islands slid past us in the distance. I watched the long wake of water folding back into the sea behind us, sipped at my champagne, and thought of an old bridge that I know in Sturminster Newton in Dorset. It still has a cast-iron notice bolted to it that warns anybody thinking of damaging or defacing the bridge in any way that the penalty is transportation. To Australia. Now, Sturminster Newton is a lovely town, but it astonishes me that the bridge is still standing.

Jane, who is much better at reading guide books than I am (I always read them on the way back to see what I missed, and it's often quite a shock), discovered something wonderful in the book she was reading. Did I know, she asked, that Brisbane was originally founded as a penal colony for convicts who committed new offences *after they had arrived in Australia?*

I spent a good half hour enjoying this single piece of information. It was wonderful. There we British sat, poor grey sodden creatures, huddling under our grey northern sky that seeped like a rancid dish cloth, busy sending those we wished to punish most severely to sit in bright sunlight on the coast of the Tasman Sea at the southern tip of the Great Barrier Reef and maybe do some surfing too. No wonder the Australians have a particular kind of smile that they reserve exclusively for use on the British.

From offshore, Hayman Island looks deserted, just a large, verdant hill fringed with pale beaches set in a dark blue sea. Only from very close to can you spot the long, low hotel nestling among the palms. There is hardly anywhere you can get a good look at it from, since it is virtually smothered with what look like giant feral pot plants. It snakes and winds its way through the greenery: pillars, fountains, shaded plazas, sun decks, discreet little shops selling heart-stoppingly expensive little things with designer labels you'd have to carefully unpick, and indiscreetly large swimming pools.

It was pretty fabulous. We adored it immediately. It was exactly the sort of place that twenty years ago I would have despised anybody for going to. One of the great things about growing older and getting things like freebie holidays is that you can finally get to do all those things that you used to despise other people for doing: sitting around on a sundeck wearing sunglasses that cost about a year's student grant, ordering up grotesque indulgences on room service, being pampered and waited on hand and foot by—and get this, this is a very important and significant part of what happens to you on Hayman Island—staff who don't just say "No worries" when you thank them for topping up your champagne glass, they actually say "No worries *at all.*" They truly and sincerely want you, specifically you, not just any old fat git lying around in a sun hat, but you *personally,* to feel that there is nothing in this best of all possible worlds that you have come to for you to concern yourself about in any way *at all.* Really. Really. We don't even despise you. *Really.* No worries *at all.*

If only it were true. I had my Sub Bug to worry about, of course. This huge great *thing* that I had lugged ten times farther than Moses had dragged the children of Israel, just in order to see how it compared with a manta ray as a means of getting about underwater. It had been quietly removed from the boat in its huge silver-coloured box and discreetly stored at the dive centre where nobody could see it or guess at its purpose.

The phone rang in our room. The room was extremely pleasant, incidentally. I'm sure you're keen to hear what the room was like, since we were staying in it at your expense. It was not enormous but it was very comfortable and sunny and tastefully decorated in Californian pastels. Our favourite item was the balcony that overlooked the sea because it had an awning that you lowered by pressing an electric switch. The switch had two settings. You could either turn it to AUTO, in which case the awning lowered itself whenever the sun came out, or you could set it to MANUEL [*sic*], in which case, we assumed, a small, incompetent Spanish waiter came and did it for you. We thought this was terribly funny. We laughed and laughed and laughed and had another glass of champagne and then laughed some more and then the phone rang.

"We have your Sub Bug," said a voice.

"Ah yes," I said. "Yes, the, er, Sub Bug. Thank you very much. Yes, is that all right?"

"No worries," said the voice, "at all."

"Ah. Good."

"So if you like, why don't you come down to the dive centre in the morning. We can check it out, see how it works, see what you need, take it out for a spin, whatever you want. We'll just do whatever we can to help you."

"Oh. Thank you. Thank you very much."

"No worries at all."

The voice was very friendly and reassuring. My jet-lagged paranoia began to subside a little. We went and had dinner.

The resort had four restaurants, and we chose the Oriental Seafood Restaurant. Seafood in Australia mostly seems to consist of barramundi, Morton Bay bugs, and everything else.

"Morton Bay bugs," said our smiling Chinese waitress, "are like lobsters, only this big." She held her two forefingers about three inches apart. "We smash their head in. Is very nice. You will like."

We didn't like that much, in fact. The restaurant was very smartly decorated in Japanese-style black and white, but the food looked better than it tasted and they played Muzak at us. For a moment I felt the ghost of the old, naff Hayman Island stalking through its glamorously tasteful new home. The other restaurants available were Polynesian, Italian, and the one to which they gave top billing, La Fontaine, a French restaurant that we decided to keep for the last of our four nights, though we had nagging doubts. I tend to like local cooking unless I'm in Wales, and the thought of French haute cuisine transported here did not fill me with confidence. I wanted to keep an open mind, though, because as it happens one of the best meals I ever had was steamed crab and chateaubriand of zebu cooked by a French-trained chef in the south of Madagascar. But then the French had infested Madagascar for seventy-five years and bequeathed it a rich legacy of culinary skills and hideous bureaucracy. We decided at least to look at La Fontaine that night. As we prowled our way toward it, we traversed acres of beautifully laid carpet, passed grand pianos, chandeliers, and reproduction Louis XVI furniture. I found myself racking my brains for any memory I might have of perhaps some schismatic eighteenth-century French court that might have been set up, however briefly, on the Great Barrier Reef. I asked Jane, who is an historian, and she assured me that I was being extremely silly, and so we went to bed.

We were woken at precisely seven-thirty the following morning and indeed every morning by a seagull that perched on our balcony and performed our regular early-morning wake-up screech. After breakfast we went to the dive centre, which was about half a mile from the hotel, and met Ian Green.

It was Ian who had called the previous evening. He was in charge of all the diving stuff on Hayman, and a more helpful and friendly person would be hard to imagine. We got the Sub Bug unpacked, and examined it as it stood gleaming in the sun.

It is, as I have said, shaped like the front half of a dolphin. The body of it is blue, and toward the front there are two small yellow fins, one on each side, that can rotate through a few degrees and direct the Sub Bug upward or downward. At the back are two large handles that you hold on to as the Sub Bug pulls you through the water. Within reach of your thumbs are buttons that make the thing go, and control its ascent and descent. Inside the Bug is a cylinder of compressed air—a normal scuba cylinder—and this provides power to spin the two propellers that push the Bug forward, and also supplies air down a flexible tube to a free-floating regulator. A regulator is the thing you stick in your mouth that gives you your air when you're diving. The point of this arrangement is that you only need your mask and flippers; you don't need to carry a scuba tank on your own back, because you're getting your air direct from the Sub Bug. The Bug is designed in such a way that you can set a maximum depth beyond which it will not go. The very maximum anyway is thirty feet.

Ian had received a flurry of faxes from Martin Pemberton about setting up the machine, and was pretty confident about it.

"No worries at all," he said, and asked me what I planned.

I said it might be an idea to take it for a shallow local try-out before taking it out into deep water.

"No worries," he said.

I said that we could then take it with us on the proper diving expedition that was going out from the island the following morning.

"No worries," he said.

"So I will then spend a little time trying it out, getting used to it, and putting it through its paces around the reef."

"No worries," he said.

"And then, er," I said, "for the purposes of this article I have to write, which is by way of being a sort of comparative test drive, I want to try the same thing on a manta ray."

"No chance," he said. "No chance *at all.*"

I suppose I should have foreseen this.

Or perhaps it was just as well that I hadn't foreseen it. If I had foreseen it, I wouldn't have been standing there half in a wet suit looking out at the glittering Tasman Sea and thinking, "Oh damn." I would have been sitting fiddling in my office in Islington wondering if I'd done enough "work" yet to justify going out and getting a bun.

The issue was very simple. As someone who has spent over two years working on ecological projects, the very first thing I should have realised was that you don't disturb the animals. It might have been all right to try and mount a manta ray ten years ago when I first heard about it, but not now. No way. You don't touch the reef. You don't take anything. No shells, no coral. You don't touch the fish, except maybe a few that it's okay to feed. And you certainly don't fuck about trying to ride manta rays.

"Hardly any chance you'd even be able to get near one anyway," said Ian. "They're very timid creatures. I guess some people have managed to get to ride on a ray in the past, but I would imagine it would be very difficult. But now we just can't allow it."

"No," I said, rather shamefacedly. "I understand, believe me. I just hadn't really thought it through, I guess."

"But we can go and have some fun with the Sub Bug," said Ian. "No worries. We can take some pictures too. That's a hell of a camera you've got there."

We now come to another rather embarrassing part of the story about which I have so far been extremely silent. Some very nice people at Nikon in England had lent me for this trip a brand-new Nikonos AF SR underwater autofocus camera, which is about £15,000 worth of the most sexy and desirable and fabulous camera equipment in the world. The camera is just wonderful, brilliant technology. Really. You want to take a photograph underwater, this is the perfect thing. It's an astounding bit of kit. Why am I going on about it like this? Well, I spend a lot of time working on a computer, and because I am used to using a Macintosh, I hardly even bother to read manuals and so—I didn't really bother to read the manual for this camera.

I realised that when I got the films back.

Please—I really don't want to say any more, except to say thank you very much, Nikon. It really is an awesome camera, and I hope very much that you will let me borrow it again one day. I won't mention the camera again in this article.

We took a small dinghy out to a tiny deserted island about ten minutes away. Ian and I spent a happy hour or so pootling around with the Bug. We dealt with a couple of problems—a grain of sand in a valve, and so on. We worked out that the Bug didn't work too well in very shallow water when it had to work against a tide. Well, we'd take it deeper tomorrow. Jane lay in the sun on the beach and read a book. After a while we got back in the dinghy and went back to Hayman. Not much of a story in all that, I suppose, but the reason I mention it is that I remember it very vividly, and one of the shortcomings, I sometimes feel, of somewhere like, for instance, Islington, is the lack of any immediately accessible tiny islands that you can spend the afternoon pootling around with Sub Bugs on. Just a bit of a poignant thought, really. We don't even have any decent bridges you can deface.

There were about ten of us on the dive boat the following morning. The hotel is so spacious and rambling that you don't often get to see many of the other guests, but it was interesting to begin to realise how many of them were Japanese. Not only Japanese, but Japanese who held hands and gazed into each other's eyes a lot. Hayman, we discovered, was a major Japanese honeymoon destination.

The Sub Bug sat up on the back of the boat, and I sat looking at it as we made the hour's journey out to the reef. Hardly any of the Barrier Reef islands are actually on the reef itself, except for Heron Island. You have to get there by boat. I was very excited. Apart from a couple of refresher dives in pools, this was my first proper scuba dive in years. I absolutely love it. I'm one of those people who has been tantalised by the flying dream for years, and scuba diving is the closest thing I know to flying. And for someone who is six foot five and less sylphlike than, to pick a name at random, the Princess of Wales, the sensation of weightlessness is an ecstatic one. Also, I usually vomit on the way back, which is a good way of working up an appetite.

We reached the reef, moored, got into our wet-suit gear, and prepared to dive. At low tide, the reef usually breaks the surface of the water. You can even walk on it, though that is now discouraged because of the damage it can cause. Even when the tide is high, though, reef diving is not a deep-diving sport. Most of what there is to see lies in the upper thirty feet, and there's rarely any cause to go deeper than sixty feet. The very deepest a sports diver can go is about ninety feet, but there's really not a lot of point. You're usually looking at bare rock rather than coral at that depth, and Boyle's law means that you use up your air much faster down there. Also, you have to spend much more time on the surface between dives if you're not going to get the bends. The Sub Bug keeps you at a safe maximum depth of thirty feet.

I wanted to do a regular dive first to get my bearings. Two at a time, we clamped our masks and regulators to our faces, did the Big Stride off the diving deck at the back of the boat, and dropped into the water in an eruption of bubbles. A moored dive boat always attracts the attention of a lot of local fish who expect, usually rightly, that they will get fed. The ones you'll get to see if you're lucky are the Maori wrasses, which are extraordinary pale olive-green creatures about the size of a Samsonite suitcase. They have large, protuberant mouths and very heavy, protuberant brows, but the reason for the name *Maori,* any Australian will assure you apologetically, is some paintlike markings on their brow. Australians are not racists anymore.

There were quite a few wrasses around the boat, and I made the mistake of getting between a couple of them and some pieces of bread that someone had thrown from the boat. The animals blithely barged past me to get at the food.

I sank down to the reef in the huge space of water and light beneath the boat, and drifted easily round it for a while to get used to being underwater again, then came back to the boat to divest myself of my scuba tank and collect the Sub Bug. Together, Ian and I hauled it into the water. I got myself into position behind the thing, and started it up. One of the curious features of scuba diving is that your suit and equipment seem so heavy and cumbersome and unwieldy on the surface—which is one of the things that tend to frighten beginners—but once you descend below water level, everything begins to flow smoothly and easily, and the trick is to exert yourself absolutely as little as possible, in order to conserve oxygen. It is, almost by definition, the least aerobic sport there is. It won't make you fit.

At first I was disappointed that the Sub Bug wouldn't move me faster than I could swim. We were gently pulling our way down, but as I started to get used once more to the slowness with which everything happens underwater, I began to relish the long, slow, balletic curves it let you make through the water, stretched out at full length behind it instead of swimming in the normal position with your arms by your side or on your chest. Following the contours of the reef became like skiing in ultra slow motion—an almost Zenlike idea. I began to enjoy it a lot, though after fifteen minutes of experimenting with it, I began to feel I had exhausted its repertoire and began to look forward to swimming under my own power again. I suspect that it's probably a machine best suited to people who want to experience a dive but don't want to bother with the business of learning to use buoyancy jackets and so on.

I returned to the boat and we hauled the thing back up out of the water. Well, I'd driven the Sub Bug. But over lunch I was worried about the total collapse of my absurd comparative test-drive plan, and discussed my thoughts with Ian and Jane.

"I think we just have to think about the comparative test drive on a kind of conceptual basis," I said. "And we have to award some points. Obviously the Sub Bug wins some points for being portable up to a point. You can take it on a plane, which you wouldn't do with a manta ray, or at least not with a manta ray you liked, and I think that we probably like all manta rays on principle really, don't we? Your manta ray is going to be a lot faster and more manoeuvrable, and you don't need to change its tank every twenty minutes. But the big points that the Sub Bug wins are for the fact that you can actually get on it. I think it has to get a lot of credit for that, if you're thinking of it as transport. But then, let's turn the whole thing around again. The reason you can't actually ride a manta ray is a sound ecological one, and on just about every ecological criterion the manta ray wins hands down. In fact, any form of transport that you *can't actually use* would be a major ecological benefit, don't you think?"

Ian nodded understandingly.

"Can I get on and read my book now, please?" said Jane.

For the afternoon dive, Ian said he wanted to take me in a different direction from the boat. I asked him why, and he looked noncommittal. I followed him down into the water and slowly we flippered our way across to a new part of the reef. When we reached it, the flat top of the reef was about four feet below the surface, and the sunlight dappled gently over the extraordinary shapes and colours of the brain coral, the antler coral, the sea ferns and anemones. The stuff you see beneath the water often seems like a wild parody of the stuff you see above it. I remember the thought I had when first I dived on the Barrier Reef years ago, which was that this was all the stuff that people used to have on their mantelpieces in the fifties. It took me a while to rid myself of the notion that the reef was a load of kitsch.

I've never learnt the names of a lot of fish. I always swot them up on the boat and forget them a week later. But watching the breathtaking variety of shape and movement keeps me entranced for hours, or would if the oxygen allowed. If I were not an atheist, I think I would have to be a Catholic because if it wasn't the forces of natural selection that designed fish, it must have been an Italian.

I was moving forward slowly in the shallows. A few feet in front of me the reef gradually dipped down into a broad valley. The valley floor was wide and dark and flat. Ian was directing my attention toward it. I didn't know why. There seemed to be just an absence of interesting coral. And then, as I looked, the whole black floor of the valley slowly lifted upward and started gently to waft its way away from us. As it moved, its edges were rippling softly and I could see that underneath it was pure white. I was transfixed by the realisation that what I was looking at was an eight-foot-wide giant manta ray.

It banked away in a wide, sweeping turn in the deeper water. It seemed to be moving breathtakingly slowly, and I was desperate to keep up with it. I came down the side of the reef to follow it. Ian motioned me not to alarm the creature, but just move slowly. I had quickly realised that its size was deceptive and it was moving much more swiftly than I realised. It banked again round the contour of the reef, and I began to see its shape more clearly. It was very roughly diamond-shaped. Its tail is not long, like a sting ray's. The most extraordinary thing is its head. Where you would expect its head to be, it's almost as if something has taken a bite out of it instead. From the two forward points—the outer edges of the "bite," if you see what I mean—

depend two horns, folded downward. And on each of these horns is a single large black eye.

As it moved, shimmering and undulating its giant wings, folding itself through the water, I felt that I was looking at the single most beautiful and unearthly thing I had ever seen in my life. Some people have described them as looking like living stealth bombers, but it is an evil image to apply to a creature so majestic, fluid, and benign.

I followed it as it swam around the outside of the reef. I couldn't follow fast or well, but it was making such wide, sweeping turns that I only had to move relatively short distances round the reef to keep it in sight. Twice, even three times it circled round the reef and then at last it disappeared and I thought I had lost it for good. I stopped and looked around. No. It had definitely gone. I was saddened, but exhilarated with wonder at what I had seen. Then I became aware of a shadow moving on the sea floor at the periphery of my vision. I looked up, unprepared for what I then saw.

The manta ray soared over the top of the reef above me, only this time it had two more in its wake behind it. Together the three vast creatures, moving in perfect, undulating harmony of line, as if following invisible rollercoaster rails, sped off and away till they were lost at last in the darkening distance of the water.

I was very quiet that evening as we packed the Sub Bug back into its big silver box. I thanked Ian for finding the manta rays. I said I understood about not riding them.

"Ah, no worries, mate," he said. "No worries at all."

—1992

* * *

Who are your favorite authors?

Charles Dickens, Jane Austen, Kurt Vonnegut, P. G. Wodehouse, Ruth Rendell.

*

Sunset at Blandings

This is P. G. Wodehouse's last—and unfinished—book. It is unfinished not just in the sense that it suddenly, heartbreakingly for those of us who love this man and his work, stops in midflow, but in the more important sense that the text up to that point is also unfinished. A first draft for Wodehouse was a question of getting the essential ingredients of a story organised—its plot structure, its characters and their comings and goings, the mountains they climb and the cliffs they fall off. It is the next stage of writing—the relentless revising, refining, and polishing—that turned his works into the marvels of language we know and love. When he was writing a book, he used to pin the pages in undulating waves around the wall of his workroom. Pages he felt were working well would be pinned up high, and those that still needed work would be lower down the wall. His aim was to get the entire manuscript up to the picture rail before he handed it in. Much of *Sunset at Blandings* would probably still have been obscured by the chair backs. It was a work in progress. Many of the lines in it are just placeholders for what would come in later revisions—the dazzling images and conceits that would send the pages shooting up the walls.

Will you, anyway, find much evidence of the great genius of

Wodehouse here? Well, to be honest, no. Not just because it is an unfinished work in progress, but also because at the time of writing he was what can only be described as ninety-three. At that age I think you are entitled to have your best work behind you. In a way, Wodehouse was condemned by his extreme longevity (he was born the year that Darwin died and was still working well after the Beatles had split up) to end up playing Pierre Menard to his own Cervantes. (I'm not going to unravel that for you. If you don't know what I'm talking about, you should read Jorge Luis Borges's short story "Pierre Menard, Author of *Don Quixote.*" It's only six pages long, and you'll be wanting to drop me a postcard to thank me for pointing it out to you.) But you will want to read *Sunset* for completeness, and for that sense you get, from its very unfinishedness, of being suddenly and unexpectedly close to a Master actually at work—a bit like seeing paint pots and scaffolding being carried in and out of the Sistine Chapel.

Master? Great genius? Oh yes. One of the most blissful joys of the English language is the fact that one of its greatest practitioners ever, one of the guys on the very top table of all, was a jokesmith. Though maybe it shouldn't be that big a surprise. Who else would be up there? Austen, of course, Dickens and Chaucer. The only one who couldn't make a joke to save his life would be Shakespeare.

Oh come on, let's be frank and fearless for a moment. There's nothing worse than watching a certain kind of English actor valiantly trying to ham it up as, for instance, Dogberry in *Much Ado.* It's desperate stuff. We even draw a veil over the whole buttock-clenching business by calling the comic device he employs in that instance *malapropism*—after Sheridan's character Mrs. Malaprop, who does exactly the same thing only funny in *The Rivals.* And it's no good saying it's something to do with the fact that Shakespeare was writing in the sixteenth century. What difference does that make? Chaucer had no difficulty being funny as hell way back in the fourteenth century when the spelling was even worse.

Maybe it's because our greatest writing genius was incapable of being funny that we have decided that being funny doesn't count. Which is tough on Wodehouse (as if he could have cared less) because his entire genius was for being funny, and being funny in such a sublime way as to put mere poetry in the shade. The precision with which he plays upon every aspect of a word's character simultaneously—its meaning, timbre, rhythm, the range of its idiomatic connections and flavours, would make Keats whistle. Keats would have been proud to have written "the smile vanished from his face like breath off a razor-blade," or of Honoria Glossop's laugh that it sounded like "cavalry on a tin bridge." Speaking of which, Shakespeare, when he wrote "A man may smile, and smile and be a villain" might have been at least as impressed by "Many a man may look respectable, and yet be able to hide at will behind a spiral staircase."

What Wodehouse writes is pure word music. It matters not one whit that he writes endless variations on a theme of pig kidnappings, lofty butlers, and ludicrous impostures. He is the greatest *musician* of the English language, and exploring variations of familiar material is what musicians do all day. In fact, what it's *about* seems to me to be wonderfully irrelevant. Beauty doesn't have to be *about* anything. What's a vase about? What's a sunset or a flower about? What, for that matter, is Mozart's Twenty-third Piano Concerto *about*? It is said that all art tends toward the condition of music, and music isn't *about* anything—unless it's not very good music. Film music is about something. "The Dam Busters' March" is about something. A

Bach fugue, on the other hand, is pure form, beauty, and playfulness, and I'm not sure that very much, in terms of human art and achievement, lies beyond a Bach fugue. Maybe the quantum electrodynamic theory of light. Maybe *Uncle Fred Flits By*, I don't know.

Evelyn Waugh, I think, compared Wodehouse's world to a pre-fall Eden, and it's true that in Blandings, Plum—if I may call him that—has managed to create and sustain an entirely innocent and benign Paradise, a task that, we may recall, famously defeated Milton, who was probably trying too hard. Like Milton, Wodehouse reaches outside his Paradise for the metaphors that will make it real for his readers. But where Milton reaches, rather confusingly, into the world of classical gods and heroes for his images (like a TV writer who only draws his references from other TV shows), Wodehouse is vividly real. "She was standing scrutinising the safe, and heaving gently like a Welsh rarebit about to come to the height of its fever." "The Duke's moustache was rising and falling like seaweed on an ebb-tide." When it comes to making metaphors (well, all right, similes if you insist), you don't mess with the Master. Of course, Wodehouse never burdened himself with the task of justifying the ways of God to Man, but only of making Man, for a few hours at a time, inextinguishably happy.

Wodehouse better than Milton? Well, of course it's an absurd comparison, but I know which one I'd keep in the balloon, and not just for his company, but for his art.

We Wodehouse fans are very fond of phoning each other up with new discoveries. But we may do the great man a disservice when we pull out our favourite quotes in public, like "Ice formed on the butler's upper slopes," or ". . . like so many substantial Americans, he had married young and kept on marrying, springing from blonde to blonde like the chamois of the Alps leaping from crag to crag" or (here I go again) my current favourite, "He spun round with a sort of guilty bound, like an adagio dancer surprised while watering the cat's milk" because, irreducibly wonderful though they are, by themselves they are a little like stuffed fish on a mantelpiece. You need to see them in action to get the full effect. There is not much in Freddie Threepwood's isolated line "I have here in this sack a few simple rats" to tell you that when you read it in context you are at the pinnacle of one of the most sublime moments in all English literature.

Shakespeare? Milton? Keats? How can I possibly mention the author of *Pearls, Girls and Monty Bodkin* and *Pigs Have Wings* in the same breath as these men? He's just not serious!

He doesn't need to be serious. He's better than that. He's up in the stratosphere of what the human mind can do, above tragedy and strenuous thought, where you will find Bach, Mozart, Einstein, Feynman, and Louis Armstrong, in the realms of pure, creative playfulness.

> From the Introduction to *Sunset at Blandings* (Penguin Books)

✳

Tea

One or two Americans have asked me why the English like tea so much, which never seems to them to be a very good drink. To understand, you have to make it properly.

There is a very simple principle to the making of tea, and it's this—to get the proper flavour of tea, the water has to be boilING (not boilED) when it hits the tea leaves. If it's merely hot, then the tea will be insipid. That's why we English have these odd rituals, such as warming the teapot first (so as not to cause the boiling water to cool down too fast as it hits the pot). And that's why the American habit of bringing a teacup, a tea bag, and a pot of hot water to the table is merely the perfect way of making a thin, pale, watery cup of tea that nobody in their right mind would want to drink. The Americans are all mystified about why the English make such a big thing out of tea because most Americans HAVE NEVER HAD A GOOD CUP OF TEA. That's why they don't understand. In fact, the truth of the matter is that most English people don't know how to make tea anymore either, and most people drink cheap instant coffee instead, which is a pity, and gives Americans the impression that the English are just generally clueless about hot stimulants.

So the best advice I can give to an American arriving in England is this: Go to Marks and Spencer and buy a packet of Earl Grey tea. Go back to where you're staying and boil a kettle of water. While it is coming to the boil, open the sealed packet and sniff. Careful—you may feel a bit dizzy, but this is in fact perfectly legal. When the kettle has boiled, pour a little of it into a teapot, swirl it around, and tip it out again. Put a couple (or three, depending on the size of the pot) of tea bags into the pot. (If I was really trying to lead you into the paths of righteousness, I would tell you to use free leaves rather than bags, but let's just take this in easy stages.) Bring the kettle back up to the boil, and then pour the boiling water as quickly as you can into the pot. Let it stand for two or three minutes, and then pour it into a cup. Some people will tell you that you shouldn't have milk with Earl Grey, just a slice of lemon. Screw them. I like it with milk. If you think you will like it with milk, then it's probably best to put some milk into the bottom of the cup before you pour in the tea.* If you pour milk into a cup of hot tea, you will scald the milk. If you think you will prefer it with a slice of lemon, then, well, add a slice of lemon.

Drink it. After a few moments you will begin to think that the place you've come to isn't maybe quite so strange and crazy after all.

MAY 12, 1999

✳

The Rhino Climb

Great wumps of equatorial heat are coming up at me from off the tarmac. It's the short rainy season in Kenya, but the sun burned off the morning dampness in minutes. I'm slathered in sunblock, the road stretches off into the distant heat haze, and my legs are settling in nicely. Dotted along the road ahead and behind me are other walkers, some striding vigorously, others appearing just to amble, but all in fact moving at the same speed. One of them is wearing a large, grey, sculptural edifice, made out of a painted woven plastic fabric stretched over a metal frame. A large horn bobs along in front of it. The thing is a grotesque but oddly beautiful caricature of a rhinoceros moving along with

---

*This is socially incorrect. The socially correct way of pouring tea is to put the milk in after the tea. Social correctness has traditionally had nothing whatever to do with reason, logic, or physics. In fact, in England it is generally considered socially incorrect to know stuff or think about things. It's worth bearing this in mind when visiting.

swift, busy strides. The sun beats down. Lopsided lorries grind their way dangerously past us. The drivers shout and grin at our rhinoceros. When we pass, as we frequently do, lorries that have clearly just rolled over and collapsed on the side of the road, we wonder if it was anything to do with us.

The other walkers have all been walking for several days now, from the shore at Mombasa along the main highway to the truck stop at Voi, the local centre of the universe. I joined them here last night, rattling in by Land-Rover from Nairobi with my sister Jane, who's been doing some work for Save the Rhino International, which is what we are all here to support. From here we will follow the road on as the tarmac gradually peters out toward the Tanzanian border.

Over the border lies Mount Kilimanjaro, the tallest mountain in the world. It is to the peak of Kilimanjaro that the expedition is intending to climb—a small bunch of Englishman out walking miles a day in the midday sun and taking turns at wearing a large rhino costume. Mad dogs have thrown in the towel long ago.

What's all this, I expect you're thinking, about "the tallest mountain in the world"? Everest, surely, deserves at least an honourable mention in this category? Well, it all depends on your point of view. Certainly, Everest stands a sturdy 29,028 feet above sea level, which is, in its way, impressive. But if you were going to climb Everest, you would probably start, if you were using a reliable guide, somewhere in the Himalayas. Anywhere in the Himalayas is pretty damn high to start with, and so, to hear some people tell it, it's just a smartish jog to do the last little bit to the actual top of Everest. The way to keep it interesting these days is to do it without oxygen or in your underpants or something.

But Kilimanjaro is not part of a widespread upheaval like

Everest. It was a long time before people managed to work out which bit of the Himalayas was actually the highest, and the discovery was finally made, as I recall, on a desk in London. No such problem with Kilimanjaro. It's volcanic and stands on its own, surrounded by a few footling little hills. When you finally get to see Killy, searching among the befuddling clouds on the horizon, your blood suddenly runs cold. "Oh," you say at last, "you mean above the clouds." Your whole head tilts upward. "Oh my god . . ." From base to apex, it is the tallest mountain in the world. It's certainly a hell of a thing to climb in a rhino costume. This crackpot idea was first put to me months earlier by the founders of Save the Rhino International, David Stirling and Johnny Roberts, and I didn't realise at first that they meant it. They raved on for a bit about having acquired a whole set of rhino costumes that Ralph Steadman had designed for an opera, and that they would be just the thing for making the ascent of Kilimanjaro in. They had already been used, David told me by way of reassurance, for running in the New York Marathon. "It'll have enormous impact," they said, "believe me. Really."

I began to realise the truth of this as we approached our first village of the day, and perhaps now would be a good point to explain what the purpose of the whole expedition was. It was not, in fact, to raise money directly for rhino conservation. Rhinos, which used to be plentiful on the plains of East Africa, are now hideously rare, but in Kenya they are about as well conserved as they can be anywhere in Africa. Richard Leakey's Kenya Wildlife Service consists of eight thousand well-trained, well-equipped, well-armed, highly motivated soldiers, and represents a formidable force. Too formidable, some of his opponents feel. Poaching in Kenya is, officially, "no longer a problem." But conservation is a continually evolving business, and we have begun to realise that just wading into Africa and telling the local people that they mustn't do to their wildlife what we've done to ours, and that we are there to make sure they don't, is an attitude that, to say the least, needs a little refining.

The communities that live along the margins of the great national parks have a tough time. They are poor and undernourished, their lands are restricted by the parks, and when from time to time the odd lion or elephant breaks out of the park, they are the ones who suffer. Arguments about preserving the genetic diversity of the planet can seem a little abstract to someone who has just lost the crops he needs to feed his family or, worse, has just lost one of his family. In the long run, conservation can't be imposed by outsiders, overriding the needs of local people. If anyone is going to take care of the wildlife, then, in the end, it must be the local people—and someone must take care of them.

Our route took us alongside and sometimes through the great national parks of Tsavo East and Tsavo West, and it was the people who lived on these perimeters that we had come to visit, and also to help. The £100,000 we were hoping to raise from the walk would be spent on building school classrooms, stocking libraries, and paying for other community projects. We wanted to encourage them to see that whatever problems the wildlife may pose to them, it was of benefit to them as well.

As we were approaching our first village of the day, the rhino, with Todd Jones inside it, was in the lead. All the walkers took turns at wearing the thing for an hour at a time, and you quickly learned to tell who was in it at any moment from the way in which it moved. If the rhino sauntered, then it was Giles inside. Giles was an ex-Gordonstoun Hugh Grant lookalike who had spent the last few years hitchhiking languidly around Africa with his own parachute. His technique was to turn up at airfields with this parachute, find someone who was flying in the general direction he wanted to go, hitch a lift, and then, when the fancy took him, just jump out of the plane. Apparently his girlfriend was a top supermodel who, every few months, would find out where he was, fly out there, and then (I'm guessing here) have him washed and sent up to her hotel room.

If the rhino ambled along in a genial way, then it was Tom inside. Tom was a tall, Wodehousian man with exactly the wrong complexion for Africa. He had the amiable air of a member of the landed gentry, and when I asked him where he lived he said, in a vague kind of way, "Shropshire."

If the rhino bustled along busily, it was Todd inside. Todd was not a mad Englishman because he was Welsh. He was in charge of the rhino costumes, had worn them originally in the opera for which they had been designed, during which he had had to carry enormously heavy sopranos on his back. He told me that he had originally wanted to be a vet, but had ended up being a succession of animals instead. Any time you see a film or TV show or a commercial that features someone dressed up as an animal, it's probably Todd inside. "I was in *The Lion, the Witch and the Wardrobe*," he told me. "Guess," he added, "which one I was." One evening he showed me pictures of his family. Here was a beautiful picture of his wife, another of his young daughter, a sweet picture of his baby son, and here was one of Todd himself. Todd was done up, very convincingly, as a bright blue centaur.

As Todd/rhino bustled along, suddenly huge crowds of children erupted onto the road ahead of us, and hurried toward us, singing and dancing and chanting, "Rhino! Rhino! Rhino!" We were quickly surrounded and escorted the last few hundred yards to where they had prepared a reception for us in the village square. The whole village had turned out to greet us with enormous enthusiasm. We sat and watched, panting in the heat and sluicing ourselves down with bottled water, as the children of the village put on a display of dancing and choral singing that was, frankly, amazing. When I say children, I'm not just talking about seven-year-olds, I'm talking about seventeen-year-olds as well. It's odd that we don't anymore have a comfortable word that covers the whole range. "Youngsters"? Patronising. "Kids"? No. "Youths"? Sounds as if they've just broken into a warehouse and stolen something. Children, then. The children had written a song about rhinos, which they then sang for us. In the background Giles had quietly taken over from Todd in the rhino suit, and after a while he joined in the dancing, lolloping, and swaying around, chasing and playing with the children before finally dodging off behind a tree for a quick ciggy. We then, with slightly less enthusiasm, sat through a series of speeches that some local dignitaries had turned up to deliver. Wherever we went, there were local dignitaries keen to be seen to be associated with us.

Gradually the whole point of the rhino suit was beginning to dawn on me. The arrival of the rhino and the Rhino Climb team was something that the village had been looking forward to and preparing for for months. It was the biggest event of the year, a carnival, a festival, a holiday. Being visited by a rhino was something that would be remembered by the villagers, and particularly the children, for years in a way that being visited by a bunch of English toffs in hats would not.

We were then taken to see the village school. Like most of the village, it was made of breezeblocks, and was half-finished. The doors and windows were empty holes, the furniture was just a few rickety benches and some trestle tables, and laid out on these were dozens of pictures of the local wildlife that the children had drawn, and which we were to judge and give prizes for. The prizes were Rhino Climb baseball hats, and, whoever won the prizes, we had to make sure that every member of the village actually got a hat. And once we have collected our sponsorship money, we will be able to complete the building of their schoolroom for them.

When at last we left, the children danced along with us for several miles, laughing and singing improvised songs—one of them would start, and the others would quickly pick it up and join in.

The words seem oddly dated, don't they? It all sounds rather naïve and sentimental to be talking about children laughing and dancing and singing together when we all know perfectly well that what children do in real life is snarl and take drugs. But these children/kids/youths, and all the ones we came across on our journey, were happy in a way that we in the West are almost embarrassed by.

The last of the children drop away from us. Our support Land Rover drives slowly past, distributing Cokes and Fantas. Jim, our photographer, is sitting on its tailgate, taking pictures of us with his Canon EOS 1, which I've been coveting ever since I saw it. Keis, our Dutch video cameraman, hoists his lightweight Sony three-chip up to his shoulder and pans along the line of walkers. I wonder if there's anywhere in the West that you could find a hundred children to sing and dance like that.

The following day is my first stint in the rhino suit. I'm much too big for it, and my legs stick out absurdly from the bottom, so that I look like a giant prawn tempura. Inside, the heat and the stench of stale sweat and old Dettol are almost overpowering until you get into the swing of things. Todd walks along beside me, determinedly keeping me engaged in conversation. After a while I realise he's monitoring me to make sure I don't faint. Todd's a good man and I like him a lot. He takes good care of people, and takes even better care of his beloved rhino suit.

I stop for a moment to pour some water into and over my face, and catch a glimpse of myself in the window of the Land-Rover. I look unimaginably stupid, and I reflect that there is something very odd about this sponsored walking business. It's always undertaken for good causes: cancer research, famine relief, wildlife conservation, and so on, but the deal seems to be this: "Okay, you are trying to raise funds for this very worthwhile cause, and I can see that it's an important and crucial matter and that lives or indeed whole species are at stake and something needs to be done as a matter of urgency, but, well . . . I don't know . . . Tell you what—do something really pointless and stupid and maybe a bit dangerous, *then* I'll give you some money."

I only spent a week on the walk. I didn't get to climb Kilimanjaro, though I did get to see it. I was very sorry not to get to go up it, though, having seen it, I have to say that I wasn't very, *very* sorry. I did get to see one rhino, briefly, out of the thousands that used to roam in this area, and I wondered if it had any sense at all that all was not right with its world. Human beings have been on this planet for a million years or so, and in that time we have faced all sorts of threats to our survival: famine, plague, warfare, AIDS. Rhinoceroses have been here for 40 million years, and just one threat has brought them to the brink of extinction: human beings. We are not the only species to have caused devastation to the rest of the world, and it must be said in our favour that we are the only one that has become aware of the consequences of its behaviour and tried to do something about it. However, I reflect as I shift the costume back into a comfortable walking posture and squint forward over its bobbing plastic horn, we do go about it in some odd ways.

Esquire, MARCH 1995

✳

For Children Only

You will need to know the difference between Friday and a fried egg. It's quite a simple difference, but an important one. Friday comes at the end of the week, whereas a fried egg comes out of a hen. Like most things, of course, it isn't quite that simple. The fried egg isn't properly a fried egg till it's been put in a frying pan and fried. This is something you wouldn't do to a Friday, of course, though you might do it *on* a Friday. You can also fry eggs on a Thursday, if you like, or on a cooker. It's all rather complicated, but it makes a kind of sense if you think about it for a while.

It's also good to know the difference between a lizard and a blizzard. This is quite an easy one. Though the two things sound very much alike, you find them in such very different parts of the world that it is a very simple matter to tell them apart. If you are somewhere inside the Arctic circle then what you are looking at is probably a blizzard, whereas if you are in a hot and dry place like Madagascar or Mexico, it's more likely to be a lizard.

This animal is a lemur. There are lots of different kinds of lemurs, and they nearly all live in Madagascar. Madagascar is an island—a very large island: much, much larger than your hat, but not as large as the moon.

The moon is much larger than it appears to be. This is worth remembering because next time you are looking at the moon you can say in a deep and mysterious voice, "The moon is *much* larger than it appears to be," and people will know that you are a wise person who has thought about this a lot.

This particular kind of lemur is called a ring-tailed lemur. Nobody knows why it is called this, and generations of scientists have been baffled by it. One day a very wise person indeed will probably work out why it is called a ring-tailed lemur. If this person is *exceedingly* wise, then he or she will only tell very close friends, in *secret,* because otherwise everybody will know it, and then nobody will realise how wise the first person to know it really was.

Here are two more things you should know the difference between: road and woad. One is a thing that you drive along in a car, or on a bicycle, and the other is a kind of blue body paint that British people used to wear thousands of years ago instead of clothes. Usually it's quite easy to tell these two apart, but if you find it at all difficult to say your *r*'s properly, it can lead to terrible confusion: imagine trying to ride a bicycle on a small patch of blue paint, or having to dig up an entire street just to have something to wear if you fancy spending the evening with some Druids.

Druids used to live thousands of years ago. They used to wear long white robes and had very strong opinions about what a wonderful thing the sun was. Do you know what an opinion is? I expect someone in your family has probably got one, so you could ask them to tell you about it. Asking people about their opinions is a very good way of making friends. Telling them about your own opinions can also work, but not always quite as well.

Nowadays most people know what a wonderful thing the sun is, so there aren't many Druids around anymore, but there are still a few just in case it slips our mind from time to time. If you find someone who has a long white robe and talks about the sun a lot, then you might have found a Druid. If he turns out to be about two thousand years old, then that's a sure sign.

If the person you've found has got a slightly shorter white coat, with buttons up the front, then it may be that he is an astronomer and not a Druid. If he is an astronomer, then one of the things you could ask him is how far away the sun is. The answer will probably startle you a lot. If it doesn't, then tell him from me that he hasn't explained it very well. After he's told you how far away the sun is, ask him how far away some of the stars are. That will *really* surprise you. If you can't find an astronomer yourself, then ask your parents to find one for you. They don't all wear white coats, which is one of the things that sometimes make them hard to spot. Some of them wear jeans or even suits.

When we say that something is startling, we mean that it surprises us a very great deal. When we say that something is a starling, we mean that it is a type of migratory bird. *Bird* is a word we use quite often, which is why it's such an easy word to say. Most of the words we use often, like *house* and *car* and *tree,* are easy to say. *Migratory* is a word we don't use nearly so much, and saying it can sometimes make you feel as if your teeth are stuck together with toffee. If birds were called "migratories" rather than "birds," we probably wouldn't talk about them nearly so much. We'd all say, "Look, there's a dog!" or "There's a cat!" but if a migratory went by, we'd probably just say, "Is it teatime yet?" and not even mention it, however nifty it looked.

But *migratory* doesn't mean that something is stuck together with toffee, however much it sounds like it. It means that something spends part of the year in one country and part of it in another.

Brandenburg 5

Whatever new extremities of discovery or understanding we reach, we always seem to find the footsteps of Bach there already. When we see images of the strange mathematical beasts lurking at the heart of the natural world—fractal landscapes, the infinitely unfolding paisley whorls of the Mandelbrot Set, the Fibonacci series, which describes the pattern of leaves growing on the stem of a plant, the Strange Attractors that beat at the heart of chaos—it is always the dizzying, complex spirals of Bach that come to mind.

Some people say that the mathematical complexity of Bach renders it unemotional. I think the opposite is true. As I listen to the interplay of parts in a piece of Bach polyphony, each individual strand of music gathers hold of a different feeling in my mind, and takes them on simultaneous interweaving roller-coasters of emotion. One part may be quietly singing to itself, another on an exhilarating rampage, another is sobbing in the corner, another dancing. Arguments break out, laughter, rage. Peace is restored. The parts can be utterly different, yet all belong indivisibly together. It's as emotionally complex as a family.

And now, as we discover that each individual mind is a family of different parts, all working separately but together to create the fleeting shimmers we call consciousness, it seems that, once again, Bach was there before us.

When you listen to the Fifth Brandenburg Concerto, you don't need a musicologist to tell you that something new and different is happening. Even two and three quarter centuries after it actually was new, you can hear the unmistakable thrumming energy of a master at the height of his powers doing something wild and daring with absolute self-confidence. When Bach wrote it, he put himself at the harpsichord instead of the viola he more usually played in ensembles. It was at a happy, productive time of his life when he was at last surrounded by some good musicians. The harpsichord traditionally played a supporting role in this kind of group, but not this time. Bach let rip.

As you listen to the first movement, you hear something strange, new, and terrifying giving birth to itself. Or maybe it's a giant engine, or even a great horse being prepared for a Herculean task, surrounded by (you can't help jumbling metaphors when language tries to keep up with music) a flotilla of helpers fussing around it. You hear it ticking over, trotting, having a little canter here and there, getting a bit frisky, and then taking a trial run as its helpers encourage it onward, keening with bated breath. It hauls itself back in again, does another quick circuit . . . and then the other instruments fall silent. It stands free and alone, pawing at the ground, breathing deeply, gathering its strength, trotting forward . . .

And then it makes its move—running . . . hurtling . . . fly-

ing . . . climbing . . . clambering . . . pushing . . . panting . . .
twisting . . . thrashing . . . pounding at the ground . . . pounding . . . pounding . . . suddenly breaking away, running onward
desperately, and then, with one last little unexpected step up in
the bass, it's home and free—the main tune charges in tri-
umphantly and it's all over bar the weeping and dancing (i.e.,
the second and third movements).

The familiarity of the Brandenburgs should not blind us to
their magnitude. I'm convinced that Bach is the greatest genius
who ever walked among us, and the Brandenburgs are what he
wrote when he was happy.

> —Penguin Classics Vol. 27: Bach—
> Brandenburg Concertos 5 & 6,
> Violin Concerto in A Minor (English
> Chamber Orchestra, conducted by
> Benjamin Britten)

THE
UNIVERSE

Frank the Vandal

The Macintosh came out five years ago, and I seem to have had the builders in my house for almost that long. Someone asked me the other day what they were doing, and I explained that I had been trying to pluck up the courage to ask them that myself.

Things are rather complicated by the fact that one of them is an electrician called Frank the Vandal. That is, his friends, if he has any that aren't in hospital, call him Frank, and I call him Frank the Vandal because every time he needs to get at any bit of wiring, he tends to hack his way through anything else that's in the way to get at it—plasterwork, woodwork, plumbing, telephone lines, furniture, even other bits of wiring that he's put in himself on previous raids. He is, I am assured, very good as an electrician, though I think he is maybe not very good as a human being. But I'm digressing here from the point I was trying to make, and have rather lost the thread because Frank just cut the power off since I did the last save. So, where was I? Ah yes.

The house was virtually a complete wreck when I bought it. Not quite as much a wreck as it is when Frank's been here, but nevertheless, it was pretty much an empty shell into which walls, floors, plumbing, and so on had to be put. When the walls have to be built, an expert (or so I'm told—not so sure about that myself, but in principle an expert) bricklayer comes into the house and builds them. I need floors and stairs and cupboards and things, so a carpenter, whistling a merry carpenter's tune, comes round and plies his trade. Then a plumber comes round and dittoes. Then Frank the Vandal comes round to wrench some wiring into place, and of course the carpenter and plumber and so on have to come round again and make extensive repairs. I'm going to have to drop the subject of Frank because he's not a part of the analogy I am by slow degrees attempting elegantly to construct. It's just that he preys on my mind a bit at the moment and it's difficult not to sit here feeling nervous while he's in the house. So forget Frank. You're lucky. You can.

Now the point is this. The house is here. Building this house is the purpose of the whole exercise. If I want anything done in it, I pick up the phone (assuming Frank hasn't hacked through the line trying to get at a light switch) and someone comes round to the house and does it.

If I want to have some cupboards installed, I don't have to do the following: I don't have to have the house completely dismantled, shipped up to Birmingham where the carpenter is, put together again in a way that a carpenter understands, then have the carpenter work on it, and then have the whole thing dismantled again, shipped back down to Islington, and put together again so that it works as a house that I can live in.

So why do I have to do that with my computer? Let me put that another way so that it makes sense. Why, when I'm working in a document in one word processor, do I keep on finding that if I want to do something else to the document, I have virtually to dismantle the document and ship it over to another word processor that has a feature I need that the first one doesn't? (Why don't I just use the second word processor? Well, because it doesn't have other features that the first one does, of course.) Or, if I want to put a picture in it, why do I have to go off to another program entirely and do the picture there, and then go through all the mind-numbing palaver of discovering that for some reason the WP I'm using doesn't know how to handle graphics in that particular format, or claims that it does but then just goes all black and sulky or makes the machine go bing when I actually ask it to. In the end I have to paste all the various bits into PageMaker, which then refuses to print for some reason. I know that MultiFinder has made all this a bit easier, but it's really just the equivalent of making Birmingham easier to get to, if you follow me.

I don't want to know about PICT files. I don't want to know about TIFF files (I don't. They give me the willies.) I don't want to have to worry about what file type to ask MacWrite II to save my work in so that I can get Nisus to read it and run one of its interminable macros over it. I'm a Mac user, for heaven's sake. This is meant to be easy.

The Mac started out as a wonderfully simple and elegant idea (give them so little memory that they won't be able to do anything anyway), and it's time that that degree of simplicity could be brought to bear on the much, much more powerful and complex system that the Mac has now become.

What I want to be able to do is this:

1. Turn on the machine.
2. Work.
3. Have a bit of fun provided I've done enough of 2, which is rarely, but that's another issue.

When I say "work," I mean I want to be able to start typing on the screen, and if I feel like putting in a drawing, I draw on the screen. Or I bring something from my scanner onto the screen, or I send something from my screen to someone else. Or I get my Mac to play the tune I've just written on the screen on a synthesiser. Or, well, the list obviously is endless. And if I need any particular tool to enable me to do anything complicated, I simply ask for it. And I mean simply. I should never have to put away the thing I'm working on unless I've actually finished it (fat chance, say my publishers) or want to do something else entirely.

What I'm talking about is the death of the "application." I don't mean just when they "unexpectedly" quit, I mean it's time we simply got rid of them. And getting hold of the tools I need should be as simple as pasting a button into HyperCard.

Ah! HyperCard!

I know it's unfashionable to say this, because a lot of people feel that HyperCard simply isn't powerful enough to do useful work in. It is, after all, a first stab at an idea that's in its infancy. The list of things you can't do with it is almost as long as the list of macros in Nisus. (What are all those things? The very act of pulling down the macros menu causes lights to dim all over North London.) But it's a sensationally good idea, and I would dearly love to see something like it become the whole working environment for the Mac. You want the number-crunching power of Excel? Paste it in. You want animation? Paste in Director. You don't like the way Director works? (You must be mad. It's brilliant.) Paste in the bits you like of any other animation tools you find lying about.

Or even rewrite it.

If it's properly written in object-oriented code, it should be as easy as writing HyperTalk. (All right. You can't write HyperTalk. It should be easier to write than HyperTalk. Just point at the bits you like and click.) We should not have to be tyrannised by application designers who don't know the first thing about how actual people do their actual work, we should be able to just pick up the bits we like and paste them in.

I've gone on a bit about electricians. I would now like to talk about cupboards. One particular cupboard. It's a cupboard in the corner of my study, and I daren't go into it, because I know that if I go into it I will not emerge till the end of the afternoon and I will emerge from it a sad and embittered man who has done battle with a seething black serpentine monster and lost. The seething black serpentine monster is a three-foot-high pile of cables, and it both taunts me and haunts me. It taunts me because it knows that whatever cable it is that I want at any particular moment to connect one particular arcane device to another particular arcane device is not to be found anywhere in its tangled entrails, and it haunts me because I know it's right.

I hate cables. They hate me too, because they know that one day I will simply be able to go into that cupboard with a flamethrower and get rid of the lot of them. In the meantime they are determined to extract from me the last ounce of frustrated misery that they can. We do not need the bastards. We shouldn't need the bastards.

Take my current situation as an example. In order to be safe from Frank the Vandal, I have transferred this article onto my portable Mac (I know, I know, you hate me. Listen. We'll all have one in the end. They'll bring the price down, trust me. Or rather, don't trust me, trust Apple. Well, yes, I see your point. Please can I get back to what I was saying anyway?) and I have taken the additional precaution of taking it round to a friend's house which is entirely electrically isolated from anything that Frank may be up to.

When I get back home with the finished piece, I can either copy it onto a floppy disk, assuming I can find one under the debris of half-finished chapters on my desk, then put that into my main Mac and print it (again assuming that Frank hasn't been near my AppleTalk network with his chainsaw). Or I can try to do battle with the monster in the cupboard till I find another AppleTalk connector somewhere in its innards. Or I can crawl around under my desk and disconnect AppleTalk from the IIx and connect it to the portable. Or . . . you get the picture, this is ridiculous. Dickens didn't have to crawl around under his desk trying to match plugs. You look at the sheer yardage of Dickens's output on a shelf and you know he never had to match plugs.

All I want to do is print from my portable. (Poor baby.) That isn't all I want, in fact. I want to be able regularly to transfer my address book and diary stacks backward and forward between my portable and my IIx. And all my current half-finished chapters. And anything else I'm tinkering with, which is the reason why my half-finished chapters are half-finished. In other words, I want my portable to appear on the desktop of my IIx. I don't want to have to do battle with cupboard monsters and then mess about with TOPS every time I want that to happen. I'll tell you all I want to have to do in order to get my portable to appear on the Desktop of my IIx.

I just want to carry it into the same room.

Bang. There it is. It's on the Desktop.

This is Infra-Red talk. Or maybe it's microwave talk. I don't really care any more than I want to care about PICTs and TIFFs and RTFs and SYLKs and all the other acronyms, which merely say, "We've got a complicated problem, so here's a complicated answer to it."

Let me make one thing clear. I adore my Macintosh, or rather my family of however many Macintoshes it is that I've recklessly accumulated over the years. I've adored it since I first saw one at Infocom's offices in Boston in 1983. The thing that has kept me enthralled and hypnotised by it in all that time is the perception that lies at the heart of its design, which is this: "There is no problem so complicated that you can't find a very simple answer to it if you look at it the right way." Or, to put it another way, "The future of computer power is pure simplicity." So my two major wishes for the 1990s are that the Macintosh systems designers get back to that future, and that Frank the Vandal gets out of my house.

MacUser magazine, 1 9 8 9

✳

Build It and We Will Come

I remember the first time I ever saw a personal computer. It was at Lasky's, on the Tottenham Court Road, and it was called a Commodore PET. It was quite a large pyramid shape, with a screen at the top about the size of a chocolate bar. I prowled around it for a while, fascinated. But it was no good. I couldn't for the life of me see any way in which a computer could be of any use in the life or work of a writer. However, I did feel the first tiniest inklings of a feeling that would go on to give a whole new meaning to the words "disposable income."

The reason I couldn't imagine what use it would be to me was that I had a very limited idea of what a computer actually was—as did we all. I thought it was a kind of elaborate adding machine. And that is exactly how "personal" computers (a misleading term as applied to almost any machine we've seen so far) were for a while developed—as super adding machines with a long feature list.

Then, as our ability to manipulate numbers with these machines became more sophisticated, we wondered what might happen if we made the numbers stand for something else, like for instance the letters of the alphabet.

Bingo! An extraordinary, world-changing breakthrough! We realised we had been myopically shortsighted to think this thing was just an adding machine. It was something far more exciting. It was a typewriter!

So we began to develop it as a super typewriter. With a long and increasingly incomprehensible feature list. Users of Microsoft Word will know what I'm talking about.

The next breakthrough came when we started to make these numbers, which were now flying round inside these machines at insane speeds, stand for the picture elements of a graphic display. Pixels.

Aha! we thought. This machine turns out to be much more exciting even than a typewriter. It's a television! With a typewriter stuck in front of it!

And now we have the World Wide Web (the only thing I know of whose shortened form—www—takes three times longer to say than what it's short for) and we have yet another exciting new model. It's a brochure. A huge, all-singing, all-dancing, hopping, beeping, flash-ridden brochure.

Of course, the computer isn't any of these things. These are all things we were previously familiar with from the real world, which we have modelled in the computer so that we can use the damn thing.

Which should tell us something interesting.

The computer is actually a modelling device.

Once we see that, we ought to realise that we can model anything in it. Not just things we are used to doing in the real world, but the things the real world actually prevents us from doing.

What does a brochure prevent us from doing?

Well, first of all its job is to persuade people to buy what you have to sell, and do it by being as glossy and seductive as possible and only telling people what you want them to know. You can't interrogate a brochure. Most corporate websites are like that. Take BMW, for instance. Its Web site is gorgeous and whizzy and it won't answer your questions. It won't let you find out what other people's experience of owning BMWs is like, what shortcomings any particular model might or might not have, how reliable they are, what they cost to run, what they're like in the wet, or anything like that. In other words, anything you might actually want to know. You can e-mail them, but your question or their answer—or anybody else's answer—will not appear on the site. Of course, there are plenty of Web sites where people do share exactly that kind of information, and they're only a few clicks away, but you won't find a word about them on BMW's site. In fact, if you want proper, grown-up information about BMWs, the last place you'll find it is at www.bmw.com. It's a brochure.

Same with British Airways. It'll tell you anything you like about British Airways flights except who else is flying those routes. So if you want to see what the choice is, you go instead to one of the scores of other sites that will tell you. Which is bad news for British Airways because they never get to find out what you were actually looking for, or how what they were offering stacked up against the competition. And because that is very valuable information, they have to send out teams of people with clipboards to try to find out, despite the fact that everybody lies to people with clipboards.

The people who have got this spectacularly right so far are the guys at Amazon. You go to their site because it's awash with shared information. The more information there is, the more people go there, and the more people go there, the more information they generate, and the more books Amazon sells. Of course, they are not afraid of open debate because, unlike BMW, they are not responsible for the product they sell. It will take BMW and British Airways a long time and a big deep breath to realise that they are *part* of the community they sell to.

But even Amazon has only got part of the picture. Like real-world shops, they can only record the sales they actually make. What about the sales they don't make and don't know that they haven't made because they haven't made them? I went on to Amazon the other day because I wanted to order the 1968 Zeffirelli *Romeo and Juliet* on DVD. Turns out it doesn't exist. I could buy it on VHS, but I don't want it on VHS. So the whole transaction was null. There was no way of recording that I came in looking to buy something, and that the something I wanted to buy wasn't there. I only got to select (or not select) from what happened to be available, I didn't get to be able to say what I actually *wanted*. So I wrote to them about it and, guess what, now you can. They're very smart like that. They are now able to supply the studios with information about what there is actually *demand* for out there. And on the basis of another—not entirely disinterested—suggestion of mine, they are going to start a running poll on which books people would most like to see turned into movies. This is information that no one has ever been able to collect before.

But let us take this one stage further. How often have you looked through a brochure or a catalogue and thought, "I wish somebody would write a book about . . ." or "If only somebody made a bicycle with a . . ." Or "Why doesn't somebody make a screwdriver that . . ." or "Why don't they make that in blue?" A brochure can't answer you, but the Web can.

What is the thing you'd really love to have, if only someone had the sense to make one? Suggestions, please, to www.h2g2.com.

—*The Independent on Sunday*,
NOVEMBER 1999

✳   ✳   ✳

I've come up with a set of rules that describe our reactions to technologies:

1. Anything that is in the world when you're born is normal and ordinary and is just a natural part of the way the world works.
2. Anything that's invented between when you're fifteen and thirty-five is new and exciting and revolutionary and you can probably get a career in it.
3. Anything invented after you're thirty-five is against the natural order of things.

✳

Interview, American Atheists

AMERICAN ATHEISTS: Mr. Adams, you have been described as a "radical Atheist." Is this accurate?

DNA: Yes. I think I use the term *radical* rather loosely, just for emphasis. If you describe yourself as "Atheist," some people will say, "Don't you mean 'Agnostic'?" I have to reply that I really *do* mean *Atheist*. I really do not believe that there is a god—in fact I am convinced that there is not a god (a subtle difference). I see not a shred of evidence to suggest that there is one. It's easier to say that I am a radical Atheist, just to signal that I really mean it, have thought about it a great deal, and that it's an opinion I hold seriously. It's funny how many people are genuinely surprised to hear a view expressed so strongly. In England we seem to have drifted from vague, wishy-washy Anglicanism to vague, wishy-washy Agnosticism—both of which I think betoken a desire not to have to think about things too much.

People will then often say, "But surely it's better to remain an Agnostic just in case?" This, to me, suggests such a level of silliness and muddle that I usually edge out of the conversation rather than get sucked into it. (If it turns out that I've been wrong all along, and there is in fact a god, and if it further turned out that this kind of legalistic, cross-your-fingers-behind-your-back, Clintonian hair-splitting impressed him, then I think I would choose not to worship him anyway.)

Other people will ask how I can possibly claim to know. Isn't *belief-that-there-is-not-a-god* as irrational, arrogant, etc., as *belief-that-there-is-a-god*? To which I say *no* for several reasons. First of all I do not *believe-that-there-is-not-a-god*. I don't see what belief has got to do with it. I believe or don't believe my four-year-old daughter when she tells me that she didn't make that mess on the floor. I believe in justice and fair play (though I don't know exactly how we achieve them, other than by continually trying against all possible odds of success). I also believe that England should enter the European Monetary Union. I am not remotely enough of an economist to argue the issue vigorously with someone who is, but what little I do know, reinforced with a hefty dollop of gut feeling, strongly suggests to me that it's the right course. I could very easily turn out to be wrong, and I know that. These seem to me to be legitimate uses for the word *believe*. As a carapace for the protection of irrational notions from legitimate questions, however, I think that the word has a lot of mischief to answer for. So, I do not *believe-that-there-is-no-god*. I am, however, *convinced* that there is no god, which is a totally different stance and takes me on to my second reason.

I don't accept the currently fashionable assertion that any view is automatically as worthy of respect as any equal and opposite view. My view is that the moon is made of rock. If someone says to me, "Well, you haven't been there, have you? You haven't seen it for yourself, so my view that it is made of Norwegian beaver cheese is equally valid"—then I can't even be bothered to argue. There is such a thing as the burden of proof, and in the case of god, as in the case of the composition of the moon, this has shifted radically. God used to be the best explanation we'd got, and we've now got vastly better ones. God is no longer an explanation of anything, but has instead become something that would itself need an insurmountable amount of explaining. So I don't think that being convinced that there is no god is as irrational or arrogant a point of view as belief that there is. I don't think the matter calls for even-handedness at all.

AMERICAN ATHEISTS: How long have you been a nonbeliever, and what brought you to that realization?

DNA: Well, it's a rather corny story. As a teenager I was a committed Christian. It was in my background. I used to work for the school chapel, in fact. Then one day when I was about eighteen I was walking down the street when I heard a street evangelist and, dutifully, stopped to listen. As I listened it began to be borne in on me that he was talking complete nonsense, and that I had better have a bit of a think about it.

I've put that a bit glibly. When I say I realized he was talking nonsense, what I mean is this. In the years I'd spent learning history, physics, Latin, math, I'd learnt (the hard way) something about standards of argument, standards of proof, standards of logic, etc. In fact we had just been learning how to spot the different types of logical fallacy, and it suddenly became apparent to me that these standards simply didn't seem to apply in religious matters. In religious education we were asked to listen respectfully to arguments that, if they had been put forward in support of a view of, say, why the Corn Laws came to be abolished when they were, would have been laughed at as silly and childish and—in terms of logic and proof—just plain wrong. Why was this?

Well, in history, even though the understanding of events, of cause and effect, is a matter of interpretation, and even though interpretation is in many ways a matter of opinion, nevertheless those opinions and interpretations are honed to within an inch of their lives in the withering crossfire of argument and counterargument, and those that are still standing are then subjected to a whole new round of challenges of fact and logic from the next generation of historians—and so on. *All opinions are not equal.* Some are a very great deal more robust, sophisticated, and well-supported in logic and argument than others.

So I was already familiar with and (I'm afraid) accepting of, the view that you couldn't apply the logic of physics to religion, that they were dealing with different types of "truth." (I now think this is baloney, but to continue . . .) What astonished me, however, was the realization that the arguments in favor of religious ideas were so feeble and silly next to the robust arguments of something as interpretive and opinionated as history. In fact they were embarrassingly childish. They were never subject to the kind of outright challenge which was the normal stock in trade of any other area of intellectual endeavor whatsoever. Why not? Because they wouldn't stand up to it. So I became an Agnostic. And I thought and thought and thought. But I just did not have enough to go on, so I didn't really come to any resolution. I was extremely doubtful about the idea of god, but I just didn't know enough about anything to have a good working model of any other explanation for, well, life, the universe, and everything to put in its place. But I kept at it, and I kept reading and I kept thinking. Sometime around my early thirties I stumbled upon evolutionary biology, particularly in the form of Richard Dawkins's books *The Selfish Gene* and then *The Blind Watchmaker,* and suddenly (on, I think the second reading of *The Selfish Gene*) it all fell into place. It was a concept of such stunning simplicity, but it gave rise, naturally, to all of the infinite and baffling complexity of life. The awe it inspired in me made the awe that people talk about in respect of religious experience seem, frankly, silly beside it. I'd take the awe of understanding over the awe of ignorance any day.

AMERICAN ATHEISTS: You allude to your Atheism in your speech to your fans (". . . that was one of the few times I actually believed in god"). Is your Atheism common knowledge among your fans, friends, and coworkers? Are many people in your circle of friends and co-workers Atheists as well?

DNA: This is a slightly puzzling question to me, and I think there is a cultural difference involved. In England there is no big deal about being an Atheist. There's just a slight twinge of discomfort about people strongly expressing a particular point of view when maybe a detached wishy-washiness might be felt to be more appropriate—hence a preference for Agnosticism over Atheism. And making the move from Agnosticism to Atheism takes, I think, much more commitment to intellectual effort than most people are ready to put in. But there's no big deal about it. A number of the people I know and meet are scientists, and in those circles Atheism is the norm. I would guess that most people I know otherwise are Agnostics, and quite a few are Atheists. If I was to try and look amongst my friends, family, and colleagues for people who believed there was a god, I'd probably be looking amongst the older and (to be perfectly frank) less well-educated ones. There are one or two exceptions. (I nearly put, by habit, "honorable exceptions," but I don't really think that.)

AMERICAN ATHEISTS: How often have fans, friends, or co-workers tried to "save" you from Atheism?

DNA: Absolutely never. We just don't have that kind of fundamentalism in England. Well, maybe that's not absolutely true. But (and I'm going to be horribly arrogant here) I guess I just tend not to come across such people, just as I tend not to come across people who watch daytime soaps or read the *National Enquirer*. And how do you usually respond? I wouldn't bother.

AMERICAN ATHEISTS: Have you faced any obstacles in your professional life because of your Atheism (bigotry against Atheists), and how did you handle it? How often does this happen?

DNA: Not even remotely. It's an inconceivable idea.

AMERICAN ATHEISTS: There are quite a few lighthearted references to god and religion in your books (". . . two thousand years after some guy got nailed to a tree"). How has your Atheism influenced your writing? Where (in which characters or situations) are your personal religious thoughts most accurately reflected?

DNA: I am fascinated by religion. (That's a completely different thing from believing in it!) It has had such an incalculably huge effect on human affairs. What is it? What does it represent? Why have we invented it? How does it keep going? What will become of it? I love to keep poking and prodding at it. I've thought about it so much over the years that that fascination is bound to spill over into my writing.

AMERICAN ATHEISTS: What message would you like to send to your Atheist fans?

DNA: Hello! How are you?

From *The American Atheist* 37, No. 1
(interview conducted by David Silverman)

✻ ✻ ✻

What are the benefits of speaking to your fans via e-mail?

It's quicker, easier, and involves less licking.

*

Predicting the Future

Trying to predict the future is a mug's game. But increasingly it's a game we all have to play because the world is changing so fast and we need to have some sort of idea of what the future's actually going to be like because we are going to have to live there, probably next week.

Oddly, the industry that is the primary engine of this incredible pace of change—the computer industry—turns out to be rather bad at predicting the future itself. There are two things in particular that it failed to foresee: one was the coming of the Internet, which, in an astonishingly short time, has become what the computer industry is now all about; the other was the fact that the century would end.

So, as we stand on the brink of a new millennium, peering up at the shiny cliff face of change that confronts us, like Kubrick's apes gibbering in front of the great black monolith, how can we possibly hope to guess what's to come? Molecular computers, quantum computers—what can we dare to say about them? We were wrong about trains, we were wrong about planes, we were wrong about radio, we were wrong about phones, we were wrong about . . . well, for a voluminous list of the things we have been wrong about, you could do worse than dig out a copy of a book called *The Experts Speak* by Christopher Cerf and Victor Navasky.

It's a compendium of authoritative predictions made in the past that turned out to be wonderfully wrong, usually almost immediately. You know the kind of thing. Irving Fisher, professor of economics at Yale University, said on October 17, 1929, that "stocks have reached what looks like a permanently high plateau." Then there was the Decca record executive who said of the Beatles in 1962, "We don't like their sound. Groups of guitars are on the way out," and so on. Ah, here's another one: "Bill Clinton will lose to any Republican who doesn't drool on stage," said *The Wall Street Journal,* in 1995. It's a very fat book you can read happily in the loo for hours.

The odd thing is that we don't get any better at it. We smile indulgently when we hear that Lord Kelvin said in 1897, "Radio has no future." But it's more surprising to discover that Ken Olsen, the president of the Digital Equipment Corporation, said in 1977, "There is no reason for any individual to have a computer in their home." Even Bill Gates, who specifically set out to prove him completely and utterly wrong, famously said that he couldn't conceive of anybody needing more than 640k of memory in their computers. Try running Word in even twenty times that.

It would be interesting to keep a running log of predictions and see if we can spot the absolute corkers when they are still just pert little buds. One such that I spotted recently was a statement made in February by a Mr. Wayne Leuck, vice-president of engineering at USWest, the American phone company. Arguing against the deployment of high-speed wireless data connections, he said, "Granted, you could use it in your car going sixty miles an hour, but I don't think too many people are going to be doing that." Just watch. That's a statement that will come back to haunt him. Satellite navigation. Wireless Internet. As soon as we start mapping physical location back into shared information space, we will trigger yet another explosive growth in Internet applications.

At least—that's what *I* predict. I could, of course, be wildly wrong. Stewart Brand, in his excellent book *The Clock of the Long Now,* proposes keeping a record of society's predictions and arguments in a ten-thousand-year library, but it would also be interesting to see how things work out in the short term. At the beginning of each new year the media tend to be full of predictions of what is going to happen over the course of the following year. Two days later, of course, they're forgotten and we never get to test them. So I'd like to invite readers to submit their own predictions—or any others they come across in print—of what is going to happen in the next five years, and when. Will we set off to Mars? Will we get peace in Ireland or the Middle East? Will the e-commerce bubble burst?

We'll put them up on the Web, where they will stay for that whole period, so we can track them against what actually happens. Predicting the future is a mug's game, but any game is improved when you can actually keep the score.

The Independent on Sunday,
NOVEMBER 1999

* * *

There's now a new generation of smarter office chair beginning to arrive that makes a virtue of doing away with all the knobs and levers. All the springing and bracing we learned about is still there, but it adjusts to your posture and movement automatically, without your having to tell it how to. All right, here's a prediction for you: when we have software that works like that, the world will truly be a better and happier place.

*

The Little Computer That Could

My favourite piece of information is that Branwell Brontë, brother of Emily and Charlotte, died standing up leaning against a mantelpiece, in order to prove it could be done.

This is not quite true, in fact. My *absolute* favourite piece of information is the fact that young sloths are so inept that they frequently grab their own arms and legs instead of tree limbs, and fall out of trees. However, this is not relevant to what is currently on my mind because it concerns sloths, whereas the Branwell Brontë piece of information concerns writers and feeling like death and doing things to prove they can be done, all of which are pertinent to my current situation to a degree that is, frankly, spooky.

I'm a writer and I'm feeling like death, as you would too, if you'd just flown into Grand Rapids, Michigan, at some ungodly hour of the morning only to discover that you can't get into your hotel room for another three hours. In fact, it's enough just to have flown into Grand Rapids, Michigan. If you are a native of Grand Rapids, Michigan, then please assume that I am just kidding. Anyone else will surely realise that I am not.

Having nowhere else to go, I am standing up, leaning against a mantelpiece. Well, a kind of mantelpiece. I don't know what it is, in fact. It's made of brass and some kind of plastic and was probably drawn in by the architect after a nasty night on the town. That reminds me of another favourite piece of information: there is a large kink in the Trans-Siberian Railway because when the tsar (I don't know which tsar it was because I am not in my study at home, I'm leaning against something shamefully ugly in Michigan and there are no books) decreed that the

Trans-Siberian railway should be built, he drew a line on a map with a ruler. The ruler had a nick in it.

I'm writing this article leaning against some nameless architectural mistake, and I am not writing the article on a Mac. I would, but my PowerBook is fresh out of power (funny notion, to name the thing after its only major shortcoming; it's rather like Greenland in that respect). I have the power cable with me but I can't plug it in anywhere. Though the power cable very cleverly has a universal power supply, it doesn't have a universal plug. It has a large, clunky, British-style three-pin plug built right into it, which means that if you forget to buy an adapter plug before you leave Heathrow, you are completely and utterly screwed. You cannot buy an adapter for British plugs outside Britain. I know. I tried that when I ran into a similar problem with the old Mac Portable. (I am not going to make any Mac Portable jokes. Apple made quite enough of them to be getting on with. Damn. I said I wasn't going to do that.) In the end I had to buy a U.S. power cable. Or rather, I had to try to buy one. Couldn't be done. They only came with new Mac Portables. I heaved a dead Mac Portable around with me for ten days and occasionally ate my sandwiches off it because it was slightly lighter than carrying a table. (Damn, there goes another one.)

I don't have the same problem with my PowerBook, though. I am not totally stupid. I brought an adapter with me this time. However, I am slightly stupid because it's in my suitcase, which I've just checked in with the bellman while I wait three hours for my room to be ready.

So what am I doing? Handwriting? You must be joking. After ten years of word processing, I can't even do handwriting anymore. I know I ought to be able to: handwriting is supposed to be one of those things like using chopsticks: once you get the hang of it, it never really deserts you. The thing is that I've had much more practice with chopsticks than with pens, so no, I'm not handwriting. I'm not talking into one of those horrible little Dictaphones, either, that keep on recording relentlessly while you're desperately trying to think of something to say. Pressing the off switch is the thing that turns your brain back on.

No. What I'm doing is sitting on a chair somewhere writing this on a new Psion Series 3a palmtop computer. I got one at the duty-free shop at Heathrow, just for the sheer unadulterated hell of it, and I have to say it's good. It works.

May I just say one thing about duty-free shops before I go on to talk about the Psion? It's not that things aren't cheaper in the duty-free shops. They are. Infinitesimally. You do save a very small amount of money if you shop at them. Of course you can then lose a very hefty sum of money in fines if you fail to realise that you have to declare anything you've bought duty-free to customs when you come back into the country. The stuff is only really duty-free if you intend to spend the rest of your life on an aeroplane. So what happens when you buy stuff at the duty-free shop for very slightly less than you would in the high street? It means that most of the money saved on duty is going into the coffers of the duty-free shops rather than helping to pay for the National Health Service (and Trident nuclear submarines). So why did I buy my Psion at the duty-free shop? Because I'm a complete idiot, that's why.

Anyway. Status update. They've found me a room. I've unpacked my adapter plug. My PowerBook is charging itself up. I'm still not using it, though, because I am now lying in the bath. So I'm still using the Psion. I have never ever written anything in the bath before. Paper gets damp and steamy, pens won't write upside down, typewriters hurt your tummy, and if you are prepared to use a PowerBook in the bath, then I assume that it isn't your own PowerBook.

So the thing is, it can be done. You can actually write on a palmtop computer, which is something I didn't realise before. I had tried to do it on a Sharp Wizard, but it wasn't possible because the keyboard was laid out alphabetically, which is hopeless. The principle behind the decision to have an alphabetical keyboard is based on a misunderstanding. I believe that the idea is this: not everybody knows qwerty (it's an odd feeling, actually typing *qwerty* as a word; try it and you'll see what I mean), but everybody knows the alphabet. This is true but irrelevant. People know the alphabet as a one-dimensional string, not as a two-dimensional array, so you're going to have to hunt and peck anyway. So why not use qwerty and let people who know it have the benefit?

I also tried the larger Sharp Wizard, the 8200, which does have a qwerty keyboard, but no word wrap. Can you believe that? Even Etch-a-Sketch has word wrap these days.

The other problem with all palmtops is, of course, that the keyboard is too small for your fingers. This is a tricky one. You can't win. If the machine's small enough to go in your pocket, it's too small to type on. Well, I've found the answer. Forgive me if you knew this already, perhaps I'm the last person in the world to find this out. Anyway, the answer is this: you grip the palmtop between both hands and you type with your thumbs. Seriously. It works. It feels a bit awkward to begin with, and your hands ache a little from using unaccustomed muscles, but you get used to it surprisingly quickly. I've clocked up a thousand words now.

Now, this raises some interesting questions. (Well, interesting to me. You can please yourselves.) What about this input business, then? I am, of course, as out of my mind with excitement as the next person about the prospect of voice input and pen input, but you know and I know, and anybody who has fooled around with a Caere Typist or the like will know, that things rarely work as smoothly in practice as they do in theory, or at least not yet. Most of the time spent wrestling with technologies that don't quite work yet is just not worth the effort for end users, however much fun it is for nerds like us. The days when you can say, "Open pod bay number 2, Hal," and be confident that Hal understands that you want to be stranded on the outskirts of Jupiter are still a way away. And I suspect that it will be a very long time before I am able to dictate an article like this and for the result to be even decipherable, let alone accurate. We've all seen the old sketch in which a secretary writes down absolutely everything the boss says, including the bit where he says, "Don't write this bit down," or "Cross out that last sentence." I think there's going to be a lot of stupid-secretary-type grief to go through before we get it working smoothly. As for pen input devices, well, as I said above, ten years of word processing has meant that my handwriting has deteriorated to the point where even I can't read it, so what chance a computer stands I really don't know. Can I be bothered to tease out the irony involved in all that? No.

So for the moment that leaves us back with the keyboard input, and keyboard input, for the moment, means qwerty. But qwerty, as we know, was originally designed to slow down typists so the keys wouldn't jam. It's deliberately inefficient. However, all attempts to replace it with something more efficient, like the Dvorak keyboard, have failed. People know qwerty already, and they don't have any pressing incentive to change. Dvorak et al. may be better, but qwerty is, or has been till now, good enough. "If it ain't busted, don't fix it" is a very sound principle and remains so despite the fact that I have slavishly ignored it all my life.

I think, though, that we might finally have arrived at a point at which there is a strong incentive to reinvent the keyboard. Palmtop computers are where all the new action is. Apple and Microsoft and everybody are suddenly beginning to get revved up about personal digital assistants and stuff, and, having been using this Psion Series 3a for a few hours now, so am I. It's terrific technology, and this is just the beginning of that crucial moment at which something stops being just an entertaining new toy and starts being something you can seriously use in the bath. We've all known for years that qwerty isn't good. I think we've now got to that important point where it isn't even good enough. The point where it isn't even good enough. (Yes, this is exact copy typing!) I hope that systems designers have not been put off by the failure of the Dvorak keyboard. I hope they are carefully studying the way that people hold palmtop computers, where their fingers naturally fall and fit and how the whole idea of how a keyboard works can be rethought. I would very much like it if my thumb joints were not now stiff and aching. I've proved it can be done, but, like Branwell Brontë, I'm not expecting to do the same trick again tomorrow.

*   *   *

We notice things that don't work. We don't notice things that do. We notice computers, we don't notice pennies. We notice e-book readers, we don't notice books.

✳

Little Dongly Things

Time to declare war, I think, on little dongly things. More of them turned up in the post this morning. I'd ordered a new optical disk drive from an American mail-order company and, because I live in that strange and remote place called "Foreign," and also because I travel like a pigeon, I was keen to know, when ordering it, if it had an international power supply.

An international power supply is the device that means it doesn't matter what country you're in, or even if you know what country you're in (more of a problem than you might suspect)—you just plug your Mac in and it figures it out for itself. We call this principle Plug and Play. Or at least Microsoft calls it that because it hasn't got it yet. In the Mac world we've had it for so long we didn't even think of giving it a name. Nowadays a lot of peripherals come with international power supplies as well—but not all. Which is why I asked.

"Yes, it does," said Scott, the sales assistant.

"You're sure it has an international power supply?"

"Yes," repeated Scott. "It has an international power supply."

"Absolutely sure?"

"Yes."

This morning it arrived. The first thing I noticed was that it didn't have an international power supply. Instead it had a little dongly thing. I have rooms full of little dongly things and don't want any more. Half the little dongly things I've got, I don't even know what gizmo they're for. More importantly, half the gizmos I've got, I don't know where their little dongly thing is. Most annoyingly, an awful lot of the little dongly things, including the one that arrived this morning, are little dongly things that run on 120-volt AC—American voltage, which means I can't use them here in Foreign (state code FN), but I have to keep them in case I ever take the gizmo to which they fit—provided I know which gizmo it is they fit to—to the U.S.A.

What, you may ask, the hell am I talking about?

The little dongly things I am concerned with (and they are by no means the only species of little dongly things with which the microelectronics world is infested) are the external power adapters that laptops and palmtops and external drives and cassette recorders and telephone answering machines and powered speakers and other incredibly necessary gizmos need to step down the AC supply from either 120 volts or 240 volts to 6 volts DC. Or 4.5 volts DC. Or 9 volts DC. Or 12 volts DC. At 500 milliamps. Or 300 milliamps. Or 1,200 milliamps. They have positive tips and negative sleeves on their plugs, unless they are the type that has negative tips and positive sleeves. By the time you multiply all these different variables together, you end up with a fairly major industry that exists, so far as I can tell, to fill my cupboards with little dongly things, none of which I can ever positively identify without playing gizmo pelmanism. The usual method of finding a little dongly thing that actually matches a gizmo I want to use is to go and buy another one, at a price that can physically drive the air from your body.

Now, why is this? Well, there's one possible theory, which is that just as Xerox is really in the business of selling toner cartridges, Sony is really in the little dongly power supply business.

Another possible reason is that it is sheer blinding idiocy. It couldn't possibly be that, could it? I mean, could it? It's hard to imagine that some of the mightiest brains on the planet, fueled by some of the finest pizza that money can buy, haven't at some point thought, "Wouldn't it be easier if we all just standardised on one type of DC power supply?" Now, I'm not an electrical engineer, so I may be asking for the impossible. Maybe it is a sine qua non of the way in which a given optical drive or CD Walkman works that it has to draw 600 milliamps rather than 500, or have its negative terminal on the tip rather than the sleeve, and that it will either whine or fry itself if presented with anything faintly different. But I strongly suspect that if you stuck a hardware engineer in a locked room for a couple of days and taunted him with the smell of pepperoni, he'd probably be able to think of a way of making whatever gizmo (maybe even the new gizmo Pro, which I've heard such good things about) he's designing work to a standard DC low-power supply.

In fact there already is a kind of rough standard, but it's rather an odd one. Not many people actually smoke in their cars these days, and the aperture in the dashboard that used to hold the cigar lighter is now more likely to be powering a mobile phone, CD player, fax machine, or, according to a recent and highly improbable TV commercial, an instant coffee-making gizmo. Because the socket originally had a different purpose, it's the wrong size and in the wrong place for what we now want to do with it, so perhaps it's time to start adapting it for its new job.

The important thing this piece of serendipitous pre-adaptation has given us is a possible DC power standard. An arbitrary one, to be sure, but perhaps we should probably just be grateful that it was designed by a car mechanic in an afternoon and not a computer industry standards committee in a lifetime. Keep the voltage level and design a new, small, plug, and you have a new standard.

The immediate advantage of adopting it would be that you would need only one DC power adapter! Think of that! Well, not exactly one, you might need a dozen of them, but they would all be exactly the same! Just get a box of 'em! They'll just be a commodity item like, um, well, I was going to say lightbulbs, but lightbulbs come in all sorts of different wattages and fittings. The great thing about having a DC power standard is that it would be much better than lightbulbs.

Apart from doing away with endless confusion and inconvenience, the arrival of a new standard would encourage all sorts of other new features to emerge. Power points in convenient places in cars. DC power points in homes and offices and, most important, DC power points in the armrests of airplane seats . . .

I have to own up and say that, much as I love my PowerBook, which now does about 97.8 percent of what I used to use the lumbering old desktop dinosaurs for, I've given up trying to use it on planes. Yes, yes, I know that there are all sorts of power-user strategies you can use to extend your battery life—dimming modes, RAM disks, processor-resting, and so on—but the point is that I really can't be bothered. I'm perfectly capable of just reading the in-flight magazine if I want to be irritated. However, if there was a DC power supply in my armrest, I would actually be able to do some work, or at least fiddle with stuff. I know that the airline companies will probably say, "Yes, but if we do that, our aeroplanes will fall out of the sky," but they always say that. I know that sometimes their planes do fall out of the sky, but, and here's the point, not nearly as often as the airline companies say they will. I for one would be willing to risk it. In the great war against little dongly things, no sacrifice, I think, is too great.

MacUser, SEPTEMBER 1996

✳   ✳   ✳

We are stuck with technology when what we really want is just stuff that works. How do you recognize something that is still technology? A good clue is if it comes with a manual.

✳

What Have We Got to Lose?

Some of the most revolutionary new ideas come from spotting something old to leave out rather than thinking of something new to put in. The Sony Walkman, for instance, added nothing significantly new to the cassette player, it just left out the amplifier and speakers, thus creating a whole new way of listening to music and a whole new industry. Sony's new Handycam rather brilliantly leaves out the zoom function on the grounds that all a zoom does is cost money, add a lot of bulk, and render every amateur video ever made unwatchable. (They might, while they're following this line of thought, consider marketing a record-only video player, and video companies might consider releasing movies that are actually *recorded* in fast-forward mode.) The RISC chip works by the brilliant, life-enhancing prin-

ciple of getting on with the easy stuff and leaving all the difficult bits for someone else to deal with. (I know it's a little more
complicated than that, but you have to admit it's a damned
attractive idea). A well-made dry martini works by the brilliant,
life-enhancing principle of leaving out the martini.

You also get dramatic advances when you spot that you can
leave out part of the *problem*. Algebra, for instance (and hence
the whole of computer programming), derives from the realisation that you can leave out all the messy, intractable numbers.
Then there's the new, improved U.K. directory enquiries service.
A couple of years or so ago, something radical changed: when
you dialed 192, you actually got a civil, helpful answer, usually—and here was the clue—delivered in a Scots accent. The
whole operation had been rounded up and moved to Aberdeen,
where they had a plentiful supply of civil, helpful people who
didn't have to be compensated for living in London. Somebody
bright at British Telecom had spotted that the location was
immaterial—the problem of distance could simply be left out of
the model (something they have yet to come to terms with in
their pricing structures). With a little extra cable-laying, it seems
to me that they could have moved U.K. directory enquiries to
St. Helena or the Falklands, thus bringing whole new possibilities of employment to areas that were previously limited to the
things you could do with sheep. The Falklands could, while they
were about it, put in a bid to run Argentina's directory enquiry
service as well, which would give the foreign offices of both
countries something to think about.

Almost everything to do with the Net involves spotting the
things we can now leave out of the problem, and location—or
distance—is one of them. Wandering around the Web is like
living in a world in which every doorway is actually one of

those science-fiction devices that deposit you in a completely different part of the world when you walk through them. In fact it isn't like it, it *is* it. Trying to work out all the implications of this is as difficult as it was for early filmmakers to work out all the implications of being able to *move* the camera. What else is going to fall out of the model?

Over the last few years I've regularly been cornered by nervous publishers or broadcasters or journalists or filmmakers and asked about how I think computers will affect their various industries. For a long time, most of them were desperately hoping for an answer that translated roughly into "not very much." ("People like the *smell* of books, they like popcorn, they like to see programmes at exactly the same moment as their neighbours, they like at least to *have* lots of articles that they've no interest in reading," etc.) But it's a hard question to answer because it's based on a faulty model. It's like trying to explain to the Amazon River, the Mississippi, the Congo, and the Nile how the coming of the Atlantic Ocean will affect them. The first thing to understand is that river rules will no longer apply.

Let's think about what might happen when magazine publishing is no longer a river in its own right, but is just a current in the digital ocean. Magazines are starting to appear on the Web, but since they are just a number of interconnected pages in a world of interconnected pages, the boundaries between "magazine" and "not-magazine," or indeed between "magazine A" and "magazine B" are, from the Web browser's point of view, rather vague. Once we drop the idea of discretely bound and sold sheaves of glossily processed wood pulp from the model, what do we have left? Anything useful?

From the point of view of readers, it's useful in much the same way that a paper magazine is: it's a concentration of the sort of stuff they're interested in, in a form that's easy to locate, with the added advantage that it will be able to point seamlessly at all kinds of related material in a way that a paper magazine cannot. All well and good.

But what about the magazine publishers? What do they have to sell? What are they going to do now that they don't have stacks of glossy paper that people are going to want to hand over wads of greenies to acquire? Well, it all depends on what sort of business you think they're in. Lots of people are not in the business you think they're in. Xerox, for instance, is in the business of selling toner cartridges. All that mucking about they do developing high-tech copying and printing machines is just creating a commodity market in toner cartridges, which is where their profit lies. Television companies are not in the business of delivering television programmes to their audience, they're in the business of delivering audiences to their advertisers. (This is why the BBC has such a schizophrenic time—it's actually in a different business from all its competitors.) And magazines are very similar: each actual sale across the newsagent's counter is partly an attempt to defray the ludicrous cost of manufacturing the damn thing, but is also, more significantly, a very solid datum point. The full data set represents the size of the audience the publisher can deliver to its advertisers.

Now, I regard magazine advertising as a big problem. I really hate it. It overwhelms the copy text, which is usually reduced to a dull, grey little stream trickling its way through enormous, glaring, billboard-like pages, all of which are clamouring to draw your attention to stuff you don't want; and the first thing you have to do when you buy a new magazine is shake it over a bin in order to shed all the coupons, sachets, packets, CDs, and free Labrador puppies that make them as fat and unwieldy as a grandmother's scrapbook. And then, when you *are* interested in buying something, you can't find any information about it because it was in last month's issue, which you've now thrown away. I bought a new camera last month, and bought loads of camera magazines just to find ads and reviews for the models I was interested in. So I resent about 99 percent of the advertising I see, but occasionally I want it enough to actually *buy* the stuff. There's a major mismatch— something is ripe to fall out of the model.

If you browse around an online magazine (HotWired, for instance, springs unbidden to mind), you will find a few discreet little sponsor icons here and there that you *choose* to click on. You only get to see the proper ad if you're actually interested in it, and that ad will then lead you directly toward solid, helpful information about the product. It is of course much more valuable for advertisers to reach one interested potential customer than it is to irritate the hell out of ninety-nine others. Furthermore, the advertiser gets astonishingly precise feedback. They will know exactly how many people have chosen to look at their ad and for how long, with the result that an unwelcome ad for something no one's interested in will quickly wither away, whereas one that catches people's attention will thrive. The advertisers pay the magazine for the opportunity to put links to their ads on popular pages of the magazine and—well, you see the way it works. It is, I am told by people with seriously raised eyebrows, astonishingly effective. The thing which drops out of the problem is the notion that advertising need be irritating and intrusive.

That's one model of how online magazines work, and it is, of course, absolutely free to readers. There's another that will probably arrive as soon as it becomes possible to move virtual cash around the Internet, and that will involve readers being billed tiny amounts of money for the opportunity to read popular Web pages. Much less than you would, for instance, regularly spend on your normal newspapers and magazines because you wouldn't have to be paying for all the trees that have to be pulped, the vans that have to be fueled, and the marketing people whose job it is to tell you how brilliant they are. The reader's money goes straight to the writer, with a proportion to the publisher of the Web site, and all the wood can stay in the forests, the oil can stay in the ground, and all the marketing people can stay out of the Groucho Club and let decent folk get to the bar.

Why doesn't all the money go to the writer, I hear you (and indeed myself) asking. Well, maybe it will if he's happy just to drop his words into the digital ocean in the hope that someone out there will find them. But like any ocean, the digital one has streams and eddies and currents, and publishers will quickly have a role finding good material to draw into those currents where readers will naturally be streaming through looking for stuff, which is more or less what they do at the moment. The difference will lie in the responsiveness of the market, the speed with which those streams will shift and surge, and the way in which power and control will shift to those who are actually contributing something useful rather than just having lunch.

The thing we leave out of the model is, essentially, just a lot of dead wood.

Wired, UK edition; Issue No. 1, 1995

∗

Time Travel

Time travel? I believe there are people regularly travelling back from the future and interfering with our lives on a daily basis. The evidence is all around us. I'm talking about how every time we make an insurance claim we discover that somehow mysteriously the exact thing we're claiming for is now precisely excluded from our policy.

✷

Turncoat

I'm often asked if I'm not a bit of a turncoat. Twenty years (help!) ago in *The Hitchhiker's Guide to the Galaxy*, I made my reputation making fun of science and technology: depressed robots, uncooperative lifts, doors with ludicrously overdesigned user interfaces (what's wrong with just pushing them?), and so on. Now I seem to have become one of technology's chief advocates, as is apparent from my recent series on Radio 4, *The Hitchhiker's Guide to the Future*. (I wish we hadn't ended up with that title, incidentally, but sometimes events have a momentum of their own.)

Two things:

First of all, I wonder if we don't have too much comedy these days. When I was a kid I used to hide under the bedclothes with an old radio I'd got from a jumble sale, and listen enraptured to *Beyond Our Ken*, *Hancock*, *The Navy Lark*, even the *Clitheroe Kid*, anything that made me laugh. It was like showers and rainbows in the desert. Then there was *I'm Sorry I'll Read That Again* and a few short years later the full glories of *Monty Python*. The thing about Python that hit me like a thunderbolt, and I really don't give a toss if this ends up in "Pseud's Corner," was that comedy was a medium in which extremely intelligent people could express things that simply couldn't be expressed any other way. From where I was sitting in my boarding school in deepest Essex, it was a thrilling beacon of light. It's curious to me that the Pythons came along just as those other great igniters of a young imagination, the Beatles, were fading. There was a sense of a baton being passed. I think George Harrison once said something similar.

But nowadays everybody's a comedian, even the weather girls and continuity announcers. We laugh at everything. Not intelligently anymore, not with sudden shock, astonishment, or revelation, just relentlessly and meaninglessly. No more rain showers in the desert, just mud and drizzle everywhere, occasionally illuminated by the flash of paparazzi.

Creative excitement has gone elsewhere—to science and technology: new ways of seeing things, new understandings of the universe, continual new revelations about how life works, how we think, how we perceive, how we communicate. So this is my second point.

Where, thirty years ago, we used to start up rock bands, we now start up start-ups and experiment with new ways of communicating with each other and playing with the information we exchange. And when one idea fails, there's another, better one right behind it, and another and another, cascading out as fast as rock albums used to in the sixties.

There's always a moment when you start to fall out of love, whether it's with a person or an idea or a cause, even if it's one you only narrate to yourself years after the event: a tiny thing, a wrong word, a false note, which means that things can never be quite the same again. For me it was hearing a stand-up comedian make the following observation: "These scientists, eh? They're so stupid! You know those black-box flight recorders they put on aeroplanes? And you know they're meant to be indestructible? It's always the thing that doesn't get smashed? *So why don't they make the planes out of the same stuff?*"

The audience roared with laughter at how stupid scientists were, couldn't think their way out of a paper bag, but I sat feeling uncomfortable. Was I just being pedantic to feel that the joke didn't really work because flight recorders are made out of titanium and that if you made planes out of titanium rather than aluminium, they'd be far too heavy to get off the ground in the first place? I began to pick away at the joke. Supposing Eric Morecambe had said it? Would it be funny then? Well, not quite, because that would have relied on the audience seeing that Eric was being dumb—in other words, they would have had to know as a matter of common knowledge about the relative weights of titanium and aluminium. There was no way of deconstructing the joke (if you think this is obsessive behaviour, you should try living with it) that didn't rely on the teller and the audience complacently conspiring together to jeer at someone *who knew more than they did*. It sent a chill down my spine, and still does. I felt betrayed by comedy in the same way that gangsta rap now makes me feel betrayed by rock music. I also began to wonder how many of the jokes I was making were just, well, ignorant.

My turn toward science came one day in about 1985 when I was walking through a forest in Madagascar. My companion on the walk was the zoologist Mark Carwardine (with whom

I later collaborated on the book *Last Chance to See*), and I asked him, "So come on then, what's so special about the rain forest that we're supposed to care about it so much?"

And he told me. Took about two minutes. He explained the difference between temperate forest and rain forest and how it came to be that the latter produced such bewildering diversity of life but was at the same time so terribly fragile. I fell silent for a few moments as I began to realise that one simple piece of new understanding had just changed the way I saw the world. I had just been handed a single thread I could now follow into the tangled ball of a bewilderingly complex world. For the next few years I hungrily devoured everything I could lay my hands on about evolutionary science and realised that nothing I'd ever understood about it at school had prepared me for the enormity of what was now swimming into my view. The thing about evolution is that if it hasn't turned your brain inside out, you haven't understood it.

Then to my surprise I discovered that it was converging with my growing interest in computers. There was nothing particularly profound about that enthusiasm—I just unashamedly love playing with gadgets. The connection lies in the counterintuitive observation that complex results arise from simple causes, iterated many times over. It's terribly simple to see this happening in a computer. Whatever complexities a computer produces—modeling wind turbulence, modeling economies or the way light dances in the eye of an imaginary dinosaur—it all grows out of simple lines of code that start with adding one and one, testing the result, and then doing it again. Being able to watch complexity blossom out of this primitive simplicity is one of the great marvels of our age, greater even than watching man walk on the moon.

It's much more difficult to see it happening in the case of the evolution of life. The time scales are so vast and our perspective so much complicated by the fact that it's ourselves we're looking at, but our invention of the computer has for the first time let us get a real feel for how it works—just as our invention of the hydraulic pump first gave us an insight into what the heart was doing and how the circulation of the blood worked.

That is also why it's impossible to divorce pure science from technology: they feed and stimulate each other. So the latest software gizmo for transferring an mp3 sound file from one computer to another across continents is, when you peer into its innards and at the infrastructure that has given rise to it and that it, in turn, becomes part of, is, in its way, every bit as interesting as the way in which a cell replicates, an idea is formed within a brain, or a beetle deep in the heart of the Amazonian rain forest digests its prey. It's all part of the same underlying process that we in turn are part of, it's where our creative energies are being poured, and I'll happily take it over comedians, television, and football any day.

OCTOBER 2000

✱   ✱   ✱

Present somebody with a questionnaire clipboard, and they lie. A friend of mine once had a job preparing a questionnaire for people to fill in on the Web. He said the information they got back was enormously heartening about the state of the world. For instance, did you know that almost 90 percent of the population are CEOs of their own companies and earn over a million dollars a year?

✳

Is There an Artificial God?

This was originally billed as a debate only because I was a bit anxious coming here. I didn't think I was going to have time to prepare anything and also, in a room full of such luminaries, I thought, "What could I, as an amateur, possibly have to say?" So I thought I would settle for a debate. But after having been here for a couple of days, I realised you're just a bunch of guys! It's been rife with ideas, and I've had so many myself through talking with and listening to people, that I'd thought what I'd do was stand up and have an argument and debate with myself. I'll talk for a while and hope sufficiently to provoke and inflame opinion that there'll be an outburst of chair-throwing at the end.

Before I embark on what I want to try to tackle, may I warn you that things may get a little bit lost from time to time, because there's a lot of stuff that's just come in from what we've been hearing today, so if I occasionally sort of go . . . I was telling somebody earlier today that I have a four-year-old daughter and was very, very interested watching her face when she was in her first two or three weeks of life and suddenly realising what nobody would have realised in previous ages—she was rebooting!

I just want to mention one thing, which is completely meaningless, but I am terribly proud of—I was born in Cambridge in 1952 and my initials are DNA!

The topic I want to introduce to you this evening, the subject of the debate that we are about to sort of not have, is a slightly facetious one (you'll be surprised to hear, but we'll see where we go with it)—"Is there an artificial God?" I'm sure most of the people in this room will share the same view, but even as an out-and-out atheist, one can't help noticing that the role of a god has had an enormously profound impact on human history over many, many centuries. It's very interesting to figure out where this came from and what, in the modern scientific world we sometimes hope against hope that we live in, it actually means.

I was thinking about this earlier today when Larry Yaeger was talking about "What Is Life?" and mentioned at the end something I didn't know, about a special field of handwriting recognition. The following strange thought went through my mind: that trying to figure out what is life and what isn't, and where the boundary is, has an interesting relationship with how you recognise handwriting. We all know, when presented with any particular entity, whether it's a bit of mould from the fridge or whatever—we instinctively know when something is an example of life and when it isn't. But it turns out to be tremendously hard exactly to define it. I remember once, a long time ago, needing a definition of life for a speech I was giving. Assuming there was a simple one and looking around the Internet, I was astonished at how diverse the definitions were and how very, very detailed each one had to be in order to include "this" but not include "that." If you think about it, a collection that includes a fruit fly and Richard Dawkins and the Great Barrier Reef is an awkward set of objects to try to compare. When we try to figure out what the rules are that we are looking for, trying to find a rule that's self-evidently true, that turns out to be very, very hard.

Compare this with the business of recognising whether

something is an *A* or a *B* or a *C*. It's a similar kind of process, but it's also a very, very different process, because you may say of something that you're "not quite certain whether it counts as life or not life, it's kind of there on the edge, isn't it, it's probably a very low example of what you might call life, it's maybe just about alive or maybe it isn't." Or maybe you might say about something that's an example of digital life, "Does that count as being alive?" Is it something, to coin someone's earlier phrase, that'll go squish if you step on it? Think about the controversial Gaia hypothesis; people say, "Is the planet alive?" "Is the ecosphere alive or not?" In the end it depends on how you define such things.

Compare that with handwriting recognition. In the end you are trying to say "Is this an *A* or is it a *B*?" People write *A*s and *B*s in many different ways; floridly, sloppily, or whatever. It's no good saying, "Well, it's sort of *A*-ish but there's a bit of *B* in there," because you can't write the word "apple" with such a thing. It is either an *A* or a *B*. How do you judge? If you're doing handwriting recognition, what you are trying to do is not to assess the relative degrees of *A*-ness or *B*-ness of the letter, but trying to define the intention of the person who wrote it. It's very clear in the end—is it an *A* or a *B*?—ah! it's an *A*, because the person writing it was writing the word "apple" and that's clearly what it means. So, in the end, in the absence of an intentional creator, you cannot say what life is, because it simply depends on what set of definitions you include in your overall definition. Without a god, life is only a matter of opinion.

I want to pick up on a few other things that came around today. I was fascinated by Larry (again), talking about tautology, because there's an argument that I remember being stumped by once, to which I couldn't come up with a reply, because I was so puzzled by the challenge and couldn't quite figure it out. A guy said to me, "Yes, but the whole theory of evolution is based on a tautology: That which survives, survives." This is tautological, therefore it doesn't mean anything. I thought about that for a while and it finally occurred to me that a tautology is something that means nothing, not only that no information has gone into it, but that no consequence has come out of it. So we may have accidentally stumbled upon the ultimate answer; it's the only thing, the only force, arguably the most powerful of which we are aware, which requires no other input, no other support from any other place, is self-evident, hence tautological, but nevertheless astonishingly powerful in its effects. It's hard to find anything that corresponds to that, and I therefore put it at the beginning of one of my books. I reduced it to what I thought were the bare essentials, which are very similar to the ones you came up with earlier, which were *"Anything that happens happens, anything that in happening causes something else to happen causes something else to happen and anything that in happening causes itself to happen again, happens again."* In fact you don't even need the second two because they flow from the first one, which is self-evident and there's nothing else you need to say; everything else flows from that. So I think we have in our grasp here a fundamental, ultimate truth, against which there is no gainsaying. It was spotted by the guy who said this is a tautology. Yes, it is, but it's a unique tautology in that it requires no information to go in, but an infinite amount of information comes out of it. So I think that it is arguably therefore the prime cause of everything in the universe. Big claim, but I feel I'm talking to a sympathetic audience.

Where does the idea of God come from? Well, I think we have a very skewed point of view on an awful lot of things, but let's try to see where our point of view comes from. Imagine early man. Early man is, like everything else, an evolved creature and he finds himself in a world that he's begun to take a little charge of; he's begun to be a toolmaker, a changer of his environment with the tools that he's made, and he makes tools, when he does, in order to make changes in his environment. To give an example of the way man operates compared to other animals, consider speciation, which, as we know, tends to occur when a small group of animals gets separated from the rest of the herd by some geological upheaval, population pressure, food shortage, or whatever, and finds itself in a new environment with maybe something different going on. Take a very simple example; maybe a bunch of animals suddenly finds itself in a place where the weather is rather colder. We know that in a few generations those genes that favour a thicker coat will have come to the fore and we'll come and we'll find that the animals have now got thicker coats. Early man, who's a toolmaker, doesn't have to do this: he can inhabit an extraordinarily wide range of habitats on earth, from tundra to the Gobi Desert—he even manages to live in New York, for heaven's sake—and the reason is that when he arrives in a new environment he doesn't have to wait for several generations; if he arrives in a colder environment and sees an animal that has those genes which favour a thicker coat, he says, "I'll have it off him." Tools have enabled us to think intentionally, to make things and to do things to create a world that fits us better. Now imagine an early man surveying his surroundings at the end of a happy day's toolmaking. He looks around and he sees a world that pleases him mightily: behind him are mountains with caves in them—mountains are great because you can go and hide in the caves and you are out of the rain and the bears can't get you; in front of him there's the forest—it's got nuts and berries and delicious food; there's a stream going by, which is full of water—water's delicious to drink, you can float your boats in it and do all sorts of stuff with it; here's cousin Ug and he's caught a mammoth—mammoths are great, you can eat them, you can wear their coats, you can use their bones to create weapons to catch other mammoths. I mean this is a *great* world, it's fantastic. But our early man has a moment to reflect and he thinks to himself, "Well, this is an interesting world that I find myself in," and then he asks himself a very treacherous question, a question that is totally meaningless and fallacious, but only comes about because of the nature of the sort of person he is, the sort of person he has evolved into, and the sort of person who has thrived because he thinks this particular way. Man the maker looks at his world and says, "So who made this, then?" Who made this?—you can see why it's a treacherous question. Early man thinks, "Well, because there's only one sort of being I know about who makes things, whoever made all this must therefore be a much bigger, much more powerful and necessarily invisible, one of me, and because I tend to be the strong one who does all the stuff, he's probably male." And so we have the idea of a God. Then, because when we make things, we do it with the intention of doing something with them, early man asks himself, "If he made it, what did he make it *for*?" Now the real trap springs, because early man is thinking, "This world fits me very well. Here are all these things that support me and feed me and look after me; yes, this world fits me nicely," and he reaches the inescapable conclusion that whoever made it, made it for him.

This is rather as if you imagine a puddle waking up one morning and thinking, "This is an interesting world I find myself in—an interesting *hole* I find myself in—fits me rather neatly, doesn't it? In fact it fits me staggeringly well, must have been made to have me in it!" This is such a powerful idea that as the sun rises in the sky and the air heats up and as, gradually, the puddle gets smaller and smaller, it's still frantically hanging on to the notion that everything's going to be all right, because this world was *meant* to have him in it, was *built* to have him in it; so the moment he disappears catches him rather by surprise. I think this may be something we need to be on the watch-out for. We all know that at some point in the future the universe will come to an end, and at some other point, considerably in advance from that but still not immediately pressing, the sun will explode. We feel there's plenty of time to worry about that, but on the other hand that's a very dangerous thing to say. Look at what's supposed to be going to happen on the first of January 2000—let's not pretend that we didn't have a warning that the century was going to end! I think that we need to take a larger perspective on who we are and what we are doing here if we are going to survive in the long term.

There are some oddities in the perspective with which we see the world. The fact that we live at the bottom of a deep gravity well, on the surface of a gas-covered planet going around a nuclear fireball 90 million miles away, and think this to be normal, is obviously some indication of how skewed our perspective tends to be, but we have done various things over intellectual history to slowly correct some of our misapprehensions. Curiously enough, quite a lot of these have come from sand, so let's talk about the four ages of sand.

From sand we make glass, from glass we make lenses, and from lenses we make telescopes. When the great early astronomers, Copernicus, Galileo, and others, turned their telescopes on the heavens and discovered that the universe was an astonishingly different place than we expected and that, far from the world being most of the universe, with just a few little bright lights going around it, it turned out—and this took a long, long, long time to sink in—that it is just one tiny little speck going round a little nuclear fireball, which is one of millions and millions and millions that make up this particular galaxy and our galaxy is one of millions or billions that make up the universe, and that then we are also faced with the possibility that there may be billions of universes, that applied a little bit of a corrective to the perspective that the universe was ours.

I rather love that notion, and, as I was discussing with someone earlier today, there's a book I thoroughly enjoyed recently by David Deutsch, who is an advocate of the multiple-universe view of the universe, called *The Fabric of Reality,* in which he explores the notion of a quantum multiple-universe view of the universe. This came from the famous wave/particle dichotomy about the behaviour of light—that you couldn't measure it as a wave when it behaves as a wave, or as a particle when it behaves as a particle. How does this come to be? David Deutsch points out that if you imagine that our universe is simply one layer and that there is an infinite multiplicity of universes spreading out on either side, not only does it solve the problem, but the problem simply goes away. This is exactly how you expect light to behave under those circumstances. Quantum mechanics has claims to be predicated on the notion that the universe behaves as if there were a multiplicity of universes, but it rather strains our credulity to think that there actually would be.

This goes straight back to Galileo and the Vatican. In fact, what the Vatican said to Galileo was, "We don't dispute your readings, we just dispute the explanation you put on them. It's all very well for you to say that the planets sort of do that as they go round and it is as if we were a planet and those planets were all going round the sun; it's all right to say it's *as if* that were happening, but you're not allowed to say that's what *is* happening, because we have a total lockhold on universal truth and also it simply strains our personal credulity." Just so, I think that the idea that there are multiple universes currently strains our credulity, but it may well be that it's simply one more strain that we have to learn to live with, just as we've had to learn to live with a whole bunch of them in the past.

The other thing that comes out of that vision of the universe is that it turns out to be composed almost entirely, and rather worryingly, of nothing. Wherever you look there is nothing, with occasional tiny, tiny little specks of rock or light. But nevertheless, by watching the way these tiny little specks behave in the vast nothingness, we begin to divine certain principles, certain laws, like gravity and so forth. So that was, if you like, the macroscopic view of the universe, which came from the first age of sand.

The next age of sand is the microscopic one. We put glass lenses into microscopes and started to look down at the microscopic view of the universe. Then we began to understand that when we get down to the subatomic level, the solid world we live in also consists, again rather worryingly, of almost nothing and that wherever we do find something it turns out not to be actually something, but only the probability that there may be something there.

One way or another, this is a deeply misleading universe. Wherever we look, it's beginning to be extremely alarming and extremely upsetting to our sense of who we are—great, strapping, physical people living in a universe that exists almost entirely for us—that it just isn't the case. At this point we are still divining from this all sorts of fundamental principles, recognising the way that gravity works, the way that strong and weak nuclear forces work, recognising the nature of matter, the nature of particles and so on, but having got those fundamentals, we're still not very good at figuring out how it works, because the math is really rather tricky. So we tend to come up with almost a clockwork view of the way it all works, because that's the best our math can manage. I don't mean in any way to disparage Newton, because I guess he was the first person who saw that there were principles at work that were different from anything we actually saw around us. His first law of motion—that something will remain in its position of either rest or motion until some other force works on it—is something that none of us, living in a gravity well, in a gas envelope, had ever seen, because everything we move comes to a halt. It was only through very, very careful watching and observing and measuring and divining the principles underlying what we could all see happening that he came up with the principles that we all know and recognise as being the laws of motion, but nevertheless it is, by modern terms, still a somewhat clockwork view of the universe. As I say, I don't mean that to sound disparaging in any way at all, because his achievements, as we all know, were absolutely monumental, but it still kind of doesn't make sense to us.

Now there are all sorts of entities we are also aware of, as well as particles, forces, tables, chairs, rocks, and so on, that are almost invisible to science; almost invisible, because science has almost nothing to say about them whatsoever. I'm talking about dogs and cats and cows and each other. We living things are so far beyond the purview of anything science can actually say, almost beyond even recognising ourselves as things that science might be expected to have something to say about.

I can imagine Newton sitting down and working out his laws of motion and figuring out the way the universe works and with him, a cat wandering around. The reason we had no idea how cats worked was because, since Newton, we had proceeded by the very simple principle that essentially, to see how things work, we took them apart. If you try to take a cat apart to see how it works, the first thing you have in your hands is a nonworking cat. Life is a level of complexity that almost lies outside our vision; is so far beyond anything we have any means of understanding that we just think of it as a different class of object, a different class of matter; "life," something that had a mysterious essence about it, was God-given—and that's the only explanation we had. The bombshell comes in 1859 when Darwin publishes *The Origin of Species*. It takes a long time before we really get to grips with this and begin to understand it, because not only does it seem incredible and thoroughly demeaning to us, but it's yet another shock to our system to discover that not only are we not the centre of the universe and we're not made of anything, but we started out as some kind of slime and got to where we are via being a monkey. It just doesn't read well. But also, we have no opportunity to see this stuff at work. In a sense Darwin was like Newton, in that he was the first person to see underlying principles that really were not at all obvious, from the everyday world in which he lived. We had to think very hard to understand the nature of what was happening around us, and we had no clear, obvious everyday examples of evolution to point to. Even today that persists as a slightly tricky problem if you're trying to persuade somebody who doesn't believe in all this evolution stuff and wants you to show him an example—they are hard to find in terms of everyday observation.

So we come to the third age of sand. In the third age of sand we discover something else we can make out of sand—silicon. We make the silicon chip—and suddenly what opens up to us is a universe not of fundamental particles and fundamental forces, but of the things that were missing in that picture that told us how they work; what the silicon chip revealed to us was the *process*. The silicon chip enables us to do mathematics tremendously fast, to model the—as it turns out—very, very simple processes that are analogous to life in terms of their simplicity; iteration, looping, branching, the feedback loop that lies at the heart of everything you do on a computer and at the heart of everything that happens in evolution—that is, the output stage of one generation becomes the input stage of the next. Suddenly we have a working model—not for a while, because early machines are terribly slow and clunky—but gradually we accumulate a working model of this thing that previously we could only guess at or deduce—and you had to be a pretty sharp and a pretty clear thinker even to divine it happening when it was far from obvious and indeed counterintuitive, particularly to as proud a species as we.

The computer forms a third age of perspective, because suddenly it enables us to see how life works. Now, that is an extraordinarily important point because it becomes self-evident that life, that all forms of complexity, do not flow downward, they flow upward, and there's a whole grammar that anybody who is used to using computers is now familiar with, which means that evolution is no longer a particular thing, because anybody who's ever looked at the way a computer program works, knows that very, very simple iterative pieces of code, each line of which is tremendously straightforward, give rise to enormously complex phenomena in a computer—and by enormously complex phenomena, I mean a word-processing program just as much as I mean Tierra or Creatures.

I can remember the first time I ever read a programming manual, many, many years ago. I'd first started to encounter computers in about 1983, and I wanted to know a little bit more about them, so I decided to learn something about programming. I bought a C manual and I read through the first two or three chapters, which took me about a week. At the end it said, "Congratulations, you have now written the letter *a* on the screen!" I thought, "Well, I must have misunderstood something here, because it was a huge, huge amount of work to do that, so what if I now want to write a *b*?" The process of programming, the speed and the means by which enormous simplicity gives rise to enormously complex results, was not part of my mental grammar at that point. It is now—and it is increasingly part of all our mental grammars, because we are used to the way computers work.

So, suddenly, evolution ceases to be such a real problem to get hold of. It's rather like the following scenario: One Tuesday a person is spotted in a street in London, doing something criminal. Two detectives are investigating, trying to work out what happened. One of them is a twentieth-century detective and the other, by the marvels of science fiction, is a nineteenth-century detective. The problem is this: The person who was clearly seen and identified on the street in London on Tuesday was seen by someone else, an equally reliable witness, on the street in Santa Fe on the same Tuesday. How could that possibly be? The nineteenth-century detective could only think it was by some sort of magical intervention. Now, the twentieth-century detective may not be able to say, "He took BA flight this and then United flight that"—he may not be able to figure out exactly which way he did it, or by which route he traveled, but it's not a problem. It doesn't bother him; he just says, "He got there by plane. I don't know which plane and it may be a little tricky to find out, but there's no essential mystery." We're used to the idea of jet travel. We don't know whether the criminal flew BA 178, or UA 270, or whatever, but we know roughly how it was done. I suspect that as we become more and more conversant with the role a computer plays and the way in which the computer models the process of enormously simple elements giving rise to enormously complex results, then the idea of life being an emergent phenomenon will become easier and easier to swallow. We may never know precisely what steps life took in the very early stages of this planet, but it's not a mystery.

So what we have arrived at here—and although the first shock wave of this arrival was in 1859, it's really the arrival of the computer that demonstrates it unarguably to us—is "Is there really a universe that is not designed from the top downward, but from the bottom upward? Can complexity emerge from lower levels of simplicity?" It has always struck me as being bizarre that the idea of God as a creator was considered sufficient explanation for the complexity we see around us, because it simply doesn't explain where he came from. If we imagine a designer, that implies a design, and that therefore each thing he designs or causes to be designed is a level simpler than him- or herself, then you have to ask, "What is the level above the designer?" There is one peculiar model of the universe that has turtles all the way down, but here we have gods all the way up. It really isn't a very good answer—but a bottom-up solution, on the other hand, that rests on the incredibly powerful tautology that "anything that happens, happens," clearly gives you a very simple and powerful answer that needs no other explanation whatsoever.

But here's the interesting thing. I said I wanted to ask, "Is there an artificial God?" and this is where I want to address the question of why the idea of a God is so persuasive. I've already explained where I feel this kind of illusion comes from in the first place; it comes from a falseness in our perspective, because we are not taking into account that we are evolved beings, beings who have evolved into a particular landscape, into a particular environment with a particular set of skills and views of the world that have enabled us to survive and thrive rather successfully. But there seems to be an even more powerful idea than that, and this is the idea I want to propose, which is that the spot at the top of the pyramid that we previously said was whence everything flowed, may not actually be vacant just because we say the flow doesn't go that way.

Let me explain what I mean by this. We have created in the world in which we live all kinds of things; we have changed our world in all kinds of ways. That's very, very clear. We have built the room we're in, and we've built all sorts of complex stuff, like computers and so on, but we've also constructed all kinds of fictitious entities that are enormously powerful. So do we say, "That's a bad idea, it's stupid—we should simply get rid of it?" Well, here's another fictitious entity—money. Money is a completely fictitious entity, but it's very powerful in our world; we all have wallets, which have got notes in them, but what can those notes do? You can't breed them, you can't stir-fry them, you can't live in them, there's absolutely nothing you can do with them that's any use, other than exchange them with each other—and as soon as we exchange them with each other, all sorts of powerful things happen, because it's a fiction that we've all subscribed to. We don't think this is wrong or right, good or bad; but the thing is that if money vanished, the entire cooperative structure that we have would implode, but if we were all to vanish, money would simply vanish too. Money has no meaning outside ourselves; it is something we have created that has a powerful shaping effect on the world, because it's something we all subscribe to.

I would like somebody to write an evolutionary history of religion, because the way in which it has developed seems to me to show all kinds of evolutionary strategies. Think of the arms races that go on between one or two animals living in the same environment—for example, the race between the Amazonian manatee and a particular type of reed that it eats. The more of the reed the manatee eats, the more the reed develops silica in its cells to attack the teeth of the manatee, and the more silica in the reed, the stronger and bigger the manatee's teeth get. One side does one thing and the other counters it. As we know, throughout evolution and history, arms races are something that drive evolution in the most powerful ways, and in the world of ideas you can see similar kinds of things happening.

Now, the invention of the scientific method and science is, I'm sure we'll all agree, the most powerful intellectual idea, the most powerful framework for thinking and investigating and understanding and challenging the world around us that there is, and it rests on the premise that any idea is there to be attacked and if it withstands the attack, then it lives to fight another day and if it doesn't withstand the attack then down it goes. Religion doesn't seem to work like that; it has certain ideas at the heart of it which we call sacred or holy or whatever. That's an idea we're so familiar with, whether we subscribe to it or not, that it's kind of odd to think what it actually means, because really what it means is "Here is an idea or a notion that you're not allowed to say anything bad about; you're just not. Why not? Because you're not!" If somebody votes for a party that you don't agree with, you're free to argue about it as much as you like; everybody will have an argument, but nobody feels aggrieved by it. If somebody thinks taxes should go up or down, you are free to have an argument about it, but if on the other hand somebody says, "I mustn't move a light switch on a Saturday," you say, "Fine, I respect that." The odd thing is, even as I am saying that, I am thinking, "Is there an Orthodox Jew here who is going to be offended by the fact that I just said that?" but I wouldn't have thought, "Maybe there's somebody from the left wing or somebody from the right wing or somebody who subscribes to this view or the other in economics," when I was making the other points. I just think, "Fine, we have different opinions." But the moment I say something that has something to do with somebody's (I'm going to stick my neck out here and say *irrational*) beliefs, then we all become terribly protective and terribly defensive and say, "No, we don't attack that; that's an irrational belief, but no, we respect it."

It's rather like, if you think back in terms of animal evolution, an animal that's grown an incredible carapace around it, such as a tortoise—that's a great survival strategy because nothing can get through it; or maybe like a poisonous fish that nothing will come close to, which therefore thrives by keeping away any challenges to what it is. In the case of an idea, if we think, "Here is an idea that is protected by holiness or sanctity," what does it mean? Why should it be that it's perfectly legitimate to support the Labour Party or the Conservative Party, Republicans or Democrats, this model of economics versus that, Macintosh instead of Windows, but to have an opinion about how the universe began, about who created the universe, no, that's holy? What does that mean? Why do we ring-fence that for any other reason other than that we've just got used to doing so? There's no other reason at all, it's just one of those things that crept into being, and once that loop gets going, it's very, very powerful. So we are used to not challenging religious ideas, but it's very interesting how much of a furor Richard creates when he does it! Everybody gets absolutely frantic about it because you're not allowed to say these things. Yet when you look at it rationally, there is no reason why those ideas shouldn't be as open to debate as any other, except that we have agreed somehow between us that they shouldn't be.

There's a very interesting book—I don't know if anybody here's read it—called *Man on Earth,* by an anthropologist who used to be at Cambridge, called John Reader, in which he describes the way that . . . I'm going to back up a little bit and tell you about the whole book. It's a series of studies of different cultures in the world that have developed within somewhat isolated circumstances, on islands or in a mountain valley or wherever, so it's possible to treat them to a certain extent as a test-tube case. You see therefore exactly the degree to which their environment and their immediate circumstances have affected the way in which their culture has arisen. It's a fascinating series of studies. The one I have in mind at the moment is the culture and economy of Bali, which is a small, very crowded island that subsists on rice. Now, rice is an incredibly efficient food and you can grow an awful lot in a relatively small space, but it's hugely labour-intensive and requires a lot of very, very precise cooperation amongst the people there, particularly when you have a large population on a small island needing to bring its harvest in. People now looking at the way in which rice agriculture works in Bali are rather puzzled by it, because it is intensely religious. The society of Bali is such that religion permeates every single aspect of it and everybody in that culture is very, very carefully defined in terms of who they are, what their status is, and what their role in life is. It's all defined by the church; they have very peculiar calendars and a very peculiar set of customs and rituals, which are precisely defined, and, oddly enough, they are fantastically good at being very, very productive with their rice harvest. In the seventies, people came in and noticed that the rice harvest was determined by the temple calendar. It seemed to be totally nonsensical, so they said, "Get rid of all this, we can help you make your rice harvest much, much more productive than even you're, very successfully, doing at the moment. Use these pesticides, use this calendar, do this, that and the other." So they started, and for two or three years the rice production went up enormously, but the whole predator/prey/pest balance went completely out of kilter. Very shortly the rice harvest plummeted again, and the Balinese said, "Screw it, we're going back to the temple calendar!" and they reinstated what was there before and it all worked again absolutely perfectly. It's all very well to say that basing the rice harvest on something as irrational and meaningless as a religion is stupid—they should be able to work it out more logically than that. They might just as well say to us, "Your culture and society work on the basis of money and that's a fiction, so why don't you get rid of it and just cooperate with each other." We know that's not going to work!

So there is a sense in which we build meta-systems above ourselves to fill in the space that we previously populated with an entity that was supposed to be the intentional designer, the creator (even though there isn't one) and because we—I don't necessarily mean we in this room, but we as a species—design and create one and then allow ourselves to behave as if there *was* one, all sorts of things begin to happen that otherwise wouldn't happen.

Let me try to illustrate what I mean. This is very speculative; I'm really going out on a limb here, because it's something I know nothing about whatsoever, so think of this more as a thought experiment than a real explanation of something. I want to talk about feng shui, which is something I know very little about, but there's been a lot of talk about it recently in terms of figuring out how a building should be designed, built, situated, decorated, and so on. Apparently we need to think about the building being inhabited by dragons and look at it in terms of how a dragon would move around it. So, if a dragon wouldn't be happy in the house, you have to put a red fishbowl here or a window there. This sounds like complete and utter nonsense, because anything involving dragons must be nonsense—there aren't any dragons, so any theory based on how dragons behave is nonsense. What are these silly people doing, imagining that dragons can tell you how to build your house? Nevertheless, it occurs to me that if you disregard for a moment the explanation that's actually offered for it, it may be there is something interesting going on that goes like this: we all know from buildings that we've lived in, worked in, been in, or stayed in, that some are more comfortable, more pleasant, and more agreeable to live in than others. We haven't had a real way of quantifying this, but in this century we've had an awful lot of architects who thought they knew how to do it, so we've had the horrible idea of the house as a machine for living in, we've had Mies van der Rohe and others putting up glass stumps and strangely shaped things that are supposed to form some theory or other. It's all carefully engineered, but nonetheless, their buildings are not actually very nice to live in. An awful lot of theory has been poured into this, but if you sit and work with an architect (and I've been through that stressful time, as I'm sure a lot of people have), then when you are trying to figure out how a room should work, you're trying to integrate all kinds of things about lighting, about angles, about how people move and how people live—and an awful lot of other things you don't know about that get left out. You don't know what importance to attach to one thing or another; you're trying, very consciously, to figure out something when you haven't really got much of a clue, but there's this theory and that theory, this bit of engineering practice and that bit of architectural practice; you don't really know what to make of them. Compare that to somebody who tosses a cricket ball at you. You can sit and watch it and say, "It's going at seventeen degrees," start to work it out on paper, do some calculus, etc., and about a week after the ball's whizzed past you, you may have figured out where it's going to be and how to catch it. On the other hand, you can simply put your hand out and let the ball drop into it, because we have all kinds of faculties built into us, just below the conscious level, able to do all kinds of complex integrations of all kinds of complex phenomena, which therefore enable us to say, "Oh look, there's a ball coming; catch it!"

What I'm suggesting is that feng shui and an awful lot of other things are precisely of that kind of problem. There are all sorts of things we know *how* to do, but don't necessarily know *what* we do, we just do them. Go back to the issue of how you figure out how a room or a house should be designed, and instead of going through all the business of trying to work out the angles and trying to digest which genuine architectural principles you may want to take out of what may be a passing architectural fad, just ask yourself, "How would a dragon live here?" We are used to thinking in terms of organic creatures; an organic creature may consist of an enormous complexity of all sorts of different variables that are beyond our ability to resolve, but we know *how* organic creatures live. We've never seen a dragon, but we've all got an idea of what a dragon is like, so we can say, "Well, if a dragon went through here, he'd get stuck just here and a little bit cross over there because he couldn't see that and he'd wave his tail and knock that vase over." You figure out how the dragon's going to be happy here, and lo and behold, you've suddenly got a place that makes sense for other organic creatures, such as ourselves, to live in.

So, my argument is that as we become more and more scientifically literate, it's worth remembering that the fictions with which we previously populated our world may have some function that it's worth trying to understand and preserve the essential components of, rather than throwing out the baby with the bath water; because even though we may not accept the reasons given for them being here in the first place, it may well be that there are good practical reasons for them, or something like them, to be there. I suspect that as we move farther and farther into the field of digital or artificial life, we will find more and more unexpected properties begin to emerge out of what we see happening and that this is a precise parallel to the entities we create around ourselves to inform and shape our lives and enable us to work and live together. Therefore, I would argue that though there isn't an *actual* God, there is an *artificial* God, and we should probably bear that in mind. That is my debating point, and you are now free to start hurling the chairs around!

Q. What is the fourth age of sand?

Let me back up for a minute and talk about the way we communicate. Traditionally, we have a bunch of different ways in which we communicate with each other. One way is one-to-one; we talk to each other, have a conversation. Another is one-to-many, which I'm doing at the moment, or someone could stand up and sing a song, or announce we've got to go to war. Then we have many-to-one communication; we have a pretty patchy, clunky, not-really-working version we call democracy, but in a more primitive state I would stand up and say, "Okay, we're going to go to war," and some may shout back, "No, we're not!"—and then we have many-to-many communication in the argument that breaks out afterwards!

In this century (and the previous century) we modelled one-to-one communications in the telephone, which I assume we are all familiar with. We have one-to-many communication—boy, do we have an awful lot of that—broadcasting, publishing, journalism, etc. We get information poured at us from all over the place, and it's completely indiscriminate as to where it might land. It's curious, but we don't have to go very far back in our history until we find that all the information that reached us was relevant to us and therefore anything that happened, any news, whether it was about something that's actually happened to us, in the next house, or in the next village, within the boundary or within our horizon, it happened in our world, and if we reacted to it, the world reacted back. It was all relevant to us, so, for example, if somebody had a terrible accident, we could crowd round and really help. Nowadays, because of the plethora of one-to-many communication we have, if a plane crashes in India we may get terribly anxious about it, but our anxiety doesn't have any impact. We're not very well able to distinguish between a terrible emergency that's happened to somebody a world away and something that's happened to someone round the corner. We can't really distinguish between them anymore, which is why we get terribly upset by something that has happened to somebody in a soap opera that comes out of Hollywood and maybe less concerned when it's happened to our sister. We've all become twisted and disconnected and it's not surprising that we feel very stressed and alienated in the world because the world impacts on us but we don't impact the world. Then there's many-to-one; we have that, but not very well yet, and there's not much of it about. Essentially, our democratic systems are a model of that, and though they're not very good, they will improve dramatically.

But the fourth, the many-to-many, we didn't have at all before the coming of the Internet, which, of course, runs on fiberoptics. It's communication between us that forms the fourth age of sand. Take what I said earlier about the world not reacting to us when we react to it; I remember the first moment, a few years ago, at which I began to take the Internet seriously. It was a very, very silly thing. There was a guy, a computer research student at Carnegie Mellon, who liked to drink Dr Pepper Light. There was a drinks machine a couple of storeys away from him, where he used to regularly go and get his Dr Pepper, but the machine was often out of stock, so he had quite a few wasted journeys. Eventually he figured out, "Hang on, there's a chip in there and I'm on a computer and there's a network running around the building, so why don't I just put the drinks machine on the network, then I can poll it from my terminal whenever I want, and tell if I'm going to have a wasted journey or not?" So he connected the machine to the local network, but the local net was part of the Internet—so suddenly anyone in the world could see what was happening with this drinks machine. Now, that may not be vital information but it turned out to be curiously fascinating; everyone started to know what was happening with the drinks machine. It began to develop, because the chip in the machine didn't just say, "The slot which has Dr Pepper Light is empty," but had all sorts of information; it said, "There are seven Cokes and three Diet Cokes, the temperature they are stored at is this and the last time they were loaded was that." There was a lot of information in there, and there was one really fabulous piece of information: it turned out that if someone had put their fifty cents in and not pressed the button, i.e., if the machine was pregnant, then you could, from your computer terminal wherever you were in the world, log on to the drinks machine and drop that can! Somebody could be walking down the corridor when suddenly, bang!—there was a Coca-Cola can! What caused that? Well, *obviously* somebody five thousand miles away! Now that was a very, very silly but fascinating story, and what it said to me was that this was the first time we could reach back into the world. It may not be terribly important that from five thousand miles away you can reach into a university corridor and drop a

Coca-Cola can, but it's the first shot in the war of bringing to us a whole new way of communicating. So that, I think, is the fourth age of sand.

Extemporaneous speech given at Digital
Biota 2, Cambridge, SEPTEMBER 1998

*

Cookies

This actually did happen to a real person, and the real person is me. I had gone to catch a train. This was April 1976, in Cambridge, U.K. I was a bit early for the train. I'd gotten the time of the train wrong. I went to get myself a newspaper to do the crossword, and a cup of coffee and a packet of cookies. I went and sat at a table. I want you to picture the scene. It's very important that you get this very clear in your mind. Here's the table, newspaper, cup of coffee, packet of cookies. There's a guy sitting opposite me, perfectly ordinary-looking guy wearing a business suit, carrying a briefcase. It didn't look like he was going to do anything weird. What he did was this: he suddenly leaned across, picked up the packet of cookies, tore it open, took one out, and ate it.

Now this, I have to say, is the sort of thing the British are very bad at dealing with. There's nothing in our background, upbringing, or education that teaches you how to deal with someone who in broad daylight has just stolen your cookies. You know what would happen if this had been South Central Los Angeles. There would have very quickly been gunfire, helicopters coming in, CNN, you know . . . But in the end, I did what any red-blooded Englishman would do: I ignored it. And I stared at the newspaper, took a sip of coffee, tried to do a clue in the newspaper, couldn't do anything, and thought, *What am I going to do?*

In the end I thought, *Nothing for it, I'll just have to go for it,* and I tried very hard not to notice the fact that the packet was already mysteriously opened. I took out a cookie for myself. I thought, *That settled him.* But it hadn't because a moment or two later he did it again. He took another cookie. Having not mentioned it the first time, it was somehow even harder to raise the subject the second time around. "Excuse me, I couldn't help but notice . . ." I mean, it doesn't really work.

We went through the whole packet like this. When I say the whole packet, I mean there were only about eight cookies, but it felt like a lifetime. He took one, I took one, he took one, I took one. Finally, when we got to the end, he stood up and walked away. Well, we exchanged meaningful looks, then he walked away, and I breathed a sigh of relief and sat back.

A moment or two later the train was coming in, so I tossed back the rest of my coffee, stood up, picked up the newspaper, and underneath the newspaper were my cookies. The thing I like particularly about this story is the sensation that somewhere in England there has been wandering around for the last quarter-century a perfectly ordinary guy who's had the same exact story, only he doesn't have the punch line.

From a speech to Embedded Systems, 2001

AND
EVERYTHING

Interview with the Onion A. V. Club

I think the idea of art kills creativity.
—D.N.A.

THE ONION. You've got a lot of stuff going on. What do you want to talk about first?

DOUGLAS ADAMS. I guess there are two main things. One is that we are imminently about to finish this thing that I've been laboring over for what seems like two years now, called *Starship Titanic,* which is a CD-ROM. It's coming out in a couple months' time. The other thing is that I've just agreed to the sale of *Hitchhiker's Guide* to Disney. So I guess over the next couple of years, that's what I'm going to be doing. I'm making that movie.

O. Tell me about *Starship Titanic.*

D.A. Well, it's a CD-ROM, and the most important thing is that it started as a CD-ROM. People wanted me to do a CD-ROM of *Hitchhiker's,* and I thought, "No, no." I didn't want to just sort of reverse-engineer yet another thing from a book I'd already written. I think that the digital media are interesting enough in their own right to be worth originating something in. Because, really, the moment you have any idea, the second thought that enters your mind after the original idea is "What is this? Is it a book, is it a movie, is it a this, is it a that, is it a short story, is it a breakfast cereal?" Really, from that moment, your decision about what kind of thing it is then determines how it develops. So something will be very, very different if it's developed as a CD-ROM than if it's developed as a book. Now, in fact, I tell a slight lie, because the idea as such, in a sort of single-paragraph form, actually was what it was in one of the *Hitchhiker* books—I think *Life, the Universe, and Everything*. Because whenever I'd get sort of stuck on the story line in *Hitchhiker*, I'd always invent a couple of other quick story lines and give them to *The Guide* to talk about. So here was one little idea that was sitting there, and a number of people said to me, "Oh, you should turn that into a novel." It just seemed like too much of a good idea, and I tend to resist those. But in fact I discovered there was a very good reason why I wasn't interested in doing *Starship Titanic* as a book, which was that essentially it was a story about a *thing*. I just thought of this idea and didn't have any people attached to it, and you can only really tell stories about people. So, later, when I was thinking, "Okay, now I want to do a CD-ROM, because I want to justify the fact that I spend all my time sitting fiddling around with computers," I actually wanted to turn it into proper grown-up work. So I was thinking, what would be a good thing? Then I suddenly remembered that the problem with turning *Starship Titanic* into a book—that it was about a thing, about a place, about a ship—suddenly became very much to its advantage. When you're doing a CD-ROM, what you're eventually going to create is a place, an environment.

o. And the user becomes the character.

D.A. Yeah, exactly. Once the place begins to develop, you then put characters in it. But it isn't about the characters, it's about the ship. What I then wanted to do was something . . . Well, it was either very old-fashioned or very radical, depending on which way you look at it; I wanted to build a conversation engine into the game. Years and years ago, I did a game based on *Hitchhiker's Guide* with a company called Infocom, which was a great company. They were doing witty, intelligent, literate games based on text. You know, there are several thousand years of human culture telling you you can do quite a lot with text, and putting in the extra element of interactivity should just add to the possibilities. You turn the computer into the storyteller and the player into the audience, like in the old days when the storyteller would actually respond to the audience, rather than just having the audience respond to the storyteller. I had an enormous amount of fun, actually, working on that. I just loved constructing these virtual conversations between the player and the machine. So I just thought it'd be lovely to try to extend that and do more with it in a modern graphics game. Because what I would like to do is see if one can take that old conversation technology and make characters really speak. Put them in an environment and see where you go from there. So we started to tackle this problem of being able to speak to the characters. Of course, everything you do with language just balloons as a problem. To begin with, we wanted to do it whereby it would be text-to-speech, which gives you the advantage that you have much more flexibility in constructing sentences on the fly. On the other hand, all of your characters sound like semi-concussed Norwegians, which I felt was a downside. So we eventually realized we were going to have to do prerecorded speech. And I thought, "That's terrible, because you only have a limited number of responses. It's just going to be . . . Oh, I'm not sure about that." So the way we eventually solved the problem, or gradually solved the problem, was that the amount of prerecorded speech just got bigger, and bigger, and bigger, and bigger. We just did another two-hour recording session this morning. We've now got something like sixteen hours of little conversational snippets: little phrases, sentences, half-sentences, and all the things the machine puts together on the fly in response to what you type in. For a long time it wasn't working very well. And now, just really in the last two or three weeks, it's started to come together, and it's started to be spooky. People come in and say, "Yeah, yeah, yeah, I don't see how this is going to work. How 'bout if you ask it this?" And they do, and their jaw drops. It's just wonderful. People come in and spend hours just sitting, locked in conversation with these characters. I hasten to add that with the sixteen hours of dialogue, it was a small team of us who wrote it. I did part of the dialogue writing, and other people did some, and we all pulled it together. It's pretty remarkable when it works. You suddenly have this populated world. Very strange, damaged robots crawling around the place, all of whom have a wide range of opinions and attitudes and ideas and strange histories, and know about some entirely unexpected things. You can engage them all in conversation.

O. Do you feel concerned that after all this work, people won't treat it with the gravity of, say, a movie or a book? That they won't treat it as an art form?

D.A. I hope that's the case, yes. I get very worried about this idea of art. Having been an English literary graduate, I've been trying to avoid the idea of doing art ever since. I think the idea of art kills creativity. That was one of the reasons I really wanted to go and do a CD-ROM: because nobody will take it seriously, and therefore you can sneak under the fence with lots of good stuff. It's funny how often it happens. I guess when the novel started, most early novels were just sort of pornography: Apparently, most media actually started as pornography and sort of grew from there. This is not a pornographic CD-ROM, I hasten to add. Before 1962, everybody thought pop music was sort of . . . Nobody would have ever remotely called it art, and then somebody comes along and is just so incredibly creative in it, just because they love it to bits and think it's the greatest fun you can possibly have. And within a few years, you've got *Sgt. Pepper's* and so on, and everybody's calling it art. I think media are at their most interesting before anybody's thought of calling them art, when people still think they're just a load of junk.

O. But, say, twenty years from now, would you like to be recognized as one of the earliest practitioners of CD-ROM as art?

D.A. Well, I would just like a lot of people to have bought it. One, for the extremely obvious reason. But the other is that if it's popular and people really like it and have fun with it, you feel you've done a good job. And if somebody wants to come along and say, "Oh, it's art," that's as it may be. I don't really mind that much. But I think that's for other people to decide after the fact. It isn't what you should be aiming to do. There's nothing worse than sitting down to write a novel and saying, "Well, okay, I'm going to do something of high artistic worth." It's funny. I read something the other day, just out of absolute curiosity; I read *Thunderball*, which is one of the James Bond books that I would love to have read when I was, I don't know, about fourteen, just sort of thumbing through it for the bits where he puts his left hand on her breast and saying, "Oh my God, how exciting." But I just thought, Well, James Bond has become such an icon in our pop culture of the last forty years, it would be interesting to see what it actually was like. And what prompted me to do this, apart from the fact that I happened to find a copy lying around, was reading someone talking about Ian Fleming and saying that he had aimed not to be literary, but to be literate. Which is a very, very big and crucial difference. So I thought, well, I'll see if he managed to do that. It's interesting, because it was actually very well written as a piece of craft. He knew how to use the language, he knew how to make it work, and he wrote well. But obviously nobody would call it literature. But I think you get most of the most interesting work done in fields where people don't think they're doing art, but are merely practicing a craft, and working as good craftsmen. Being literate as a writer is good craft, is knowing your job, is knowing how to use your tools properly and not to damage the tools as you use them. I find when I read literary novels—you know, with a capital "L"—I think an awful lot is nonsense. If I want to know something interesting about a way human beings work, how they relate to each other and how they behave, I'll find an awful lot of women crime novelists who do it better, Ruth Rendell for instance. If I want to read something that's really giving me something serious and fundamental to think about, about the human condition, if you like, or what we're all doing here, or what's going on, then I'd rather read something by a scientist in the life sciences, like Richard Dawkins. I feel that the agenda of life's important issues has moved from novelists to science writers, because they know more. I tend to get very suspicious of anything that thinks it's art while it's being created. As far as being a CD-ROM is concerned, I just wanted to do the best thing I could, and have as much fun as I could doing it. I think it's pretty good. There are always bits that you fret over for being less than perfect, but you can keep on worrying over something forever. The thing is pretty damn good.

O. You've got the movie, too. I'd heard rumors of a *Hitchhiker's Guide* movie kicking around for decades.

D.A. Oh, well, yeah. Although it sort of bubbles under, there have been two previous sources of rumors. One was when I originally sold the rights about fifteen years ago to Ivan Reitman, who was not as well-known then as he is now. It really didn't work out, because once we got down to it, Ivan and I didn't really see eye-to-eye. In fact, it turned out he hadn't actually read the book before he bought it. He'd merely read the sales figures. I think it really wasn't his cup of tea, so he wanted to make something rather different. Eventually, we agreed to differ and went our respective ways, and by this time the ownership had passed from him to Columbia, and he went on to make a movie called *Ghostbusters,* so you can imagine how irritated I was by that. It sat there owned by Columbia for many years. I think Ivan Reitman then got somebody else to write a script based on it, which is, I think, the worst script I'd ever read. Unfortunately, it has my name on it *and* the other writer's, whereas I did not contribute a single comma to it. I've only just discovered that that script has been sitting in script city, or whatever it is, for a long time, and that everyone assumes I wrote it and am therefore a terrible screenwriter. Which is rather distressing to me. So then, a few years ago, I was introduced to someone who became a great friend of mine, Michael Nesmith, who has done a number of different things in his career: In addition to being a film producer, he was originally one of the Monkees. Which is kind of odd when you get to know him, because he's such a serious, thoughtful, quiet chap, but with quiet reserves of impish glee. So his proposal was that we go into partnership together to make this. He's the producer, and I do the scripts and so on. We had a very good time working on it for quite a while, but I just think Hollywood at that point saw the thing as old. It's been around the block. And basically, what I was being told an awful lot was essentially, "Science-fiction comedy will not work as a movie. And here's why not: If it could work, somebody would have done it already."

O. That logic seems kind of flawed.

D.A. So what happens, of course, is that *Men in Black* came out this past year, so suddenly somebody has done it already. And *Men in Black* is . . . How can I put this delicately? There were elements of it I found quite familiar, shall we say? And suddenly a comedy science-fiction movie that was very much in the same vein as *Hitchhiker's* became one of the most successful movies ever made. So that kind of changed the landscape a little bit. Suddenly people kind of wanted it. The project with Michael . . . In the end, we hadn't gotten it to take, so we parted company very good friends, and still are. I just hope that there will be other projects in the future that he and I will work on together, because I like him enormously and we got on very well together. And also, the more time I get to spend in Santa Fe, the better. So now the picture's with Disney—or, more specifically, with Caravan, which is one of the major independent production companies, but it's kind of joined at the hip to Disney. It's been very frustrating not to have made it in the last fifteen years; nevertheless, I feel extremely buoyed by the fact that one can make a much, much, much better movie out of it now than one could have fifteen years ago. That's in technical terms; in terms of how it will look and how it will work. Obviously the real quality of the picture is in the writing and the acting and the directing and so on and so forth, and those skills have neither risen nor sunk in fifteen years. But at least one substantial area, in how it can be made to look, has improved a great deal.

O. And Jay Roach [*Austin Powers*] is directing it, right?

D.A. That's right. He's a very interesting fellow. I've now spent quite a lot of time talking to him. The key to the whole thing, in many ways, was when I met Jay Roach, because I hit it off very well with him, and thought, "Here's a very bright, intelligent guy." Not only is he a bright, intelligent guy, but here's a measure of how bright and intelligent he is: he wants me to work very closely on his movie. Which is always something that endears a writer to a director. In fact, when I was making the original radio series, it was unheard of to do what I did. Because I'd just written it. But I kind of inserted myself in the whole production process. The producer/director was a little surprised by this, but in the end took it in very good grace. So I had a huge amount to do with the way the program developed, and that's exactly what Jay wants me to do on this movie. So I felt, "Great, here's somebody I can do business with." Obviously I'm saying that at the beginning of a process that's going to take two years. So who knows what's going to happen? All I can say is that at this point in the game, things are set as fair as they possibly could be. So I feel very optimistic and excited about that.

O. It's been nearly twenty years since the radio program, right?

D.A. Well, it's almost exactly twenty years. It'll be twenty years next month.

O. What's the enduring appeal of *Hitchhiker's Guide to the Galaxy?*

D.A. Well, I don't know. All I know is that I worked very hard at it, and I worried very much about it, and I think I made things very difficult for myself doing it. And if ever there was an easy way of doing something, I would find a much harder way to do it. And I suspect that the amount that people have liked it is not unrelated to the amount of work I put into it. That's a simplistic thing to say, but it's the best I can come up with.

O. Is the idea that the movie will cover the first book?

D.A. Yeah. It's funny, because I've been looking around the Web at what people have been saying. I've seen, "He's going to put all five books into it." People just don't understand the way a book maps onto a movie. Somebody said, and I think quite accurately, that the best source material for a movie is a short story. Which effectively means, yes, it's going to be the first book. Having said that, whenever I sit down and do another version of *Hitchhiker,* it highly contradicts whichever version went before. The best thing I can say about the movie is that it will be specifically contradicting the first book.

O. Which version of *Hitchhiker* are you happiest with?

D.A. Not the TV version, that's for sure. In different moods, I will feel either the radio or the book, which are the two other versions left, so it's got to be one of those, hasn't it? I feel differently about each of them. On the one hand, the radio series was where it originated; that's where it grew; that's where the seed grew. Also, that's where I felt that myself and the other people working on it—the producer and the sound engineers and so on, and, of course, the actors—all created something that really felt groundbreaking at the time. Or rather, it felt like we were completely mad at the time. I can remember sitting in the subterranean studio, auditioning the sound of a whale hitting the ground at three hundred miles an hour for hours on end, just trying to find ways of tweaking the sound. After hours of that, day after day, you do begin to doubt your sanity. Of course, you have no idea if anybody's going to listen to this stuff. But, you know, there was a real sense that nobody had done this before. And that was great; there's a great charge that comes with that. On the other hand, the appeal of the books to me is that that's just me. The great appeal of a book to any writer is that it is just them. That's it. There's nobody else involved. That's not quite true, of course, because the thing developed out of a radio series in the first place, and there is a sense in there of all the people who have contributed, in one way or another, to the radio show that it grew out of. But, nevertheless, there is a this-is-all-my-own-work feel about a book. And I'm pleased with the way it reads. I feel it flows nicely. It feels as if it were easy to write, and I know how difficult that was to achieve.

O. Do you ever get tired of *Hitchhiker's Guide to the Galaxy?*

D.A. There was a period where I got heartily sick of it, and I really never wanted to hear anything more about it again, and I would almost scream at anybody who used the words to me. But since then, I went off and did other things. I did the Dirk Gently books. My favorite thing that I've ever done was a thing I did about ten years ago: I went around the world with a zoologist friend of mine, and looked for various rare and endangered species of animals, and wrote a book about that called *Last Chance to See,* which is my own personal favorite. *Hitchhiker* now is something from the past that I feel very fond of; it was great, it was terrific, and it's being very good to me. I had a conversation a little while ago with Pete Townshend of The Who, and I think at that point I was saying, "Oh God, I hope I'm not just remembered as the person who wrote *Hitchhiker's Guide to the Galaxy.*" And he kind of reprimanded me a little bit. He said, "Look, I have the same thing with *Tommy,* and for a while I thought like that. The thing is, when you've got something like that in your history, it opens an awful lot of doors. It allows you to do a lot of other things. People remember that. It's something one should be grateful for." And I thought that was quite right.

o. Have you put Dirk Gently aside?

D.A. Well, I started to write another Dirk Gently book, and I just lost it. For some reason I couldn't get it going, so I had to put it aside. I didn't know what to do with it. I looked at the material again about a year later, and suddenly thought, "Actually, the reason is that the ideas and the character don't match. I've tried to go for the wrong kind of ideas, and these ideas would actually fit much better in a *Hitchhiker* book, but I don't want to write another *Hitchhiker* book at the moment." So I sort of put them on one side. And maybe one day I will write another *Hitchhiker* book, because there's an awful lot of material sitting around waiting to go in it. But going back to Dirk Gently, I sort of put Dirk aside, really. There was a student production of *Dirk Gently, Holistic Detective* in Oxford two or three months ago, so I went along to see it. And it's an enormously complicated plot . . . Part of the complexity is there to disguise the fact that the plot doesn't really quite work . . . It was funny watching it on stage, because I suddenly began to think about it again, and think, "Well, they did this well, but what they should have done was this, and they should've done that." You know, it starts the whole ball rolling in your head. What was also interesting to me was that while I was sitting there being quite critical of the production, I was astonished by how much the audience was enjoying it. It was rather sort of a peculiar situation. I suddenly thought, "I would love to see this happen as a film, because I can now see, having thought about it freshly in this context, what kind of a movie it could be, and it could be great." So maybe, once the *Hitchhiker* movie has gotten to the stage where I can turn my attention to other things as well, that's what I'd like to do next. And with that movie under way, I hope more doors will open as far as filmmaking is concerned. I would love to do movies, but this is a man saying this innocently who's never done one.

Interview conducted
with Keith Phipps, 1998

✳   ✳   ✳

Douglas Adams
48 Bloomsbury Terrace
London N1-6TS

April 14, 1999

David Vogel
Walt Disney Pictures

Dear David,

I've tried to reach you by phone a couple of times. Perhaps it would have helped if I'd explained why I was calling: I was in the States for a few days and thought it might be helpful if I came across to L.A. so that you and I could have a meeting. I didn't hear from you, so I'm on a plane back to England, where I'm typing this.

We seem to have gotten to a place where the problems appear to loom larger than the opportunities. I don't know if I'm right in thinking this, but I only have silence to go on, which is always a poor source of information.

It seems to me that we can either slip into the traditional stereotypes—you're the studio executive who has a million real-world problems to worry about, and I'm the writer who only cares about seeing his vision realised and hang the cost and consequences—or we can recognise that we both share the same goal, which is to make the most successful movie we possibly can. The fact that we may have different perspectives on how this can best be achieved should be a fertile source of debate and interactive problem solving. It's not clear to me that a one-way traffic of written "notes" interspersed with long, dreadful silences is a good substitute for this.

You have a great deal of experience nursing major motion pictures into existence. I have a great deal of experience of nursing The Hitchhiker's Guide to the Galaxy into existence in every medium other than motion pictures. I'm sure you must feel frustrated that I don't seem to understand the range of problems you have to contend with, just as I feel frustrated that I haven't had any real creative dialogue with Disney about this project yet. I have a suggestion to make: Why don't we actually meet and have a chat?

I could be in L.A. for next Monday (4/19) or early the following week. I would invite Disney to bear the cost of this extra trip over. I've appended a list of numbers you can reach me on. If you manage not to reach me, I shall know you're trying not to, very, very hard indeed.

Best wishes,

Douglas Adams

Email: dna@tdv.com
Assistant (Sophie Astin) (and voicemail): 555 171 555 1700
    (between 10 A.M. and 6:00 P.M. British Summertime)
Office fax: 555 171 555 1701
Home (no voicemail): 555 171 555 3632
Home fax: 555 171 555 5601
UK cell phone (and voicemail): 555 410 555 098
US cellphone (and voicemail): (310) 555 555 6769
Other home (France): 555 4 90 72 39 23
Jane Belson (wife) (office): 555 171 555 4715
Film agent (US) Bob Bookman: (310) 555 4545
Book agent (UK) Ed Victor (office): 555 171 555 4100
    (UK office hours)

Book agent (UK) Ed Victor (office): 555 171 555 4112
Book agent (UK) Ed Victor (home): 555 171 555 3030
Producer: Roger Birnbaum: (818) 555 2637
Director: Jay Roach (Everyman Pictures): (323) 555 3585
Jay Roach (home): (310) 555 5903
Jay Roach (cellphone): (310) 555 0279
Shauna Robertson (Everyman Pictures): (323) 555 3585
Shauna Robertson, home: (310) 555 7352
Shauna Robertson, cellphone: (310) 555 8357
Robbie Stamp, Executive Producer (UK) (office): 555 171
    555 1707
Robbie Stamp, Executive Producer (UK) (home): 555 181
    555 1672
Robbie Stamp, Executive Producer (UK) (cell phone): 555
    7885 55 8397
Janet Thrift (mother) (UK): 555 19555 62527
Jane Garnier (sister) (UK) (work): 555 1300 555 684
Jane Garnier (sister) (UK) (home): 555 1305 555 034
Jakki Kelloway (daughter's nanny) (UK): 555 171 555
    5602
Angus Deayton & Lise Meyer (next-door neighbours who
    can take a message) (UK): Work: 555 (145) 555 0464,
    Home: 555 (171) 555 0855
Restaurants I might conceivably be at:
    The Ivy (UK): 555 171 555 4751
    The Groucho Club (UK): 555 171 555 4685
    Granita (UK): 555 171 555 3222
    Sainsbury's (supermarket where I shop; they can always
        page me): 555 171 555 1789
Website forum www.douglasadams.com/forum

* * *

[Editor's Note: This letter had the desired effect. David Vogel responded, resulting in a productive meeting that pushed the movie forward.]

✳

The Private Life of Genghis Khan

The last of the horsemen disappeared into the smoke, and the thudding of their hooves receded into the grey distance.

The smoke hung on the land. It drifted across the setting sun, which lay like an open wound across the western sky.

In the ringing silence that followed the battle, very, very few, pitifully few cries could be heard from the bloody, mangled wreckage on the fields.

Ghostlike figures, stunned with horror, emerged from the woods, stumbled, and then ran forward crying—women, searching for their husbands, brothers, fathers, lovers, first amongst the dying and then amongst the dead. The flickering light by which they searched was that of their burning village, which had that afternoon officially become part of the Mongol Empire.

The Mongols.

From out of the wastes of central Asia they had swept, a savage force for which the world was utterly unprepared. They swept like a wildly wielded scythe, hacking, slashing, obliterating all that lay in their path, and calling it conquest.

And throughout the lands that feared them now or would come to fear them, no name inspired more terror than that of their leader, Genghis Khan. The greatest of the Asian warlords, he stood alone, revered as a god among warriors, marked out by the cold light of his grey-green eyes, the savage furrow of his brow, and the fact that he could beat the shit out of any of them.

Later that night the moon rose, and by its light a small party of horsemen carrying torches rode quietly out from the Mongol encampment that sprawled over a nearby hill. A casual observer would not have noticed anything remarkable about the man who rode at their centre, muffled in a heavy cloak, tense, hunched forward on his horse as if weighed down by a heavy burden, because a casual observer would have been dead.

The band rode a few miles through the moonlit woods, picking their way along the paths until they came at last to a small clearing, and here they reined their horses in and waited on their leader.

He moved his horse slowly forward and surveyed the small group of peasant huts that stood huddled together in the centre of the clearing, trying very hard at short notice to look deserted.

Hardly any smoke at all was rising from the primitive chimney stacks. Virtually no light appeared at the windows, and not a sound could be heard from any of them save that of a small child saying, "Shhhhh . . ."

For a moment a strange green fire seemed to flash from the eyes of the Mongol leader. A heavy, deadly kind of thing that you could hardly call a smile drew itself through his fine, wispy beard. The strange kind of smiley thing would signify (briefly) to anyone who was stupid enough to look that there was nothing a Mongol warlord liked better after a day hacking people to bits than a big night out.

The door flew open. A Mongol warrior surged into the hut like a savage wind. Two children ran screaming to their mother, who was cowering wide-eyed in the corner of the tiny room. A dog yelped.

The warrior hurled his torch onto the still-glowing fire, and then threw the dog onto it. That would teach it to be a dog. The last surviving man of the family, a grey and aged grandfather, stepped bravely forward, eyes flashing. With a flash of his sword the Mongol whipped off the old man's head, which trundled across the floor and fetched up leaning rakishly against a table leg. The old man's body stood tensely for a moment, not knowing what to think. As it began slowly, majestically, to topple forward, Khan strode in and pushed it brusquely aside. He surveyed the happy domestic scene and bestowed a grim kind of smile on it. Then he walked over to a large chair and sat in it, testing it first for comfort. When he was satisfied with it, he heaved a heavy sigh and sat back in front of the fire on which the dog was now blazing merrily.

The warrior grabbed at the terrified woman, pushed her children roughly aside, and brought her, trembling, in front of the mighty Khan.

She was young and pretty, with long, bedraggled black hair. Her bosom heaved and her face was stark with fright.

Khan regarded her with a slow, contemptuous look.

"Does she know," he said at length in a low, dead voice, "who I am?"

"You . . . you are the mighty Khan!" cried the woman.

Khan's eyes fixed themselves on hers.

"Does she know," he hissed, "what I want of her?"

"I . . . I'll do anything for you, O Khan," stammered the woman, "but spare my children!"

Khan said quietly, "Then begin." His eyes dropped and he gazed distantly into the fire.

Nervously, shaking with fear, the woman stepped forward and laid a tentative, pale hand on Khan's arm.

The soldier smacked her hand away.

"Not that!" he barked.

The woman started back, aflutter. She realised she would have to do better. Still shaking, she knelt down on the floor and started gently to push apart the Khan's knees.

"Stop that!" roared the soldier, and shoved her violently backwards. Bewilderment began to mix with the terror in her eyes as she cowered on the floor.

"Come on" snapped the soldier, "ask him what kind of day he's had."

"What . . . ?" she wailed, "I don't . . . I don't understand what . . ."

The soldier seized her, spun her into a half-nelson, and jabbed the point of his sword against her throat.

"I said ask him," he hissed, "what kind of day he's had!"

The woman gasped with pain and incomprehension. The sword jabbed again. "Say it!"

"Er, what sort . . . of . . . er, day . . ." she said in a hesitant, strangled squeak, "have you . . . had?"

"'Dear'!" hissed the soldier, "say 'dear'!"

Her eyes bulged in horror at the sword.

"What sort of day have you had . . . dear?" she asked querulously.

Khan looked up briefly, wearily.

"Oh, same as usual," he said. "Violent."

He gazed back at the fire again.

"Right," said the soldier to the woman, "go on."

She relaxed very slightly. She seemed to have passed some kind of test. Perhaps it would be straightforward from now on, and she could at least get it over with. She moved nervously forward and started to caress the Khan again.

The soldier hurled her savagely across the room, kicked her, and yanked her screaming to her feet again.

"I said stop that!" he bellowed. He pulled her face close to his and breathed a lungful of cheap wine and week-old rancid goat-fat fumes at her, which failed to cheer her up because it reminded her sharply of her late lamented husband who used to do the same thing to her every night. She sobbed.

"Be nice to him!" the Mongol snarled, and spat one of his unwanted teeth at her. "Ask him how his work's going!"

She gawped at him. The nightmare was continuing. A stinging blow landed on her cheek.

"Just say to him," the soldier snarled again, "'How's the work going, dear?'" He shoved her forward.

"How . . . how's the work going . . . dear?" she yelped miserably.

The soldier shook her. "Put some affection into it!" he roared.

She sobbed again. "How . . . how's the work going . . . dear?" she yelped miserably again, but this time with a kind of pathetic pout at the end.

The mighty Khan sighed.

"Oh, not too bad, I suppose," he said in a world-weary tone. "We swept through Manchuria a bit, and spilt quite a lot of blood there. That was in the morning, then this afternoon was mainly pillaging, though there was a bit of bloodshed around half past four. What sort of day have you had?"

So saying, he pulled a couple of scroll maps from out of his furs and started to study them abstractedly by the light of the smouldering dog.

The Mongol warrior pulled a glowing poker out of the fire and advanced menacingly on the woman.

"Tell him! Go on!"

She leapt back with a shriek.

"Tell him!"

"Er, my husband and father were killed!" she said.

"Oh yes, dear?" said Khan absently, not looking up from his maps.

"Dog was burnt!"

"Oh, er, really?"

"Well, er, that's about it, really . . . er . . ."

The soldier advanced on her with the poker again.

"Oh, and I was tortured a bit!" shrieked the woman.

Khan looked up at her. "What?" he said vaguely. "Sorry, dear, I was just reading this . . ."

"Right," said the soldier, "nag him!"

"What?"

"Just say, 'Look, Genghis, put that thing away while I'm talking to you. Here I am, spend all day slaving over a hot . . .'"

"He'll kill me!"

"Bleeding kill you if you don't."

"I can't stand it!" cried the woman, and collapsed on the floor. She flung herself on the great Khan's feet. "Don't torment me," she wailed. "If you mean to rape me, then rape me, but don't . . ."

The great Khan surged to his feet and glowered down at her. "No," he muttered savagely, "you'd only laugh—you're just like all the others."

He stormed out of the hut and rode off into the night in such a rage that he almost forgot to burn down the village before he left.

✳   ✳   ✳

After another particularly vicious day, the last of the horsemen disappeared into the smoke, and the thudding of their hooves receded into the grey distance.

The smoke hung on the land. It drifted across the setting sun, which lay like an open wound across the western sky.

In the ringing silence that followed the battle, very, very few, pitifully few, cries could be heard from the bloody, mangled wreckage on the fields.

Ghostlike figures, stunned with horror, emerged from the woods, stumbled, and then ran forward crying—women, searching for their husbands, brothers, fathers, lovers, first amongst the dying and then amongst the dead.

Far away, behind the screen of smoke, thousands of horsemen arrived at their sprawling camp, and with a huge amount of clatter, shouting, and comparing of backhand slashes, they dismounted and instantly started in on the cheap wine and rancid goat fat.

In front of his splendidly bedraped imperial tent, a bloodstained and battle-weary Khan dismounted.

"Which battle was that?" he asked his son, Ogdai, who had ridden with him. Ogdai was a young and ambitious general, keenly interested in viciousness of all kinds. He was hoping to improve on his own Known World record for the highest number of peasants impaled on a single sword thrust, and would be getting in some practice that night.

He strode up to his father.

"It was the Battle of Samarkand, O Khan!" he proclaimed, and rattled his sword in a tremendously impressive way.

Khan folded his arms and leant on his horse, looking over it across the dreadful mess they'd made of the valley beneath them.

"Oh, I can't tell the difference anymore," he said with a sigh. "Did we win?"

"Oh yes! Yes! Yes!" exclaimed Ogdai with fierce pride. "It was a mighty victory indeed!

"Indeed it was!" he added, and waggled his sword again. He drew it excitedly and made a few practice thrusts. Yes, he thought to himself, tonight he was going to go for the six.

Khan screwed his face up at the gathering dusk.

"Oh dear," he said, "after twenty years of these two-hour battles I get the feeling that there must be more to life, you know." He turned, lifted up the front of his torn and bloodied gold-embroidered tunic and stared down at his own hairy tummy. "Here, feel this," he said. "Do you think I'm putting it on a bit?"

Ogdai gazed at the great Khan's tummy with a mixture of awe and impatience.

"Er, no," he said. "No, not at all." With a flick of his fingers, Ogdai summoned a servant to bring the maps to him, ran him through, and, as he fell, caught from his nerveless but not entirely surprised fingers the plans of the grand campaign.

"Now, O Khan," he said, spreading the map over the back of another servant who stood specially hunched over for the purpose, "we must push forward to Persia, and then we shall be poised to take over the whole world!"

"No, look, feel that," said Khan, pinching a fold of skin between his fingers. "do you think . . ."

"Khan!" interrupted Ogdai urgently. "We are on the point of conquering the world!" He stabbed at the map with a knife, catching the servant beneath a nasty nick on his left lung.

"When?" said Khan with a frown.

Ogdai threw up his arms in exasperation. "Tomorrow!" he said. "We start tomorrow!"

"Ah, well, tomorrow's a bit difficult, you see," said Khan. He puffed out his cheeks and thought for a moment. "The thing is that next week I've got this lecture on carnage techniques in Bokhara, and I thought I'd use tomorrow to prepare it."

Ogdai stared at him in astonishment as the map-bearing servant slowly collapsed on his foot.

"Well, can't you put that off?" he exclaimed.

"Well, you see, they've paid me quite a lot of money for it already, so I'm a bit committed."

"Well, Wednesday?"

Khan pulled a scroll from out of his tunic and looked through it, shaking his head slowly. "Not sure about Wednesday . . ."

"Thursday?"

"No, Thursday I am certain about. We've got Ogdai and his wife coming round to dinner, and I'd kind of promised . . ."

"But I *am* Ogdai!"

"Well, there you are, then. You wouldn't be able to make it either."

Ogdai's silence was only disturbed by the sound of thousands of hairy Mongols shouting and fighting and getting pissed.

"Look," he said quietly, "will you be ready to conquer the world . . . on Friday?"

Khan sighed. "Well, the secretary comes in on Friday mornings."

"Does she."

"All those letters to answer. You'd be astonished at the demands people try to make on my time, you know." He slouched moodily against his horse. "Would I sign this, would I appear there. Would I please do a sponsored massacre for charity. So that usually takes till at least three, then I had hoped to get away early for a long weekend. Now, Monday, Monday . . ."

He consulted his scroll again.

"Monday's out, I'm afraid. Rest and recuperation, that's one thing I do insist upon. Now how about Tuesday?"

The strange keening noise that could be heard in the distance at this moment sounded like the normal everyday wailing of women and children over their slaughtered menfolk, and Khan paid it no mind. A light bobbed on the horizon.

"Tuesday—look, I'm free in the morning—no, hold on a moment, I'd sort of made a date for meeting this awfully interesting chap who knows absolutely everything about understanding things, which is something I'm awfully bad at. Now, that's a pity because that was my only free day next week. Now, next Tuesday we could usefully think about—or is that the day I . . ."

The keening sound continued, in fact it grew, but it was so lightly borne upon the evening breeze that it still did not intrude itself on Khan's senses. The approaching light was so pale as to be indistinguishable from that of the moon, which was bright that night.

". . . so that's more or less the whole of March out," said Khan, "I'm afraid."

"April?" asked Ogdai, wearily. He idly whipped out a passing peasant's liver, but the joy had gone out of it. He flipped the thing listlessly off into the dark. A dog that had grown very fat over the years by the simple expedient of staying close to Ogdai at all times leapt on it. These were not pleasant times.

"Well, no, April's out," said Khan. "I'm going to Africa in April, that's one thing I had promised myself."

The light approaching them through the night sky had now

at last attracted the attention of one or two other leading Mongols in the vicinity, who, wonderingly, stopped hitting each other and stabbing things and drew near.

"Look," said Ogdai, himself still unaware of what things were coming to pass, "can we please agree that we will conquer the world in May, then?"

The mighty Khan sucked doubtfully on his teeth. "Well, I don't like to commit myself that far in advance. One feels so tied down if one's life is completely mapped out beforehand. I should be doing more reading, for heaven's sake, when am I going to find the time for that? Anyway—" He sighed and scratched at his scroll. "'May—possible conquest of the world.' Now I've only pencilled that in, so don't regard it as absolutely definite—but keep on at me about it and we'll see how it goes. Hello, what's that?"

Slowly, with the grace of a beautiful woman stepping into a bath, a long, slim, silver craft lowered itself gently to the ground. Soft light streamed from it. From its opening doorway stepped a tall, elegant creature with a curiously fine grey-green complexion. It walked slowly towards them.

In its path lay the dark figure of a peasant who had been crying quietly to himself since he had watched his liver being eaten by Ogdai's dog and had known that no way was he going to get it back, and wondered how on earth his poor wife was going to cope now. He chose this moment finally to pass on to better things.

The tall alien stepped over him with distaste and, though you would have had to read its face very closely to realise this, a little envy. It nodded briefly to each of the gathered Mongol leaders in turn, and pulled a small clipboard out from under its heavy metallic robe.

"Good evening," it said in a small, weaselly voice, "my name is Wowbagger, also called the Infinitely Prolonged, I shall not trouble you with the reasons why. Greetings."

He turned and addressed the completely pop-eyed mighty Khan.

"You are Genghis Khan? Genghis Temüjin Khan, son of Yesügei?"

The diary scrolls slipped from Khan's hands to the ground. The pale luminesence from Wowbagger's ship suffused his wondering, ravaged, careworn yellow features. As in a dream, the mighty Emperor stepped forward in acknowledgement.

"Can I just check the spelling?" said the alien, showing him the clipboard. "I would hate to get it wrong at this stage and then have to start all over again, I really would."

Khan nodded faintly.

"Right number of aitches, then?" said the alien.

Again, the transfigured Emperor slightly inclined his face, while his eyes still boggled.

"Good," said Wowbagger, and made a little tick on his clipboard. He looked up. "Genghis Khan," he said, "you are a wanker; you are a tosspot; you are a very tiny piece of turd. Thank you." With that he retreated into his ship and flew off.

There was a nasty kind of silence.

Later that year, Genghis Khan stormed into Europe in such a rage that he almost forgot to burn down Asia before he left.

> Based in part on an original sketch devised by Graham Chapman and written by Chapman and Adams for the Graham Chapman Television Show "Out of the Trees," 1975. From *The Utterly Utterly Merry Comic Relief Christmas Book*, 1986.

✳

Young Zaphod Plays It Safe

A large flying craft moved swiftly across the surface of an astoundingly beautiful sea. From midmorning onward it plied back and forth in great, widening arcs, and at last attracted the attention of the local islanders, a peaceful, seafood-loving people who gathered on the beach and squinted up into the blinding sun, trying to see what was there.

Any sophisticated, knowledgable person who had knocked about, seen a few things, would probably have remarked on how much the craft looked like a filing cabinet—a large and recently burgled filing cabinet lying on its back with its drawers in the air and flying. The islanders, whose experience was of a different kind, were instead struck by how little it looked like a lobster.

They chattered excitedly about its total lack of claws, its stiff, unbendy back, and the fact that it seemed to experience the greatest difficulty staying on the ground. This last feature seemed particularly funny to them. They jumped up and down on the spot a lot to demonstrate to the stupid thing that they themselves found staying on the ground the easiest thing in the world. But soon this entertainment began to pall for them. After all, since it was perfectly clear to them that the thing was not a lobster, and since their world was blessed with an abundance of things that were lobsters (a good half a dozen of which were now marching succulently up the beach towards them), they saw no reason to waste any more time on the thing, but decided instead to adjourn immediately for a late lobster lunch.

At that exact moment the craft stopped suddenly in midair, then upended itself and plunged headlong into the ocean with a great crash of spray that sent the islanders shouting into the trees. When they reemerged, nervously, a few minutes later, all they were able to see was a smoothly scarred circle of water and a few gulping bubbles.

That's odd, they said to each other between mouthfuls of the best lobster to be had anywhere in the Western Galaxy, that's the second time that's happened in a year.

The craft that wasn't a lobster dived directly to a depth of two hundred feet, and hung there in the heavy blueness, while vast masses of water swayed about it. High above, where the water was magically clear, a brilliant formation of fish flashed away. Below, where the light had difficulty reaching, the colour of the water sank to a dark and savage blue.

Here, at two hundred feet, the sun streamed feebly. A large, silk-skinned sea mammal rolled idly by, inspecting the craft with a kind of half-interest, as if it had half expected to find something of this kind round about here, and then it slid on up and away towards the rippling light.

The craft waited here for a minute or two, taking readings, and then descended another hundred feet. At this depth it was becoming seriously dark. After a moment or two the internal lights of the craft shut down, and in the second or so that passed before the main external beams suddenly stabbed out, the only visible light came from a small, hazily illuminated pink sign that read, THE BEEBLEBROX SALVAGE AND REALLY WILD STUFF CORPORATION.

The huge beams switched downwards, catching a vast shoal of silver fish, which swivelled away in silent panic.

In the dim control room that extended in a broad bow from the craft's blunt prow, four heads were gathered round a computer display that was analysing the very, very faint and intermittent signals that were emanating from deep on the seabed.

"That's it," said the owner of one of the heads finally.

"Can we be quite sure?" said the owner of another of the heads.

"One hundred per cent positive," replied the owner of the first head.

"You're one hundred per cent positive that the ship which is crashed on the bottom of this ocean is the ship which you said you were one hundred per cent positive could one hundred per cent positively never crash?" said the owner of the two remaining heads. "Hey"—he put up two of his hands—"I'm only asking."

The two officials from the Safety and Civil Reassurance Administration responded to this with a very cold stare, but the man with the odd, or rather the even number of heads, missed it. He flung himself back on the pilot couch, opened a couple of beers—one for himself and the other also for himself—stuck his feet on the console, and said "Hey, baby," through the ultra-glass at a passing fish.

"Mr. Beeblebrox . . ." began the shorter and less reassuring of the two officials in a low voice.

"Yup?" said Zaphod, rapping a suddenly empty can down on some of the more sensitive instruments. "You ready to dive? Let's go."

"Mr. Beeblebrox, let us make one thing perfectly clear . . ."

"Yeah, let's," said Zaphod. "How about this for a start. Why don't you just tell me what's really on this ship."

"We have told you," said the official. "By-products."

Zaphod exchanged weary glances with himself.

"By-products," he said. "By-products of what?"

"Processes," said the official.

"What processes?"

"Processes that are perfectly safe."

"Santa Zarquana Voostra!" exclaimed both of Zaphod's heads in chorus. "So safe that you have to build a zarking fortress ship to take the by-products to the nearest black hole and tip them in! Only it doesn't get there because the pilot does a detour—is this right?—to pick up some lobster? Okay, so the guy is cool, but . . . I mean own up, this is barking time, this is major lunch, this is stool approaching critical mass, this is . . . this is . . . total vocabulary failure!

"Shut up!" his right head yelled at his left. "We're flanging!"

He got a good calming grip on the remaining beer can.

"Listen, guys," he resumed after a moment's peace and contemplation. The two officials had said nothing. Conversation at this level was not something to which they felt they could aspire. "I just want to know," insisted Zaphod, "what you're getting me into here."

He stabbed a finger at the intermittent readings trickling over the computer screen. They meant nothing to him, but he didn't like the look of them at all. They were all squiggly, with lots of long numbers and things.

"It's breaking up, is that it?" he shouted. "It's got a hold full of epsilonic radiating aorist rods or something that'll fry this whole space sector for zillions of years back, and it's breaking up. Is that the story? Is that what we're going down to find? Am I going to come out of that wreck with even more heads?"

"It cannot possibly be a wreck, Mr. Beeblebrox," insisted

the official. "The ship is guaranteed to be perfectly safe. It cannot possibly break up."

"Then why are you so keen to go and look at it?"

"We like to look at things that are perfectly safe."

"Freeeoooow!"

"Mr. Beeblebrox," said the official patiently, "may I remind you that you have a job to do?"

"Yeah, well maybe I don't feel so keen on doing it all of a sudden. What do you think I am, completely without any moral whatsits, what are they called, those moral things?"

"Scruples?"

"Scruples, thank you, whatsoever? Well?"

The two officials waited calmly. They coughed slightly to help pass the time.

Zaphod sighed a what-is-the-world-coming-to sort of sigh to absolve himself from all blame, and swung himself round in his seat.

"Ship?" he called.

"Yup?" said the ship.

"Do what I do."

The ship thought about this for a few milliseconds and then, after double-checking all the seals on its heavy-duty bulkheads, it began slowly, inexorably, in the hazy blaze of its lights, to sink to the lowest depths.

Five hundred feet.

A thousand.

Two thousand.

Here, at a pressure of nearly seventy atmospheres, in the chilling depths where no light reaches, nature keeps its most heated imaginings. Two-foot-long nightmares loomed wildly into the bleaching light, yawned, and vanished back into the blackness.

Two and a half thousand feet.

At the dim edges of the ship's lights, guilty secrets flitted by with their eyes on stalks.

Gradually the topography of the distantly approaching ocean bed resolved with greater and greater clarity on the computer displays until at last a shape could be made out that was separate and distinct from its surroundings. It was like a huge, lopsided, cylindrical fortress that widened sharply halfway along its length to accommodate the heavy ultra-plating with which the crucial storage holds were clad, and which were supposed by its builders to have made this the most secure and impregnable spaceship ever built. Before launch, the material structure of this section had been battered, rammed, blasted, and subjected to every assault its builders knew it could withstand, in order to demonstrate that it could withstand them.

The tense silence in the cockpit tightened perceptibly as it became clear that it was this section that had broken rather neatly in two.

"In fact it's perfectly safe," said one of the officials. "It's built so that even if the ship does break up, the storage holds cannot possibly be breached."

Three thousand eight hundred twenty-five feet.

Four Hi-Presh-A SmartSuits moved slowly out of the open hatchway of the salvage craft and waded through the barrage of its lights towards the monstrous shape that loomed darkly out of the sea night. They moved with a sort of clumsy grace, near weightless though weighed on by a world of water.

With his right-hand head, Zaphod peered up into the black immensities above him, and for a moment his mind sang with a silent roar of horror. He glanced to his left and was relieved to see that his other head was busy watching the Brockian Ultra-Cricket broadcasts on the helmet vid without concern. Slightly behind him to his left walked the two officials from the Safety and Civil Reassurance Administration, and slightly in front of him to his right walked the empty suit, carrying their implements and testing the way for them.

They passed the huge rift in the broken-backed starship *Billion Year Bunker,* and played their flashlights up into it. Mangled machinery loomed between torn and twisted bulkheads two feet thick. A family of large transparent eels lived in there now and seemed to like it. The empty suit preceded them along the length of the ship's gigantic, murky hull, trying the airlocks. The third one it tested ground open uneasily. They crowded inside it and waited for several long minutes while the pump mechanisms dealt with the hideous pressure that the ocean exerted, and slowly replaced it with an equally hideous pressure of air and inert gases. At last the inner door slid open and they were admitted to a dark outer holding area of the starship *Billion Year Bunker.*

Several more high-security Titan-O-Hold doors had to be passed through, each of which the officials opened with a selection of quark keys. Soon they were so deep within the heavy security fields that the Ultra-Cricket broadcasts were beginning to fade, and Zaphod had to switch to one of the rock video stations, since there was nowhere that they were not able to reach.

A final doorway slid open, and they emerged into a large, sepulchral space. Zaphod played his flashlight against the opposite wall and it fell full on a wild-eyed, screaming face.

Zaphod screamed a diminished fifth himself, dropped his light, and sat heavily on the floor, or rather on a body that had been lying there undisturbed for around six months, and that reacted to being sat on by exploding with great violence. Zaphod wondered what to do about all this and, after a brief but hectic internal debate, decided that passing out would be the very thing.

He came to a few minutes later, and pretended not to know who he was, where he was, or how he had got there, but was not able to convince anybody. He then pretended that his memory suddenly returned with a rush and that the shock caused him to pass out again, but he was helped unwillingly to his feet by the empty suit—which he was beginning to take a serious dislike to—and forced to come to terms with his surroundings.

They were dimly and fitfully lit and unpleasant in a number of respects, the most obvious of which was the colourful arrangement of parts of the ship's late lamented navigation officer over the floor, walls, and ceiling, and especially over the lower half of his, Zaphod's, suit. The effect of this was so astoundingly nasty that we shall not be referring to it again at any point in this narrative—other than to record briefly the fact that it caused Zaphod to throw up inside his suit, which he therefore removed and swapped, after suitable headgear modifications, with the empty one. Unfortunately the stench of the fetid air in the ship, followed by the sight of his own suit walking around casually draped in rotting intestines, was enough to make him throw up in the other suit as well, which was a problem that he and the suit would simply have to live with.

There. All done. No more nastiness.

At least, no more of that particular nastiness.

The owner of the screaming face had calmed down very slightly now and was bubbling away incoherently in a large tank of yellow liquid—an emergency suspension tank.

"It was crazy," he babbled, "crazy! I told him we could always try the lobster on the way back, but he was crazy. Obsessed! Do you ever get like that about lobster? Because I don't. Seems to me it's all rubbery and fiddly to eat, and not that much taste, well, I mean is there? I infinitely prefer scallops, and said so. Oh Zarquon, I said so!"

Zaphod stared at this extraordinary apparition, flailing in its tank. The man was attached to all kinds of life-support tubes, and his voice was bubbling out of speakers that echoed insanely round the ship, returning as haunting echoes from deep and distant corridors.

"That was where I went wrong," the madman yelled. "I actually said that I preferred scallops and he said it was because I hadn't had real lobster like they did where his ancestors came from, which was here, and he'd prove it. He said it was no problem, he said the lobster here was worth a whole journey, let alone the small diversion it would take to get here, and he swore he could handle the ship in the atmosphere, but it was madness, madness!" he screamed, and paused with his eyes rolling, as if the word had rung some kind of bell in his mind. "The ship went right out of control! I couldn't believe what we were doing and just to prove a point about lobster which is really so overrated as a food, I'm sorry to go on about lobsters so much, I'll try and stop in a minute, but they've been on my mind so much for the months I've been in this tank, can you imagine what it's like to be stuck in a ship with the same guys for months eating junk food when all one guy will talk about is lobster and then spend six months floating by yourself in a tank thinking about it. I promise I will try and shut up about the lobsters, I really will. Lobsters, lobsters, lobsters—enough! I think I'm the only survivor. I'm the only one who managed to get to an emergency tank before we went down. I sent out the mayday and then we hit. It's a disaster, isn't it? A total disaster, and all because the guy liked lobsters. How much sense am I making? It's really hard for me to tell."

He gazed at them beseechingly, and his mind seemed to sway slowly back down to earth like a falling leaf. He blinked and looked at them oddly, like a monkey peering at a strange fish.

He scrabbled curiously with his wrinkled-up fingers at the glass side of the tank. Tiny, thick yellow bubbles loosed themselves from his mouth and nose, caught briefly in his swab of hair, and strayed on upwards.

"Oh Zarquon, oh heavens," he mumbled pathetically to himself, "I've been found. I've been rescued . . ."

"Well," said one of the officials, briskly, "you've been found at least." He strode over to the main computer bank in the middle of the chamber and started checking quickly through the ship's main monitor circuits for damage reports.

"The aorist rod chambers are intact," he said.

"Holy dingo's dos," snarled Zaphod, "there are aorist rods on board!"

Aorist rods were devices used in a now happily abandoned form of energy production. When the hunt for new sources of energy had at one point got particularly frantic, one bright young chap suddenly spotted that one place which had never used up all its available energy was—the past. And with the sudden rush of blood to the head that such insights tend to induce, he invented a way of mining it that very same night, and within a year huge tracts of the past were being drained of all their energy and simply wasting away. Those who claimed that the past should be left unspoilt were accused of indulging in an extremely expensive form of sentimentality. The past provided a very cheap, plentiful, and clean source of energy, there could always be a few Natural Past Reserves set up if anyone wanted to pay for their upkeep, and as for the claim that draining the past impoverished the present, well, maybe it did, slightly, but the effects were immeasurable and you really had to keep a sense of proportion.

It was only when it was realised that the present really was being impoverished, and that the reason for it was that those selfish plundering wastrel bastards up in the future were doing exactly the same thing, that everyone realised that every single aorist rod, and the terrible secret of how they were made, would have to be utterly and forever destroyed. They claimed it was for the sake of their grandparents and grandchildren, but it was of course for the sake of their grandparents' grandchildren, and their grandchildren's grandparents.

The official from the Safety and Civil Reassurance Administration gave a dismissive shrug. "They're perfectly safe," he said. He glanced up at Zaphod and suddenly said with uncharacteristic frankness, "There's worse than that on board. At least," he added, tapping at one of the computer screens, "I hope it's on board."

The other official rounded on him sharply.

"What the hell do you think you're saying?" he snapped.

The first shrugged again. He said, "It doesn't matter. He can say what he likes. No one would believe him. It's why we chose to use him rather than do anything official, isn't it? The more wild the story he tells, the more it'll sound like he's some hippy adventurer making it up. He can even say that we said this and it'll make him sound like a paranoid." He smiled pleasantly at Zaphod, who was seething in a suit full of sick. "You may accompany us," he told him, "if you wish."

*   *   *

"You see?" said the official, examining the ultra-titanium outer seals of the aorist rod hold. "Perfectly secure, perfectly safe."

He said the same thing as they passed holds containing chemical weapons so powerful that a teaspoonful could fatally infect an entire planet.

He said the same thing as they passed holds containing zeta-active compounds so powerful that a teaspoonful could blow up a whole planet.

He said the same thing as they passed holds containing theta-active compounds so powerful that a teaspoonful could irradiate a whole planet.

"I'm glad I'm not a planet," muttered Zaphod.

"You'd have nothing to fear," assured the official from the Safety and Civil Reassurance Administration. "Planets are very safe. Provided," he added—and paused. They were approaching the hold nearest to the point where the back of the starship *Billion Year Bunker* was broken. The corridor here was twisted and deformed, and the floor was damp and sticky in patches.

"Ho-hum," he said, "ho very much hum."

"What's in this hold?" demanded Zaphod.

"By-products," said the official, clamming up again.

"By-products . . ." insisted Zaphod, quietly, "of what?"

Neither official answered. Instead they examined the hold door very carefully and saw that its seals were twisted apart by the forces that had deformed the whole corridor. One of them touched the door lightly. It swung open to his touch. There was darkness inside, with just a couple of dim yellow lights deep within it.

"Of what?" hissed Zaphod.

The leading official turned to the other.

"There's an escape capsule," he said, "that the crew were to use to abandon ship before jettisoning it into the black hole," he said. "I think it would be good to know that it's still there." The other official nodded and left without a word.

The first official quietly beckoned Zaphod in. The large dim yellow lights glowed about twenty feet from them.

"The reason," he said quietly, "why everything else in this ship is, I maintain, safe, is that no one is really crazy enough to use them. No one. At least no one that crazy would ever get near them. Anyone that mad or dangerous rings very deep alarm bells. People may be stupid, but they're not that stupid."

"By-products," hissed Zaphod again—he had to hiss in order that his voice shouldn't be heard to tremble—"of what?"

"Er, Designer People."

"What?"

"The Sirius Cybernetics Corporation were awarded a huge research grant to design and produce synthetic personalities to order. The results were uniformly disastrous. All the 'people' and 'personalities' turned out to be amalgams of characteristics which simply could not coexist in naturally occurring life-forms. Most of them were just poor pathetic misfits, but some were deeply, deeply dangerous. Dangerous because they didn't ring alarm bells in other people. They could walk through situations the way that ghosts walk through walls, because no one spotted the danger.

"The most dangerous of all were three identical ones—they were put in this hold, to be blasted, with this ship, right out of this universe. They are not evil, in fact they are rather simple and charming. But they are the most dangerous creatures that ever lived because there is nothing they will not do if allowed, and nothing they will not be allowed to do . . ."

Zaphod looked at the dim yellow lights, the two dim yellow lights. As his eyes became accustomed to the light, he saw that the two lights framed a third space where something was broken. Wet, sticky patches gleamed dully on the floor.

Zaphod and the official walked cautiously toward the lights. At that moment, four words came crashing into the helmet headsets from the other official.

"The capsule has gone," he said tersely.

"Trace it," snapped Zaphod's companion. "Find exactly where it has gone. We must know where it has gone!"

Zaphod approached the two remaining tanks. A quick glance showed him that each contained an identical floating body. He examined one more carefully. The body, that of an elderly man, was floating in a thick yellow liquid. The man was kindly looking, with lots of pleasant laugh lines round his face. His hair seemed unnaturally thick and dark for someone of his age, and his right hand seemed continually to be weaving forward and back, up and down, as if shaking hands with an endless succession of unseen ghosts. He smiled genially, babbled and burbled like a half-sleeping baby, and occasionally seemed to rock very slightly with little tremors of laughter, as if he had just told himself a joke he hadn't heard before, or didn't remember properly. Waving, smiling, chortling, with little yellow bubbles beading on his lips, he seemed to inhabit a distant world of simple dreams.

Another terse message suddenly came through his helmet headset. The planet toward which the escape capsule had headed had already been identified. It was in Galactic Sector ZZ9 Plural Z Alpha.

Zaphod found a small speaker by the tank, and turned it on. The man in the yellow liquid was babbling gently about a shining city on a hill.

He also heard the Official from the Safety and Civil Reassurance Administration issue instructions to the effect that the missing escape capsule contained a "Reagan" and that the planet in ZZ9 Plural Z Alpha must be made "perfectly safe."

> From *The Utterly Utterly Merry Comic
> Relief Christmas Book*, 1986

✳

Excerpts from an Interview conducted by Matt Newsome

D.N.A. The thing with Dirk Gently was that I felt I had lost contact with that character, I couldn't make that book viable, which is why I said, "Okay, let's go off and do something else." Then, looking back at all the ideas that were there in *Salmon of Doubt*, I looked at it again about a year later and suddenly realised what it was that I'd been getting wrong, which was that these are essentially much more like Hitchhiker ideas and not like Dirk Gently ideas.

So, there will come a point I suspect at some point in the future where I will write a sixth Hitchhiker book. But I kind of want to do that in an odd kind of way because people have said, quite rightly, that *Mostly Harmless* is a very bleak book. And it was a bleak book. The reason for that is very simple—I was having a lousy year, for all sorts of personal reasons that I don't want to go into, I just had a thoroughly miserable year, and I was trying to write a book against that background. And, guess what, it was a rather bleak book!

I would love to finish Hitchhiker on a slightly more upbeat note, so five seems to be a wrong kind of number, six is a better kind of number. I think that a lot of the stuff which was originally in *Salmon of Doubt,* was planned into *Salmon of Doubt,* and really wasn't working, I think could be yanked out and put together with some new thoughts.

M.N. Yes, because certainly some people have heard that *Salmon of Doubt* was now going to be a new Hitchhiker book.

D.N.A. Well, in a sense, because I shall be salvaging some of the ideas I couldn't make work within a Dirk Gently framework and putting them in a Hitchhiker framework, undergoing necessary changes on the way. And, for old time's sake, I may call it *Salmon of Doubt,* I may call it—well, who knows!

＊

THE
SALMON
OF
DOUBT

[Editor's Note: The version of The Salmon of Doubt *presented here has been assembled from various versions of this work-in-progress. Please read the Editor's Note at the beginning of this book for a detailed description of how this was put together. On the next page I have placed Douglas's fax to his longtime London editor, which describes his overall scheme for the novel, giving us some inkling as to where the story might have gone from here.]*

*   *   *

Fax

To: *Sue Freestone*
From: *Douglas Adams*
Re: The Salmon of Doubt *description*

Dirk Gently, hired by someone he never meets, to do a job that is never specified, starts following people at random. His investigations lead him to Los Angeles, through the nasal membranes of a rhinoceros, to a distant future dominated by estate agents and heavily armed kangaroos. Jokes, lightly poached fish, and the emergent properties of complex systems form the background to Dirk Gently's most baffling and incomprehensible case.

Chapter 1

EARLY MOST MORNINGS Dave climbed up to this isolated spot on the hill and brought small offerings to leave in the shrine of St. Clive, the patron saint of real-estate agents. Today what he'd brought was, so far as he could make out, part of a swimming-pool cleaning device, a sort of large, plastic, sucking lobsterish thing.

He laid the thing down carefully and stood back to admire the effect.

The shrine was just a small heap of rocks, really, with a little array of things that had got dug up from time to time. There was a remote-control garage opener, something that was probably part of a juice extractor, and a small, illuminated Kermit the Frog. The pool-cleaning lobsterish thing was a pretty good addition, and he arranged it so that its two feet of broken ribbed plastic tubing hung down like an elephant's trunk over Kermit.

His morning trips up to the shrine were partly just to amuse himself, but also a chance to be alone and reflect on things. This whole place had started just as somewhere to fool around by himself, but it had rapidly turned into something kind of bigger than he meant, and he needed somewhere to get away from it all and think about things. Sometimes he'd even worry. When he was worried he would start to giggle slightly, and when he was really worried he would start to hum old Carpenters tunes till the worry went away.

But today he wasn't going to worry. Today he was going to have fun. He unslung the canvas bag he'd brought up with him and dropped it on the ground for a moment.

From up here, the view was stupendous. Lush forest surrounded DaveLand in every direction, forest of extraordinary richness and diversity, teeming with life and colour. Through it wound the river Dave, which then meandered on through the hills till it met, five hundred miles away, the immense ocean, which, until recently, he had called the Dave Ocean, but which in a fit of modest embarrassment he had now renamed the Karen Ocean. He had always thought that Pacific was a really dumb name. He had been on it. It wasn't Pacific at all. He'd fixed that.

DaveLand itself was now a pretty impressive affair. Astonishing, really, when he thought about it. He brushed his hand through his lank hair and stared out at it, suppressing a very, very small giggle.

DaveLand lightly covered about ninety acres of hillside, with new outcrops already beginning to appear on nearby hills. Beautiful homes. Much more beautiful than any of the ones that his imaginary St. Clive would have sold or even understood. None of your split-level ranch-style crap with stupid conversation pits that anyone with half a brain would probably kill themselves rather than converse in. Dave's houses were of a different kind altogether.

Apart from anything else, they were smart houses. Just simple stuff, like they faced the right way. They had glass in the right places, stone in the right places, water in the right places, plants in the right places, so the air moved through them properly and was warm where you wanted it and cool where you wanted it. It was just physics. Most architects didn't know any physics, he decided. They just knew dumb stuff. In Dave's houses, prisms and fibres moved sunlight where you wanted it. Heat exchangers took heat from the food in the fridge and gave it to the food in the oven. Simple. People went into Dave's houses and would say, "Hey! This is really neat! How come other people don't build houses like this?" Answer? Because they're dumb.

And telephones. Dave had given people here much neater, smarter, altogether more fabulous telephones than they'd ever had before. Now they wanted television as well, which Dave thought was pretty dumb in the first place, and monumentally dumb in the circumstances; but that in turn had been a pretty interesting problem and Dave, of course, had solved it. But Dave had solved so many problems that he had inadvertently created a new one. DaveLand was now a community of nearly a thousand people, which made him kind of responsible. He hadn't expected to be responsible.

He pulled up a bunch of long grass and swished it around fretfully. The early-morning sunlight glinted off Dave's Place. Dave's Place was easily the largest and most gracious of all the buildings in, well, in the world. It ringed the summit of the hill opposite with elegant sweeping white stone walls and seeming acres of glass. The summit itself was laid out as a Japanese garden. Streams ran down through the house from it.

Just beneath Dave's Place, on the same hillside and contained within the same security compound (he couldn't believe he had to have stuff like security compounds now; and forty—forty—of the nine-hundred-plus inhabitants of DaveLand were now lawyers) was The Way of the Nostril.

The Way of the Nostril was probably the single smartest thing that Dave had ever thought of. Even he, to whom most things that most people would think were pretty smart were pretty dumb, thought it was pretty smart. It was the single reason that all of this was here, and it had become the single thing that made Dave hum old Carpenters tunes most, except maybe the lawyers.

The sun was now gleaming brilliantly over all of DaveLand. It was pretty neat, Dave had to admit, but he also had to admit that he had kind of liked DaveLand when it was just his own funny stupid place to come to because only he was smart enough to get there. But one thing had led to another, and now all this. Here he was, only twenty-five and already beginning to feel like he was almost thirty.

Well, screw all that. Today he was going to have some fun. He picked up the large canvas bag and slung it back over his shoulders. Sam would have a fit. The lawyers would go nuts. Good. He turned and climbed farther on up the hill. The hill was called Top of the World, and was named after the tune by the Carpenters. One of the great things about having your own world was that you could just go ahead and like the Carpenters on it.

The hill got pretty rocky and craggy higher up, and Dave had to do a bit of rock-scrambling to get to where he was going.

Within about twenty minutes he was pretty hot and a bit sweaty, but he'd made it to the top, or at least the last significant flat bit, a solid slab of deeply rutted rock on which he sat, and dumped the bag. He gathered his breath for a few moments and then started to unpack it. He pulled out aluminium struts, he pulled out orange strings, he pulled out little purple sheets of Kevlar.

After about ten minutes of assembly the thing was ready, a large, gossamer-winged insect of a contraption. The scraps of Kevlar strung between the struts of the frame were surprisingly small and oddly shaped. Dave had worked out that most of the cloth used in conventional hang gliders was redundant, and had got rid of it.

He examined the assembled frame systematically and satisfied himself that it was all as it should be, that it was Daveworthy.

He looked out nervously, but only just for a moment. He was going to do it anyway, so it was dumb to be nervous. Carefully picking up the hang glider, he carried it out to the edge of the rock, till he was standing on a ledge looking out over the whole extent of DaveLand. He noticed with satisfaction that although his glider looked like nothing more than a kind of drying frame for silk bikinis, it was very stiff and he had to pull it forcefully through the air to move it.

From here to Dave's Place was about a mile horizontally and a couple of hundred feet vertically. He could just see, glinting in the sun, his large blue swimming pool, neatly secluded within the Japanese garden on the top of Dave's Hill. The distance and the direction of the sun made details a little difficult, but he was confident that Sam would be waiting for him there beside the pool. He reckoned he could drop himself pretty neatly into that. He glanced at his watch. It was just after eight o'clock, and he'd scheduled the meeting for eight. Sam would be there.

Sam's view was that a lot of Dave's plans and schemes were reckless, crazy, irresponsible, occasionally bordering on the just plain dumb. Dropping into the pool would be something better than dumb guys could do. How tough could it be to do it if you were Dave?

He checked the wind direction, stepped into a lightweight harness belt, tightened it, clipped the belt to the glider, passed his hands through two loops, gripped the main struts, and he was ready.

All he had to do now was throw himself off into space.

Wow. Okay. Go.

No fuss, no dumb stuff. With a light heart he threw himself out forward, and sailed into empty space. The air supported him immediately, with a little rough buffeting. He braced himself against the frame, then tried to relax a little, then relaxed a little more, trying to find a good balance that was easy but responsive. He got it. He was out there. He was flying. He was just some kind of a bird.

Hey, this was good. The empty air was kind of a shock, but a good shock, like a swimming pool in the morning. And the air wasn't empty. It was like falling into enormous invisible pillows, with fingers that came out and tugged and pulled at you, ruffling your hair, rattling your T-shirt. As his brain got to grips with the huge openness around him, he felt like a little toy hanging from the end of an immense mobile slowly turning over DaveWorld. He was turning in a big, easy arc, a little bit to the right and then, in response to a small shift in his weight, a little bit to the left, but still, it seemed, moving as an arc within an arc, a wheel within a wheel. The world, his world, turned slowly around beneath him, green, rich, lush and vivid.

It was about 1.2 million years since the human race had suddenly gone extinct, and the world had really perked up a lot in that time. In geological terms it was but a fleeting moment, of course, but the forces of evolution had suddenly had tons of space to play in, huge gaps to fill, and everything had started to thrive like crazy. Everybody used to talk about saving the world—well, Dave had done it. Now it was great. The whole place was really neat now. DaveWorld. Yay.

He was riding the air pretty well now, not fighting it, but flowing along it. He was beginning to get a sense, though, that just dropping himself in his own swimming pool might be a little tougher than he had expected. But that was how he liked things to be—a little tougher than he expected.

Maybe it was even going to be a lot tougher, he began to realise. It was one thing to be staying comfortably aloft, following the currents, riding gradually down, it was quite another thing to steer in any meaningful kind of way. When he tried to turn too sharply, the delicate structure around him would start to rattle and bang in quite an alarming way.

Chapter 2

"I DON'T DO CATS," said Dirk Gently.

His tone was sharp. He felt he had come up in the world. He had no evidence to support this view, he just felt it was about time. He also had indigestion, but that had nothing whatever to do with it.

The woman—what was her name? Melinda something. He had it written on a piece of paper somewhere but had lost it, possibly under the pile of unopened bank statements on the far corner of his desk—was standing in front of his desk with her left eyebrow raised indignantly.

"Your advertisement says . . ."

"The advertisement is out of date," snapped Dirk. "I don't do cats." He waved her away and pretended to be busy with some paperwork.

"Then what do you do?" she persisted.

Dirk looked up curtly. He had taken against this woman as soon as she walked in. Not only had she caught him completely off guard, but she was also irritatingly beautiful. He didn't like beautiful women. They upset him, with their grace, their charm, their utter loveliness, and their complete refusal to go out to dinner with him. He could tell, the very instant this Melinda woman walked into the room, that she wouldn't go out to dinner with him if he was the last man on earth and had a pink Cadillac convertible, so he decided to take preemptive action. If she was going to not go out to dinner with him, then she would not go out to dinner with him on his terms.

"None of your business," he snapped. His gut gurgled painfully.

She raised her other eyebrow as well.

"Has the appointment I made with you caught you at a bad time?"

"Yes," thought Dirk, though he didn't say it. It was one of the worst months he could remember. Business had been slow, but not merely slow. What was normally a trickle had first slowed to a dribble and then dried up completely. Nothing. Nobody. No work whatever, unless you included the batty old woman who had come in with a dog whose name she couldn't remember. She had suffered, she said, a minor blow to the head and had forgotten her dog's name, as a result of which he would not come when she called. Please could he find out what his name was? Normally she would ask her husband, she explained, only he had recently died bungee jumping which he shouldn't have been doing at his age only it was his seventieth birthday and he said he'd do exactly what he wanted even if it killed him which of course it did, and though she had of course tried contacting him through a medium the only message she'd got from him was that he didn't believe in all this stupid spiritualist nonsense, it was all a damned fraud, which she thought was very rude of him, and certainly rather embarrassing for the medium. And so on.

He had taken the job. This was what it had come to.

He didn't say any of this, of course. He just gave the Melinda woman a cold look and said, "This is a respectable private investigation business. I . . ."

"Respectable," she said, "or respected?"

"What do you mean?" Dirk usually produced much sharper

retorts than this, but, as the woman said, she had caught him at a bad time. After a weekend dominated by the struggle to identify a dog, nothing at all had happened yesterday, except for one thing that had given him a very nasty turn and made him wonder if he was going mad.

"Big difference," the Melinda woman continued. "Like the difference between something that's supposedly inflatable and something that's actually inflated. Between something that's supposedly unbreakable and something that will actually survive a good fling at the wall."

"What?" said Dirk.

"I mean that however respectable your business may be, if it was actually respected you'd probably be able to afford a carpet, some paint on the walls, and maybe even another chair in here for a person to sit on."

Dirk had no idea what had happened to the other chair in his office, but he certainly wasn't going to admit it.

"You don't need a chair," he said. "I'm afraid you are here under a misapprehension. We have nothing to discuss. Good day to you, dear lady, I am not going to look for your lost cat."

"I didn't say it was a lost cat."

"I beg your pardon," said Dirk. "You distinctly . . ."

"I said it was a sort of lost cat. It's half lost."

Dirk looked at her expressionlessly. Apart from being extremely good-looking in a blondish, willowyish kind of way, she was dressed well in an "I don't care what I wear, just any old thing that's lying around" kind of way that relies on being extremely careful about what you leave lying around. She was obviously pretty bright, probably had a pretty good job, like running some sort of major textile or telecommunications company despite being clearly only thirty-two. In other words, she was exactly the sort of person who didn't mislay cats, and certainly didn't go running off to poky little private detective agencies if she did. He felt ill at ease.

"Talk sense, please," he said sharply. "My time is valuable."

"Oh yes? How valuable?"

She looked scornfully around his office. He had to admit to himself that it was grim, but he was damned if he was just going to sit there and take it. Just because he needed the work, needed the money, had nothing better to do with his time, there was no reason for anybody to think that he was at the beck and call of every good-looking woman who walked into his office offering to pay for his services. He felt humiliated.

"I'm not talking about my scale of fees, though it is, I promise you, awesome. I was merely thinking of time passing. Time that won't pass this way again."

He leaned forward in a pointed manner.

"Time is a finite entity, you know. Only about four billion years to go till the sun explodes. I know it seems like a lot now, but it will soon go if we just squander it on frivolous nonsense and small talk."

"Small talk! This is half of my cat we're talking about!"

"Madam, I don't know who this 'we' is that you are referring to, but . . ."

"Listen. You may choose, when you've heard the details of this case, not to accept it because it is, I admit, a little odd. But I made an appointment to see you on the basis of what it said in your advertisement, to whit, that you find lost cats, and if you turn me down solely on the basis that you do not find lost cats, then I must remind you that there is such a thing as the Trades Descriptions Act. I can't remember exactly what it says, but I bet you five pounds it says you can't do that."

Dirk sighed. He picked up a pencil and pulled a pad of paper towards him.

"All right," he said, "I'll take down the details of the case."

"Thank you."

"And then I'll turn it down."

"That's your business."

"The point I'm trying to make," said Dirk, "is that it isn't. So. What is this cat's name?"

"Gusty."

"Gusty."

"Yes. Short for Gusty Winds."

Dirk looked at her. "I won't ask," he said.

"You'll wish you had."

"I'll be the judge of that."

She shrugged.

"Male?" said Dirk. "Female?"

"Male."

"Age?"

"Four years."

"Description?"

"Well, um. That's a bit tricky."

"How hard can a question be? What is he, black? White? Ginger? Tabby?"

"Oh. Siamese."

"Good," said Dirk, writing down "Siamese." "And when did you last see him?"

"About three minutes ago."

Dirk laid his pencil down and looked at her.

"Maybe four, in fact," she added.

"Let me see if I understand you," said Dirk. "You say you lost your cat, er, 'Gusty,' while you've been standing here talking to me?"

"No. I lost him—or sort of half-lost him—two weeks ago. But I last saw him, which is what you asked, just before I came into your office. I just checked to see he was okay. Which he was. Well, sort of okay. If you can call it okay."

"And . . . er, where was he, exactly, when you checked to see that he was okay?"

"In his basket. Shall I bring him in? He's just out here."

She went out of the room and returned with a medium-sized wickerwork cat box. She put it down on Dirk's desk. Its contents mewed slightly. She closed the door behind her.

Dirk frowned.

"Excuse me if I'm being a little obtuse," he said, looking round the basket at her. "Tell me which bit of this I've got wrong. It seems to me that you are asking me if I will exercise my professional skills to search for and if possible find and return to you a cat . . ."

"Yes."

". . . which you already have with you in a cat basket?"

"Well, that's right up to a point."

"And which point is that?"

"Have a look for yourself."

She slid out the metal rod that held the lid in place, reached into the basket, lifted out the cat, and put him down on Dirk's desk, next to the basket.

Dirk looked at him.

He—Gusty—looked at him.

There is a particular disdain with which Siamese cats regard you. Anyone who has accidentally walked in on the Queen cleaning her teeth will be familiar with this feeling.

Gusty looked at Dirk and clearly found him reprehensible in some way. He turned away, yawned, stretched, groomed his whiskers briefly, licked down a small patch of ruffled fur, then leapt lightly off the table and started carefully to examine a splinter of floorboard, which he found to be far more interesting than Dirk.

Dirk stared wordlessly at Gusty.

Up to a point, Gusty looked exactly like a normal Siamese cat. Up to a point. The point up to which Gusty looked like a normal Siamese cat was his waist, which was marked by a narrow, cloudy grey band.

"The front half looks quite well," said Melinda whatever-her-name-was in a small voice. "Quite sleek and healthy, really."

"And the back half?" said Dirk.

"Is what I want you to look for."

Beyond the grey, cloudy band there was nothing. The cat's body simply stopped dead in midair. Everything below approximately the ninth rib was, well, absent.

The odd thing about this was that the cat seemed quite unaffected. This is not to suggest that he had learnt to live with his sad affliction, or that he was courageously making the best of things. He was, quite simply, unaffected. He didn't seem to notice. Not content with ignoring the normal requirements of biology, the cat was also in clear breach of the laws of physics. He moved, jumped, promenaded, sat, in exactly the same way as if his rear half were present.

"It isn't invisible," said Melinda, picking the cat up, awkwardly. "It's actually not there." She passed her hand back and forth through clear air, where the cat's hindquarters should have been. The cat twisted and turned in her grip, mewling crossly, then leapt nimbly to the ground and stalked about in an affronted manner.

"My, my," said Dirk, steepling his fingers under his chin. "That is odd."

"You'll take the case?"

"No," said Dirk. He pushed the pad of paper away from him. "I'm sorry, but I just can't be doing this sort of stuff. If there's anything I want less than to find a cat, it's to find half a cat. Suppose I was unfortunate enough to find it. What then? How am I supposed to go about sticking it on? I'm sorry, but I'm through with cats, and I am definitely through with anything that even smacks of the supernatural or paranormal. I'm a rational being, and I . . . excuse me." The phone was ringing. Dirk answered it. He sighed. It was Thor, the ancient Norse God of Thunder. Dirk knew immediately it was him from the long, portentous silence and the low grumblings of irritation followed by strange, distant bawling noises. Thor did not understand phones very well. He would usually stand ten feet away and shout godlike commands at them. This worked surprisingly well as far as making the connection was concerned, but made actual conversation well-nigh impossible.

Thor had moved in with an American girl of Dirk's acquaintance, and Dirk understood from the strange Icelandic proclamations echoing over the line that he, Dirk, was supposed to be turning up for tea that afternoon.

Dirk said that, yes, he knew that, that he would be there at about five, was looking forward to it and would see him later; but Thor, of course, could hear none of this from where he was standing, and was beginning to get angry and shout a lot.

Dirk had at last to give up and hesitantly put the phone down, hoping that Thor would not do too much damage in Kate's small flat. She had, he knew, managed to persuade the big god to try to crush packets of crisps in his rages rather than actual sofas and motorbikes, but it was sometimes touch-and-go when he really couldn't get the hang of what was going on.

Dirk felt oppressed. He looked up. Oh yes.

"No," he said. "Go away. I can't deal with any more of this stuff."

"But, Mr. Gently, I hear you have something of a reputation in this area."

"And that's precisely what I want to get rid of. So please get out of here and take your bifurcated feline with you."

"Well, if that's your attitude . . ."

She picked up the cat basket and sauntered out. The half-cat made a pretty good go of sauntering out as well.

Dirk sat at his desk and simmered for a minute or two, wondering why he was so out of sorts today. Looking out of his window, he saw the extremely attractive and intriguing client he had just rudely turned away out of sheer grumpiness. She looked particularly gorgeous and alluring as she hurried across the road toward a black London taxicab.

He hurried to the window and wrenched it up. He leant out.

"I suppose dinner's out of the question, then?" he yelled.

Chapter 3

"YOU JUST MISSED THOR, I'm afraid," said Kate Schechter. "He suddenly went off in a fit of Nordic angst about something or other."

She waved a hand vaguely at the gaping, jagged hole in the window that overlooked Primrose Hill. "Probably gone to the zoo to stare at elks again. He'll turn up again in a few hours, full of beer and remorse and carrying a large pane of glass that won't fit. So he'll then get upset about that and break something else."

"We had a bit of a misunderstanding on the phone, I'm afraid," said Dirk. "But I don't really know how to avoid them."

"You can't," said Kate. "He's not a happy god. It's not his world. Never will be, either."

"So what are you going to do?"

"Oh, there's plenty to do. Just repairing things keeps me busy."

It wasn't what Dirk meant, but he realised she knew that and didn't probe. She went into the kitchen to fetch the tea at that point anyway. He subsided into an elderly armchair and peered around the small flat. He noticed that there was now quite a collection of books on Norse mythology stacked on Kate's desk, all sprouting numerous bookmarks and annotated record cards. She was obviously doing her best to master the situation. But one book, buried about four inches into the wall, and obviously flung there by superhuman force, gave some idea of the sort of difficulties she was up against.

"Don't even ask," she said, when she returned bearing tea. "Tell me what's going on with you instead."

"I did something this afternoon," he said, stirring the pale, sickly tea and suddenly remembering that, of course, Americans had no idea how to make it, "that was incredibly stupid."

"I thought you seemed a bit grim."

"Probably the cause rather than the effect. I'd had an appalling week, plus I had indigestion, and I suppose it made me a bit . . ."

"Don't tell me. You met a very attractive and desirable woman and were incredibly pompous and rude to her."

Dirk stared at her. "How did you know that?" he breathed.

"You do it all the time. You did it to me."

"I did not!" protested Dirk.

"You certainly did!"

"No, no, no."

"I promise you, you . . ."

"Hang on," interrupted Dirk. "I remember now. Hmm. Interesting. And you're saying I do that all the time?"

"Maybe not all the time. Presumably you have to get some sleep occasionally."

"But you claim that, typically, I'm rude and pompous to attractive women?"

He wrestled his way up out of the armchair and fished around in his pocket for a notebook.

"I didn't mean you to get quite so serious about it, it's not exactly a major . . . well, now I come to think about it I suppose it probably is a major character flaw. What are you doing?"

"Oh, just making a note. Odd thing about being a private detective—you spend your time finding out little things about other people that nobody else knows, but then you discover that there are all sorts of things that everybody else knows about you, which you don't. For instance, did you know that I walk in an odd way? A kind of strutting waddle, someone described it as."

"Yes, of course I do. Everybody who knows you knows that."

"Except me, you see," said Dirk. "Now that I know I've been trying to catch myself at it as I walk past shop windows. Doesn't work, of course. All I ever see is myself frozen midstride with one foot in the air and gaping like a fish. Anyway, I'm drawing up a little list, to which I have now added, 'Am always extremely rude and pompous to attractive women.'"

Dirk stood and looked at the note for a second or two.

"You know," he said, thoughtfully, "that could explain an astonishing number of things."

"Oh come on," said Kate. "You're taking this a bit literally. I just meant I've noticed that when you're not feeling good, or you're on the spot in some way, you tend to get defensive, and that's when you . . . are you writing all this down as well?"

"Of course. It's all useful stuff. I might end up mounting a full-scale investigation into myself. Damn all else to do at the moment."

"No work?"

"No," said Dirk, gloomily.

Kate tried to give him a shrewd look, but he was staring out of the window.

"And is the fact that you don't have any work connected in any way to the fact that you were very rude to an attractive woman?"

"Just barging in like that," muttered Dirk, half to himself.

"Don't tell me," said Kate. "She wanted you to look for a lost cat."

"Oh no," said Dirk. "Not even as grand as that. Gone are the days when I used to have entire cats to look for."

"What do you mean?"

Dirk described the cat. "See what I have to contend with?" he added.

Kate stared at him.

"You're not serious."

"I am," he said.

"Half a cat?"

"Yes. Just the back half."

"I thought you said the front half . . ."

"No, she'd got that. That was there, all right. She only wanted me to look for the back half." He stared thoughtfully at London from over the raised rim of his china teacup.

Kate looked at him suspiciously.

"But isn't that . . ." she said, ". . . very, very, very weird?"

Dirk turned and faced her.

"I would say," he declared, "that it was the single most weird and extraordinary phenomenon I have witnessed in a lifetime of witnessing weird and extraordinary phenomena. Unfortunately," he added, turning away again, "I wasn't in the mood for it."

"What do you mean?"

"I had indigestion. I'm always bad-tempered when I've got indigestion."

"And just because of that, you . . ."

"It was more than that. I'd lost the piece of paper too."

"What piece of paper?"

"That I wrote down her appointment on. Turned up under a pile of bank statements."

"Which you never open or look at."

Dirk frowned, and opened his notebook again.

"'Never . . . open . . . bank . . . statements,'" he wrote thoughtfully. "So, when she arrived," he continued, after he'd put the book back in his pocket, "I wasn't expecting her, so I wasn't in command of the situation. Which meant that . . ."

He fished out his notebook, and wrote in it again.

"Now what are you putting?" asked Kate.

"Control freak," said Dirk. "My first instinct was to make her sit down, and then pretend to get on with something while I composed myself."

"So?"

"I looked around and I noticed there wasn't a chair. God knows where it had gone. Which meant that she had to stand over me. Which I also hate. That's when I turned really ratty." He peered at his notebook again, and flipped through it. "Strange convergence of tiny little events, don't you think?"

"What do you mean?"

"Well, here was a case of the most extraordinary kind. A beautiful, intelligent, and obviously well-off woman arrives and offers to pay me to investigate a phenomenon that challenges the very foundation of everything that we know about physics and biology, and I . . . turn it down. Astonishing. Normally you'd have to nail me to the floor to keep me away from a case like that. Unless," he added thoughtfully, waving his notebook slowly in the air, "unless you knew me this well."

"What are you suggesting?"

"Well, I don't know. The whole sequence of little obstacles would have been completely invisible except for one thing.

When I eventually found the piece of paper I'd written her details on, the phone number was missing. The bottom of the sheet of paper had been torn off. So I have no easy way of finding her."

"Well, you could try calling directory information. What's her name?"

"Smith. Hopeless. But don't you think it odd that the number had been torn off?"

"No, not really, if you want an honest answer. People tear off scraps of paper all the time. I can see you're probably in a mood to construct some massive space/time bending conspiracy theory out of it, but I suspect you just tore off a strip of paper to clean your ears out with."

"You'd worry about space/time if you'd seen that cat."

"Maybe you just need to get your contact lenses cleaned."

"I don't wear contact lenses."

"Maybe it's time you did."

Dirk sighed. "I suppose there are times when my imaginings do get a little overwrought," he said. "I've just had too little to do recently. Business has been so slow, I've even been reduced to looking up to see if they'd got my number right in the Yellow Pages and then calling it myself just to check that it was working. Kate . . . ?"

"Yes, Dirk?"

"You would tell me if you thought I was going mad or anything, wouldn't you?"

"That's what friends are for."

"Are they?" mused Dirk. "Are they? You know, I've often wondered. The reason I ask is that when I phoned myself up . . ."

"Yes?"

"I answered."

"Dirk, old friend," said Kate, "you need a rest."

"I've had nothing but rest," grumbled Dirk.

"In which case you need something to do."

"Yes," said Dirk. "But what?"

Kate sighed. "I can't tell you what to do, Dirk. No one can ever tell you anything. You never believe anything unless you've worked it out for yourself."

"Hmmm," said Dirk, opening his notebook again. "Now that is an interesting one."

Chapter 4

"JOSH," said a voice in a kind of Swedish-Irish accent.

Dirk ignored it. He unloaded his small bag of shopping into bits of his badly disfigured kitchen. It was mostly frozen pizza, so it mostly went into his small freezer cabinet, which was mostly filled with old, white, clenched things that he was now too frightened to try to identify.

"Jude," said the Swedish-Irish voice.

"Don't make it bad," hummed Dirk to himself. He turned on the radio for the six-o'clock news. It featured mostly gloomy stuff. Pollution, disaster, civil war, famine, etc., and, just as an added bonus, speculation as to whether the Earth was going to be hit by a giant comet or not.

"Julian," said the Swedish-Irish voice, tinnily. Dirk shook his head. Surely not.

More on the comet story: there was a wide range of views about precisely what was going to happen. Some authorities said that it was going to hit Sheridan, Wyoming, on the seventeenth of June. NASA scientists said that it would burn up in the upper atmosphere and not reach the surface. A team of Indian astronomers said that it would miss the Earth altogether by several million miles before going on to plunge into the sun. The British authorities said it would do whatever the Americans said it would do.

"Julio," said the voice. No response.

Dirk missed the next thing the radio said because of the noise of his front wall flapping. His front wall was made of large, thick sheets of polythene these days, because of an incident a few weeks earlier when, in a radical departure from the sort of behaviour that Dirk's neighbours liked to see, a Tornado jet fighter had exploded out of the front of Dirk's house and then plunged screaming into Finsbury.

There was, of course, a perfectly logical explanation for this, and Dirk was tired of giving it. The reason that Dirk had had a Tornado jet fighter in his hallway was that he hadn't known it was a Tornado jet fighter. Of course he hadn't known it was a Tornado jet fighter. As far as he was concerned, it was merely a large and bad-tempered eagle that he had trapped in his hallway the same way anybody would to stop it dive-bombing him the whole time. That a large Tornado jet fighter had, for a brief while, taken on the shape of an eagle was on account of an unfortunate airborne encounter with the Thunder God, Thor, of legend, and . . .

This was the part of the story where Dirk usually had to struggle a little to sustain his audience's patient attention, which he would, if successful, further strain by explaining that the Thunder God, Thor, had then thought better of his fit of temper and decided to put things right by returning the Tornado to its proper shape. Unfortunately, Thor, being a god, had had his mind on higher or at least other things, and hadn't called up, as any mere mortal might have done, to check if this was a convenient moment. He had just decreed it done and it was done, bang.

Devastation.

And also the insurance problem from hell. The insurance companies involved had all claimed that this was, by any reasonable standards, an act of God. But, Dirk had argued, which god? Britain was constitutionally a Christian monotheistic state, and therefore any "act of God" defined in a legal document must refer to the Anglican chap in the stained glass and not to some polytheistic thug from Norway. And so on.

Meanwhile, Dirk's house—not an especially grand place to start with—was propped up with scaffolding and tented with polythene, and Dirk had no idea when he was going to be able to get it repaired. If the insurance company failed to pay up—which seemed increasingly likely in light of the strategy that insurance companies had adopted in recent years, of merely advertising their services rather than actually providing them—Dirk was going to have to . . . well, he didn't quite know what. He had no money. None of his own, at least. He had some of the bank's money, but how much he had no idea.

"Justin," intoned the little voice. There was no answering response.

Dirk tipped his unopened bank statements on to the kitchen table, and stared at them with loathing. It seemed to him for a moment that the envelopes were vibrating slightly, and even that the whole of space and time was beginning to revolve slowly around them and get sucked into their event horizon, but he was probably imagining it.

"Karl." Nothing. "Karel. Keir." Nothing. Nothing.

Dirk made some coffee, taking the long route round his kitchen, in order to avoid coming too close to his bank statements, now that he had put them down. Viewed in a certain light, the entire structure of his adult life could be seen as a means of avoiding opening his bank statements. Someone else's bank statements—now that was a different matter. He was rarely happier than when poring over someone else's bank statements: he always found them to be rich in colour and narrative drive, particularly if he'd had to steam them open. But the prospect of opening his own gave him the screaming heebie-jeebies.

"Keith," said the voice, hopefully, nasally. Nothing.

"Kelvin." No.

Dirk poured his coffee as slowly as he could, for he realised that the time had finally come. He had to open the statements and learn the worst. He selected the largest knife he could find and advanced on them, theateningly.

"Kendall." Silence.

In the end he did it almost nonchalantly, with a sadistic little flick-slit movement. He quite enjoyed it, in fact, and even felt fashionably vicious. In a few seconds the four envelopes—his financial history of the last four months—were open. Dirk laid their contents out before him.

"Kendrick." Nothing.

"Kennedy." The tinny little voice was beginning to get on Dirk's nerves. He glanced at the corner of the room. Two mournful eyes looked at him in silent bewilderment.

As Dirk at last looked at the figures at the bottom of the last sheet of paper, a kind of swimmy feeling assailed him. He gasped sharply. The table began to bend and sway. He felt as if the hands of fate had started kneading his shoulders. He had imagined it was bad, in fact for the last few weeks he had imagined little else other than how bad it might be, but even in his worst imaginings he had no idea it might be this bad.

Clammy things happened in his throat. He could not possibly, possibly be over £22,000 overdrawn. He pushed his chair back from the kitchen table, and for a few moments just sat there, throbbing. £22,000 . . .

The word "Kenneth" floated mockingly through the room.

As he rapidly cast his mind back over what he could remember of his expenditures over the last few weeks—an ill-considered shirt here, a reckless bun there, a wild weekend in the Isle of Wight—he realised that he must be right. He could not possibly be £22,000 overdrawn.

He took a deep breath and looked at the figures once more.

There it was again. £22,347.43.

There must be some mistake. Some terrible, terrible mistake. The chances were, of course, that he had made it, and as he stared, trembling, at the paper he realised, quite suddenly, that he had.

He had been looking for a negative number and had therefore assumed that that was what he was looking at. In fact his account stood at £22,347.43. In credit.

Credit . . .

He'd never known such a thing. Didn't even know what it looked like. Hadn't recognised it. Slowly, carefully, almost as if the figures might fall off the page and get lost on the floor, he sifted through the sheets one by one to try to find out where on earth all this money had come from. "Kenny," "Kentigern," and "Kermit" slipped by unheard.

It was immediately clear that it was regular amounts that had been coming in, once a week. There had been seven of them—so far. The most recent one had come in the Friday before last, which was as far as these statements went. The odd thing was that though the amounts were regular, they were untidy amounts, similar each week, but not exactly the same. The previous Friday's payment was £3,267.34. The previous Thursday's (they had each come in at the end of the week, three of them on a Thursday, four on a Friday) was for £3,232.57. The week before it had been £3,319.14. And so on.

Dirk stood up and took a deep breath. What the hell was going on? He felt that his whole world was spinning very slowly in what was, as far as he could judge, an anticlockwise direction. That prompted a vague recollection that the last time he had drunk any tequila, it had made his world spin slowly in a clockwise direction. That was obviously what he needed if he was going to be able to think about this clearly. He rummaged hurriedly through a cupboard full of dusty nine-tenths empty bottles of half-forgotten rums and whiskies and found some. A half-full bottle of mezcal. He poured himself a finger in the bottom of a teacup and hurriedly returned to his statements, suddenly panicking in case the figures vanished while he wasn't looking.

They were still there. Irregularly large sums regularly paid in. His head began to swim again. What were they? Interest payments that had been accidentally credited to the wrong account? If they were interest payments, that would account for the fluctuations in the amounts. But it still didn't make sense for the simple reason that over £3,000 interest a week represented the interest on two or three million pounds and was not the sort of thing that the owner of such an amount of money was going to allow to be misplaced, let alone for seven weeks in a row. He took a pull on the mezcal. It marched around his mouth waving its fists, waited a moment or two, and then started to beat up his brain.

He wasn't thinking rationally about this, he realised. The problem was that they were his own accounts, and he was used to reading other people's. Since they were his own, it was in fact possible for him just to phone up the bank and ask. Except that, of course, they'd be closed now. And he had a horrible feeling that if he phoned them up, the response would be "Whoops, sorry, wrong account. Thank you for bringing this error to our attention. How stupid of us to imagine that this money could possibly belong to you." Obviously he had to try to work out where it was from before he asked the bank. In fact he had to get the money out of the bank before he asked them. He probably had to get to Fiji or somewhere before he asked them. Except—suppose the money continued to come in?

On reapplying his attention to the papers, he realised something else that would have occurred to him straightaway if he hadn't been so flustered. There was, of course, a code next to each entry. The purpose of the code was to tell him what kind of entry it was. He looked the code up. Easy. Each payment had reached his account by international transfer.

Hmmm.

That would also account for the fluctuations. International exchange rates. If the same amount of a foreign currency was being transferred each week, then the variations in the rate would ensure that a slightly differing amount actually arrived on each occasion. It would also explain why it didn't arrive on exactly the same day each week. Although it only took less than a second to make a computerised international transfer of money, the banks liked to make as much fuss as they possibly could about it so that the funds would swill around profitably in their system for a while.

But which country were the payments coming from? And why?

"Kevin," said the Irish-Swedish voice. "Kieran."

"Oh, shut up!" shouted Dirk suddenly.

That provoked a response. The small border terrier lying, perplexed, in a basket in the corner of the room looked up excitedly and yipped with pleasure. It had not reacted at all to any of the names that the elderly computer on the table next to it had been reciting from a text file of babies' names, but the creature obviously just enjoyed being told to shut up and was keen for more.

"Kimberly," said the computer. Nothing. The dog with no name looked disappointed.

"Kirby."

"Kirk." The dog slowly settled back down into its basket of old newspapers and resumed its previous posture of baffled distress.

Old newspapers. That was what Dirk needed.

A couple of hours later he had the answer, or at least some kind of an answer. Nothing that went so far as to make any kind of actual sense, but enough to make Dirk feel an encouraging surge of excitement: he had managed to unlock a part of the puzzle. How big a part he didn't know. As yet he had no idea how big a puzzle he was dealing with. No idea at all.

He had collected a representative sample of the newspapers of the last few weeks from under the dog, under the sofa, under his bed, scattered around the bathroom, and, crucially, had managed to secure two damp but vital copies of the *Financial Times* from an old tramp in return for a blanket, some cider, and a copy of *The Origin of Consciousness in the Breakdown of the Bicameral Mind*. An odd request, he thought, as he walked back from the tiny scrap of park, but probably no odder than his. He was constantly reminded of how startlingly different a place the world was when viewed from a point only three feet to the left.

Using the figures from the papers, he was able to construct a map of the movements of each of the world's major currencies over the last few weeks and see how they compared with the fluctuations in the amounts that had been paid into his account every week. The answer sprang into focus immediately. U.S. dollars. Five thousand of them, to be precise. If $5,000 had been transferred from the U.S. to the U.K. every week, then it would have arrived as more or less exactly the amounts that had been showing up in his account. Eureka. Time for a celebratory fridge raid.

Dirk hunkered down in front of the TV with three slices of cold pizza and a can of beer, put on the radio as well, and also a ZZ Top CD. He needed to think.

Someone was paying him $5,000 a week, and had been doing so for seven weeks. This was astounding news. He ruminated on his pizza. Not only that, but he was being paid by someone in America. He took another bite, rich in cheese, pepperoni, spicy minced beef, anchovy, and egg. He hadn't spent much time in America and didn't know anyone there—or indeed anywhere else on the Earth's crust—who would be wantonly shoveling unsolicited bucks at him like this.

Another thought struck him, but this time it wasn't about the money. A ZZ Top song about TV dinners made him think for a moment about his pizza, and he looked at it with sudden puzzlement. Cheese, pepperoni, spicy minced beef, anchovy, and egg. No wonder he'd had indigestion today. The other three slices were what he'd had for breakfast. It was a combination to which he, probably uniquely in all the world, was addicted, and which he had some months ago forsworn because his gut couldn't cope with it anymore. He hadn't thought twice about it when he'd blundered across it in the fridge this morning because it was exactly the sort of thing a person liked to find in a fridge. It hadn't occurred to him to ask who had put it there. But it hadn't been him.

Slowly, disgustingly, he removed the half-chewed portion from his mouth. He didn't believe in the pizza fairy.

He disposed of the half-masticated gungey bits and then examined the two remaining slices. There was nothing unusual or suspicious about them at all. It was exactly the pizza he regularly used to eat until he made himself give it up. He phoned his local pizza restaurant and asked them if anybody else had been in to buy a pizza with that particular combination of toppings.

"Ah, you're the bloke who has the *gastricciana,* are you?" said the pizza chef.

"The what?"

"It's what we call it. No, mate, nobody else has ever bought that wonderful combination, believe me."

Dirk felt somewhat dissatisfied with aspects of this conversation, but he let it pass. He put the phone down thoughtfully. He felt that something very strange was going on and he didn't know what.

"No one knows anything."

The words caught his attention and he glanced up at the TV. A breezy Californian in the sort of Hawaiian shirt that could serve, if needed, as a distress signal was standing in the bright sunshine and answering questions, Dirk quickly worked out, about the approaching meteor. He called the meteor Toodle Pip.

"Toodle Pip?" asked his interviewer, the BBC's California correspondent.

"Yeah. We call it Toodle Pip because anything it hits, you could pretty much say good-bye to."

The Californian grinned.

"So you're saying it is going to hit?"

"I'm saying I don't know. Nobody knows."

"Well, the scientists at NASA are saying . . ."

"NASA," said the Californian genially, "is talking shit. They don't know. If we don't know, they sure as hell don't know. Here at Similarity Engines we have the most massively powerful parallel computers on Earth, so when I say we don't know, I know what I'm talking about. We know that we don't know, and we know why we don't know. NASA doesn't even know that."

The next item on the news was also from California, and was about a lobby group called Green Shoots, which was attracting a lot of support. Its view, and it was one that spoke to the battered psyches of many Americans, was that the world was much better able to take care of itself than we were, so there was no point in getting all worked up about it or trying to moderate our natural behaviour. "Don't worry," said their slogan, quoting the title of a popular song. "Be happy."

"Great Balls of Fire," thought Dirk to himself, quoting another.

"Scientists in Australia," said someone on the radio "are trying to teach kangaroos to speak." Dirk decided that what he most needed was a good night's sleep.

In the morning, things suddenly seemed wonderfully clear and simple. He didn't know the answer to anything, but he knew what to do about it. A few phone calls to the bank had established that tracing the money back to its origins was going to be hideously difficult, partly because it was an inherently complicated business anyway, partly because it quickly became clear that whoever had been paying the money to him had taken some trouble to cover his or her tracks, but mostly because the man on the foreign desk at his bank had a cleft palate.

Life was too short, the weather too fine, and the world too full of interesting and exciting pitfalls. Dirk would go sailing.

Life, he was fond of telling himself, was like an ocean. You can either grind your way across it like a motorboat or you can follow the winds and the currents—in other words, go sailing. He had the wind: he was being paid by someone. Presumably that someone was paying him to do something, but what he had omitted to say. Well, that was a client's privilege. But Dirk felt that he should respond to this generous urge to pay him, that he should do something. But what? Well, he was a private detective, and what private detectives did when they were being paid was mostly to follow people.

So that was simple. Dirk would follow someone.

Which meant that now he had to find a good current: someone to follow. Well, there was his office window, with a whole world surging by outside it—or a few people at least. He would pick one. He began to tingle with excitement that his investigation was finally under way, or would be as soon as the next person—no, not the next person, the . . . fifth next person walked around the corner that he could see on the other side of the road.

He was immediately glad that he had decided to build in a brief period of mental preparation. Almost immediately number one, a large duvet of a woman, came around the corner with numbers two and three being dragged unwillingly along with her—her children, whom she nagged and scolded with every step. Dirk breathed a sigh of relief that it wasn't going to be her.

He stood by the side of his window, quiet with anticipation. For a few minutes no one further came round the corner. Dirk watched as the large woman bullied her two children into the newsagent opposite, despite their wails that they wanted to go home and watch TV. A minute or two later she bullied them back out into the sunshine again despite the their wails that they wanted an ice cream and a Judge Dredd comic.

She yanked them away up the road, and the scene fell quiet.

The scene was a triangular-shaped one, because of the angle at which two roads collided with each other. Dirk had recently moved to this new office—new to him, that was; the actual building was old and dilapidated and remained standing more out of habit than from any inherent structural integrity—and much preferred it to his previous one, which was miles from anywhere. In his old one he could have waited all week for five people to walk around a corner.

Number four appeared.

Number four was a postman with a pushcart. A small bead of perspiration appeared on Dirk's forehead as he began to realise how badly wrong his plan could go.

And here was number five.

Number five almost lurched into sight. He was in his late twenties, tallish, with ginger hair and a black leather bomber jacket. Having arrived round the corner, he then stopped and stood still for a moment. He looked around as if half-expecting to meet somebody. Dirk started to move, when suddenly number six walked round the corner.

Number six was a different proposition altogether: a rather delicious-looking woman in jeans, with short, thick black hair. Dirk swore to himself and wondered if he hadn't secretly meant six instead of five. But no. An undertaking was an undertaking, and he was being paid a lot of money. He owed it to whoever was paying the money to stick to whatever agreement it was that they hadn't actually got. Number five was still standing there dithering on the street corner, and Dirk hurried quickly downstairs to take up the chase.

As he opened the cracked front door he was met by number four, the postman with the pushcart, who handed him a small bundle of letters. Dirk pocketed them and hurried out into the street and the spring sunshine.

He hadn't followed anybody for quite a while, and discovered that he had lost the knack. He set off so enthusiastically in pursuit of his quarry that he realised he was walking far too quickly and would in fact have to walk straight past him. He did so, paused for a few confused seconds, turned round, and started to walk back, which caused him to collide directly with his quarry. Dirk was so flummoxed to find that he had actually physically hit the person he was supposed to be stealthily tailing that in order to allay any suspicion he jumped onto a passing bus and headed off down Rosebery Avenue.

This, he felt, was not an auspicious beginning. He sat on the bus for a few seconds, completely stunned at his own ineptness. He was being paid $5,000 a week for this. Well, in a sense he was. He became aware that people were looking at him slightly oddly. But not nearly as oddly, he reflected, as they would do if they had the slightest idea about what he was actually doing.

He twisted round in his seat and squinted back down the road, wondering what would be a good next move. Normally, if you were tailing somebody, it was a problem if they unexpectedly jumped onto a bus, but it was almost more of a problem if you unexpectedly jumped on one yourself. It was probably best if he just got off again and tried to resume the trail, though how on earth he was going to look unobtrusive now, he didn't know. As soon as the bus next came to a halt, he jumped off again and started walking back up Rosebery Avenue. Before he had gone very far, he noticed his quarry walking down the road in his direction. He reflected that he had managed to pick a remarkably helpful and cooperative subject, and better than he deserved. Time to get a grip and be a little more circumspect. He was almost at the door of a small café, so he ducked inside it. He stood at the counter pretending to dither for a moment over the sandwiches until he sensed that the subject had passed.

The subject didn't pass. The subject walked in and stood behind him at the counter. In a panic, Dirk ordered a tuna and sweetcorn roll, which he hated, and a cappuccino, which went particularly badly with fish, and hurried off to sit at one of the small tables. He wanted to be able to bury himself in a newspaper, but he didn't have one, so he had to make do with his post. He pored over it intently. Various bills of the usual preposterous and wildly overoptimistic kind. Various circulars of the strange type that private detectives tended to receive—catalogues full of tiny electronic gadgets all designed to counteract each other; ads for peculiar grades of film or revolutionary new types of thin plastic strips. Dirk couldn't be bothered with any of it, though he did pause for a moment over a flyer for a newly published book on advanced surveillance techniques. He screwed it up crossly and threw it on the floor.

The last envelope was another bank statement. His bank had long ago got into the habit of sending them to him on a weekly basis, just to make the point, really. They hadn't yet adjusted to his new sheen of solvency, or didn't trust it. Probably hadn't even noticed it, in fact. He opened the statement, still only half-believing.

Yes.

Another £3,253.29. Last Friday. Incredible. Inexplicable. But there.

There was also something else odd, though. It took him a

moment or two to spot it, because he was keeping half an eye expertly trained on his subject, who was buying coffee and a doughnut and paying for it out of a fan of twenties.

The last entry on Dirk's statement was for a cash withdrawal on his debit card: £500. Yesterday. The statement had obviously been sent out at close of business yesterday, and it had the day's transactions up to date. That was all very excellent and efficient and a fine testimony to the efficacy of modern computer technology, of course, but the fact was that Dirk hadn't withdrawn £500 yesterday, or any other day for that matter. His card must have been stolen. Hell's bells! He fished anxiously for his wallet.

No. His cards were there. Safe.

He thought about it. He couldn't envisage any way in which a fraudster could make an actual cash withdrawal without the actual card. A horrible clammy thought suddenly grabbed his stomach. These were his own bank statements he'd been getting, weren't they? He checked in alarm. Yes. His name, his address, his account number. He had double-checked the other ones last night, several times. Definitely his statements. They just didn't seem to be his financial transactions, that was all.

Time to concentrate on the job in hand. He looked up. His quarry was sitting two tables away, patiently munching his bun and staring into the middle distance.

After a moment or two he stood up, brushed some crumbs off his leather jacket, turned, and walked to the door. He paused for a moment, as if considering which way to go, and then set off the way he had been going, strolling casually. Dirk slipped his mail into his pocket and quietly followed.

He had picked a good subject, he soon realised. The man's ginger hair shone like a beacon in the spring sunshine, so whenever he was briefly swallowed up in a crowd, it would only be a matter of seconds before Dirk would catch sight of him again, meandering idly along the street.

Dirk wondered what he did for a living. Not a lot, it seemed—or at least, not a lot today. A pleasant walk through Holborn and into the West End. Loafing around in a couple of bookshops for half an hour (Dirk made a note of the titles his quarry browsed through), stopping for (another) coffee in an Italian café to glance through a copy of *The Stage* (which probably explained why he had so much free time for loafing around in bookshops and Italian cafés), and then a long, leisurely amble up through Regent's Park and then across Camden and back toward Islington—Dirk began to think that this business of following people was really a rather congenial one. Fresh air, exercise—he was feeling in such tremendously good spirits by the end of the day that as soon he strode back in through his front door—or rather, his front polythene flap—it was instantly clear to him that the dog's name was Kierkegaard.

Chapter 5

SOLUTIONS NEARLY ALWAYS come from the direction you least expect, which means there's no point trying to look in that direction because it won't be coming from there.

This was an observation that Dirk mentioned a lot to people, and he mentioned it again to Kate that evening when he phoned her.

"Wait a minute, wait a minute, wait a minute," she said, trying to wedge a phrase into his monologue and wiggle it about. "Are you telling me . . ."

"I'm telling you that the late husband of the woman who's forgotten her dog's name was a biographer."

"But . . ."

"And I expect you know that biographers often name their pets after their subjects."

"No. I . . ."

"It's so they've got someone to shout at when they get fed up. You spend hours wading through someone banging on about the teleological suspension of the ethical or whatever and sometimes you just need to be able to shout 'Oh, shut up, Kierkegaard, for Christ's sake.' Hence the dog."

"Dir . . ."

"Some biographers use a small wooden ornament or a potted plant, but most prefer something you can get a good yap out of. Feedback, you see. Speaking of which, do I sense that you have an observation to make?"

"Dirk, are you telling me that you spent all day following a total stranger?"

"Absolutely. And I intend to do the same tomorrow. I shall be skulking near his front door bright and early. Well, bright at least. No point in being early. He's an actor."

"You could get locked up for that!"

"Occupational hazard. Kate, I'm being paid $5,000 a week. You have to be prepared to . . ."

"But not to follow a total stranger!"

"Whoever is employing me knows my methods. I am applying them."

"You don't know anything about the person who's employing you."

"On the contrary, I know a great deal."

"All right, what's his name?"

"Frank."

"Frank what?"

"No idea. Look, I don't know that his name is Frank. His—or her—name has nothing to do with it. The point is that they have a problem. The problem is serious, or they wouldn't be paying me a substantial amount of money to solve it. And the problem is ineffable or they'd tell me what it is. Whoever it is knows who I am, where I am, and precisely how best to reach me."

"Or maybe the bank's just made an error. Hard to believe, I know, but . . ."

"Kate, you think I'm talking nonsense, but I'm not. Listen. In the past, people would stare into the fire for hours when they wanted to think. Or stare at the sea. The endless dancing shapes and patterns would reach far deeper into our minds than we could manage by reason and logic. You see, logic can only proceed from the premises and assumptions we already make, so we just drive round and round in little circles like little clockwork cars. We need dancing shapes to lift us and carry us, but they're harder to find these days. You can't stare into a radiator. You can't stare into the sea. Well, you can, but it's covered with plastic bottles and used condoms, so you just sit there getting cross. All we have to stare into is the white noise. The stuff we sometimes call information, but which is really just a babble rising in the air."

"But without logic . . ."

"Logic comes afterwards. It's how we retrace our steps. It's being wise after the event. Before the event you have to be very silly."

"Ah. So that's what you're doing."

"Yes. Well, it's solved one problem already. I've no idea how long it would have taken me to work out that the wretched dog was called Kierkegaard. It was only by the happiest of chances that my surveillance subject happened to pick out a biography of Kierkegaard, which I then discovered, when I checked it out myself, had been written by the man who subsequently threw himself off a crane with elastic round his legs."

"But the two cases had nothing to do with each other."

"Have I mentioned that I believe in the fundamental connectedness of all things? I think I have."

"Yes."

"Which is why I must now go and investigate some of the other books he was interested in before getting myself ready for tomorrow's expedition."

" . . . "

"I can hear you shaking your head in sorrow and bewilderment. Don't worry. Everything is getting nicely out of control."

"If you say so, Dirk. Oh, by the way, what does 'ineffable' actually mean?"

"I don't know," said Dirk tersely, "but I intend to find out."

Chapter 6

THE FOLLOWING MORNING the weather was so foul it hardly deserved the name, and Dirk decided to call it Stanley instead.

Stanley wasn't a good downpour. Nothing wrong with a good downpour for clearing the air. Stanley was the sort of thing you needed a good downpour to clear the air of. Stanley was muggy, close, and oppressive, like someone large and sweaty pressed up against you in a tube train. Stanley didn't rain, but every so often he dribbled on you.

Dirk stood outside in the Stanley.

The actor had kept him waiting for over an hour now, and Dirk was beginning to wish that he had stuck by his own opinion that actors never got up in the morning. Instead of which he had turned up rather eagerly outside the actor's flat at about 8:30 and then stood behind a tree for an hour.

Nearly an hour and a half now. There was a brief moment of excitement when a motorcycle messenger arrived and delivered a small package, but that was about it. Dirk lurked about twenty yards from the actor's door.

The Motorcycle Messenger Arrival Incident had surprised him a bit. The actor didn't seem to be a particularly prosperous one. He looked as if he were more in the still-knocking-on-people's-doors bit of his career than in the having-scripts-biked-round-to-him bit.

Time dragged by. Dirk had read through the small collection of newspapers he'd brought with him twice, and checked through the contents of his wallet and pockets several times: the usual collection of business cards for people he had no recollection of meeting, unidentifiable phone numbers on scraps of paper, credit cards, cheque book, his passport (he had suddenly remembered that he had left it in another jacket when his quarry had paused for a longish time at the window of a travel agent yesterday), his toothbrush (he never travelled without his toothbrush, with the result that it was completely unusable), and his notebook.

He even consulted his own horoscope in one of the papers, the one written by a disreputable friend of his who toiled unscrupulously under the name of The Great Zaganza. First he glanced at some of the entries under other birth signs, just to get a feel for the kind of mood the GZ was in. Mellow, it seemed, at first sight. "Your ability to take the long view will help you though some of the minor difficulties you experience when Mercury . . . ," "Past weeks have strained your patience, but new possibilities will now start to emerge as the sun . . . ," "Beware of allowing others to take advantage of your good nature. Resolve will be especially called for when . . ." Boring, humdrum stuff. He read his own horoscope. "Today you will meet a three-ton rhinoceros called Desmond."

Dirk clapped the paper shut in irritation, and at that moment the door suddenly opened. The actor emerged with a purposeful air. He was carrying a small suitcase, a shoulder bag, and a coat. Something was happening. Dirk glanced at his watch. Three minutes past ten. He made a quick note in his book. His pulse quickened.

A taxi was coming down the street towards them. The actor hailed it. Damn! Something as simple as that. He was going to get away. The actor climbed into the cab and it drove off down the street, past Dirk. Dirk swivelled to watch it, and caught a momentary glimpse of the actor looking back through the rear window. Dirk watched helplessly and then glanced up and down the street in the vain hope that . . .

Almost miraculously a second taxi appeared suddenly at the top of the street, heading towards him. Dirk shot out an arm, and it drew to a halt beside him.

"Follow that cab!" exclaimed Dirk, clambering into the back.

"I been a cabbie over twenty years now," said the cabbie as he slid back into the traffic. "Never had anybody actually say that to me."

Dirk sat perched on the edge of his seat, watching the cab in front as it threaded its way through the slow, agonising throttle of the London traffic.

"Now that may seem like a little thing to you, but it's interesting, innit?"

"What?" said Dirk.

"Anytime you see anything on the telly where someone jumps in a cab, it's always 'Follow that cab,' innit?"

"Is it? I've never noticed," said Dirk.

"Well, you wouldn't," said the cabbie. "You're not a cabbie. What you notice depends on who you are. If you're a cabbie, then what you especially notice when you watch the telly," continued the cabbie, "is the cabbies. See what the cabbies are up to. See?"

"Er, yes," said Dirk.

"But on the telly you never actually see the cabbies, see? You only see the people in the back of the cab. Like, the cabbie's never of any interest."

"Er, I suppose so," said Dirk. "Um, can you still see the cab we're supposed to be following?"

"Oh yeah, I'm following him okay. So, the only time you ever actually see the cabbie is when a fare says something to him. And when a fare says something to a cabbie in a drama, you know what it invariably is?"

"Let me guess," said Dirk. "It's 'Follow that cab!'"

"Exactly my point. So if what you see on the telly is to be believed, all cabbies ever do," continued the cabbie, "is follow other cabbies."

"Hmmm," said Dirk, doubtfully.

"Which leaves me in a very strange position, as being the one cabbie that never gets asked to follow another cabbie. Which leads me to the unmistakable conclusion that I must be the cabbie all the other cabbies are following . . ."

Dirk squinted out of the window, trying to spot if there was another cab he could switch to.

"Now, I'm not saying that's what's actually happening, but you can see how someone might get to thinking that way, can't you? It's the power of the media, innit?"

"There was," said Dirk, "an entire television series about taxi drivers. It was called, as I recall, *Taxi*."

"Yeah, well I'm not talking about that, am I?" said the cabbie, irrefutably, "I'm talking about the power of the media to selectively distort reality. That's what I'm talking about. I mean, when it comes down to it, we all live in our own different reality, don't we, I mean when it comes down to it."

"Well, yes, I think you're right as a matter of fact," said Dirk, uneasily.

"I mean, you take these kangaroos they're trying to teach language to. What does anyone think we're going to talk about? What are we going to say, then, eh? 'So—how's the hopping life treating you then?' 'Oh fine, mustn't grumble. This pocket down me front's a bit of a pain, though, always full of fluff and paper clips.' It isn't going to be like that. These kangaroos have got brains the size of a walnut. They live in a different world, see. It would be like trying to talk to John Selwyn Gummer. You see what I'm saying?"

"Can you see the cab we're following?"

"Clear as a bell. Probably be there before him."

Dirk frowned.

"Be where before him?"

"Heathrow."

"How on earth do you know he's going to Heathrow?"

"Any cabbie can tell if another cabbie's going to Heathrow."

"What do you mean?"

"You read the signs. Okay, so there's certain obvious things, like the fare's carrying luggage. Then there's the route he's taking. That's easy. But, you say, he may just be going to stay with friends in Hammersmith. All I can say is, the fare didn't get into the cab in the manner of someone going to stay with friends in Hammersmith. So, what else do you look for? Well, here's where you need to be a cabbie to know. Normal life for a cabbie is lots of little bits here and there. You don't know from minute to minute what's going to happen, what work you're going to get, how the day's going to go. You kind of prowl around in a restless kind of way. But if you get a fare to Heathrow, you're away. Good solid journey, good solid fare, wait in line for an hour or so, get a good solid fare back to town. That's your whole morning taken care of. You drive in a completely different way. You're higher up on the road, you take better lines through corners. You're on your way. You're going somewhere. It's called doing the Heathrow Hop. Any cabbie'll spot it."

"Hmm," said Dirk. "That's remarkable."

"What you notice depends on who you are."

"You couldn't happen to tell which flight he's catching, could you?" asked Dirk.

"Who do you think I am, mate," retorted the cabbie, "a bloody private detective?" Dirk sat back in his seat and stared out of the window, thoughtfully.

Chapter 7

THERE MUST BE some kind of disease that causes people to talk like that, and the name for it must be something like Airline Syllable Stress Syndrome. It's the disease that seems to kick in at about ten thousand feet and becomes more and more pronounced, if that's a good word to use in this context, with altitude until it levels out at a plateau of complete nonsense at about 35,000 feet. It makes otherwise rational people start saying things like "The captain has now turned off the seatbelt sign," as if there were someone lurking around the cockpit attempting to deny that the captain has done any such thing, that he is indeed the captain and not an impostor, and that there aren't a whole bunch of second-rate and inferior seatbelt signs that he mightn't have been fiddling about with.

Another thing that Dirk reflected on as he settled back into his seat was the curious coincidence that not only does the outside of an aircraft look like the outside of a vacuum cleaner, but also that the inside of an aircraft smells like the inside of a vacuum cleaner.

He accepted a glass of champagne from the cabin steward. He supposed that most of the words that airline staff used, or rather most of the sentences into which they were habitually arranged, had been worked so hard that they had died. The strange stresses that cabin stewards continually thumped them with were like electric shocks applied to heart-attack victims in an attempt to revive them.

Well.

What a strange and complicated hour and a half that had been. Dirk was still by no means sure that something somewhere had not gone terribly wrong, and he was tempted, now that the seatbelt sign had been turned off by the captain, to go and take a bit of a casual stroll through the aircraft to have a look for his quarry. But no one was going to be getting on or off the aircraft for a little while now, so he would probably be wiser to restrain himself for an hour. Or even longer. It was, after all, an eleven-hour flight to Los Angeles.

He had not been expecting to go to Chicago today, and the sight of his quarry making a beeline for the check-in desk for the 1330 flight to Chicago had made him lurch. However, a resolution was a resolution, so after a brief pause to make sure that his quarry hadn't merely gone up to the check-in desk to ask directions to the tie shop, Dirk had made his way light-headedly to the ticket sales desk and slammed plastic.

Overwhelmed with his sudden solvency, he had even booked himself business class. His anonymous employer was obviously someone of means who was not going to quibble over a few minor expenses. Suppose his quarry was travelling business class? Dirk would not be able to keep tabs on him from a seat stuck in the back of the plane. There was almost an argument there for travelling first class, but not, Dirk reluctantly admitted to himself, a sane one.

But, an hour and a half after the plane had taken off, Dirk was beginning to wonder. As a business-class passenger he was denied access to the first-class section up in the nose of the plane, but could wander freely wherever else he liked. He had wandered freely up and down each aisle three times now, surreptitiously watched each of the toilet doors, and seen his quarry nowhere. He returned to his seat and pondered the situation. Either his quarry was in the first-class cabin or he was not on the plane.

First class? He just didn't look it. The fare would be quite a few months rent on his flat. But who knows? Maybe he had caught the eye of a Hollywood casting director who was whisking him over for a screen test. It wouldn't be difficult to slip into the first-class cabin and have a quick look around, but it would be difficult to do it without attracting attention.

Not on the plane? Dirk had seen him heading in towards passport control, but there had been a moment when he had suddenly looked round and Dirk had ducked quickly into the bookshop.

A few seconds later, when Dirk next glanced up, his quarry had gone—into, Dirk had assumed, passport control. Dirk had lingered for a decent interval, bought some newspapers and books, and then made his way through passport control and into the departure area himself.

It had not especially surprised him that he had not spotted his quarry anywhere in the departure area: it was a shining maze of pointless shops, cafés, and lounges, and Dirk felt that there was nothing to be gained by rushing around hunting for him. They were being funnelled inexorably in the same direction anway. They'd be on the same plane.

Not on the plane? Dirk sat stock still. Thinking back, he had to admit that the last time he had actually physically seen his quarry was before he had even gone through passport control, and that everything else was based on the assumption that his quarry was going to do what he, Dirk, had decided he was going to do. This, he now realised, was actually quite a large assumption. Cold air trickled down his neck from the nozzle above him.

Yesterday he had inexpertly boarded a bus while tailing this man. Today, it seemed, he had inadvertently boarded a plane to Chicago. He put his hand to his brow and asked himself, honestly, how good a private detective he really was.

He summoned a cabin steward and ordered a glass of whisky, and nursed it as if it were very ill indeed. After a while he reached into his plastic bag of books and newspapers. He might as well just pass the time. He sighed. He drew out of the bag something he had no recollection of putting there.

It was a courier delivery packet, which had already been opened. With a slow frown developing on his forehead, he pulled out its contents. There was a book inside. He turned it over, wonderingly. It was called *Advanced Surveillance Techniques*. He recognised it. He'd had a flyer for it yesterday in the post. He'd screwed it up and thrown it to the floor. Folded between a couple of pages of the book was the exact same flyer, flattened and smoothed out. With a deep sense of foreboding, Dirk slowly unfolded it. Scrawled across it in felt tip, in handwriting that was oddly familiar, were the words "Bon Voyage!" The cabin steward leaned across him. "Can I freshen your drink, sir?" he said.

Chapter 8

THE SUN STOOD high above the distant Pacific. The day was bright, the sky blue and cloudless, the air, if you liked the smell of burnt carpets, perfect. Los Angeles. A city I have never visited.

A car, a blue convertible, sleek and desirable, came sweeping west out of Beverly Hills along the, as I understand it, gracious curves of Sunset Boulevard. Anybody seeing such a car would have wanted it. Obviously. It was designed to make you want it. If people had turned out not to want it very much, the makers would have redesigned it and redesigned it until they did. The world is now full of things like this, which is, of course, why everybody is in such a permanent state of want.

The driver was a woman, and I can tell you for a fact that she was very beautiful. She had fine dark hair cut in a bob, and as she drove, her hair riffled in the warm breeze. I would tell you about what she wore, but I'm very bad at clothes and if I started telling you that it was an Armani this or a what's-her-name Farhi that, you would know instinctively that I was faking it, and since you are taking the trouble to read what I have written, I intend to treat you with respect even if I do, occasionally and in a friendly and well-meaning kind of way, lie to you. So I'll just say that the clothes she was wearing were exactly the sort of clothes that someone who knew vastly more about clothes than I do would admire enormously, and were blue. Impossibly tall palm trees towered above her, silent Mexicans moved over impossibly perfect lawns.

The gates of Bel Air went by—and behind them, perfect houses nestling in perfect bouquets of shrubbery. I've seen exactly those houses on television and even I, sceptical and sarcastic old me, have felt that I really, really wanted one of them. Luckily, the sort of the things that people who live in such houses say to each other make me giggle until tea squirts out of my nose and so the moment passes.

The sleek, desirable blue convertible swept on. There is a set of traffic lights, I understand, on the borders of Bel Air and Brentwood, and as the car approached them, they turned red. The car drew to a halt. The woman shook her hair and adjusted her sunglasses in the mirror. As she did so, she caught sight of a brief flicker of movement in the mirror as a small, dark-haired figure emerged quietly from the shade of the roadside and snuck round the back of the car. A moment later he was leaning right over her, pointing a small handgun into her face. I know even less about handguns than I do about clothes. I'd be completely hopeless in Los Angeles. I'd be laughed at not only for my lack of dress sense but also my pitiful inability to tell a Magnum .38 from a Walther PPK or even, for heaven's sake, a derringer. I do know, however, that the gun was also blue, or at least blue-black, and that the woman was startled out of her wits to have it pointed into her left eye from a range of just under one inch. Her assailant gave her to understand that now would be an excellent moment for her to vacate her seat and, no, not to take the key out of the car or even to attempt to pick up her bag, which was lying on the seat next to her, but just to be very cool, move very easily, very gently, and just get the fuck out of the car.

The woman tried to be very cool, to move very easily and very gently, but was hampered by the fact that she was shaking with uncontrollable fear as the gun bobbed about just an inch or so from her face like a mayfly in the summer. She did, however, get the fuck out of the car. She stood trembling in the middle of the road as the thief jumped into the car in her place, gunned the engine in a quick roar of triumph, and careered sharply off along Sunset Boulevard, around the bend, and away. She twisted around on the spot in an agony of shocked helplessness. Her world had turned abruptly upside down and tipped her out of it, and she was now, suddenly and unexpectedly, that most helpless of all people in Los Angeles, a pedestrian.

She tried to wave down one or two of the other cars on the road, but they manoeuvred politely past her. One of them was an open-topped Mustang with the radio playing loudly. I'd love to be able to say that it was tuned to an oldies station and that the words "How does it feeeeel? How does it feeeeeel?" snarled out at this moment, but there are limits even to fiction. It was an oldies station, but the old song it was playing was "Sunday Girl" by Blondie, and so wasn't even remotely appropriate, seeing as this was a Thursday. What could she do?

Another perfect crime. Another perfect day in the City of Angels. And only one tiny little lie.

Forgive me.

Chapter 9

IF THERE IS an uglier building in England than Ranting Manor, then I haven't seen it. It must be hiding somewhere and not, like Ranting Manor, squatting in the middle of a hundred acres of rolling parkland. The original estate consisted of many more hundreds of acres that were the pride of Oxfordshire, but generations of syphilitic idiocy and blitheringness have reduced it to its current decrepit state—an ill-kempt bunch of woods, fields, and lawns littered with the results of various failed attempts to raise money by whatever means seemed to someone like a good idea at the time: a godforsaken fun fair, a once quite well-stocked zoo, and, of more recent provenance, a small high-technology business park, current occupant one faltering computer games company, now cast adrift by its American parent and believed to be the only such company in the world making a loss. You could find a billion-barrel oilfield in the grounds of Ranting Manor and you could pretty much guarantee that within a couple of years it would be operating at a loss, and would require the selling of the family tin to keep it going. The family silver has long since gone, of course, along with most of the family. Disease, alcohol, drugs, sexual imbecility, and poorly maintained road vehicles have combined to cut vicious swathes through the ranks of the Rantings and reduced them to almost none.

How much history would you like? Maybe just a very little. The Manor itself dates back to the thirteenth century, or at least bits of it do. The bits are all that remain of the original monastery, inhabited for a couple of centuries or so by a devout order of calligraphers and pederasts. Then Henry VIII got his mitts on it and handed it over to a courtly scumbag called John Ranting, in return for some spectacular piece of loyal villainy. He knocked it down and rebuilt it after his own pleasure, which was probably pleasing enough, seeing as the architects of the Tudor period pretty much knew what they were doing: stout beams, nice plasterwork and leaded windows, all the things we now value enormously but that John Ranting's descendants, unfortunately, did not—especially the Victorian rubber magnate Sir Percy Ranting, who, in the 1860s, tore much of it down and rebuilt it as a hunting lodge. These Victorian "hunting lodges" were built because the immensely wealthy merchants of the age were not supposed to parade their actual penises around in public, instead of which vast tracts of pretty and innocent English countryside had their erections inflicted upon them. Big, bulbous, ruddy buildings with vast ballrooms, grand, angular staircases, and as many turrets and crenellations as a recreational condom.

The nineteenth century was, in aesthetic terms, disastrous enough for Ranting Manor, but right slap-bang after it, of course, came the twentieth, with all its architectural theories and double glazing. The main additions during this period were, in the thirties, a sort of large Nazi billiard room and in the sixties an indoor swimming pool, tiled in orange and purple, to which were now added various clumps of brightly coloured fungus.

The thing that binds all these different styles together is a general air of dampness and decay and a sense that if a public-spirited citizen tried to set the place alight, it would go out well before the fire brigade arrived. What else? Oh yes. It's haunted.

Enough of the wretched building.

At about ten-thirty in the evening, which would make it roughly the same time that the car was being stolen on Sunset Boulevard, a small perimeter gate squeaked open. The main iron gates to the estate were kept locked at night, but the side gate was usually to be found unfastened. A reputation for being an unwholesome and troublesome place was usually enough to deter any intruders. An old sign on the main gate said BEWARE OF THE DOG, beneath which someone had scrawled, "Why single out the dog particularly?"

The figures of, respectively, a large dog and a small man slipped in through the side gate. Both walked with a pronounced limp. The dog limped on its left foreleg, the man on his right leg or, to be more accurate, not on his right leg because he didn't have one. It was missing beneath the knee. Instead, the man limped on a wooden leg that was a full inch longer than his left leg and made walking not merely difficult, but actually rather a trial.

The night was dull. The moon was up, or at least half of it was, but for the most part it was shrouded in clouds. The two shadowy figures limped their way in unison along the driveway, resembling, from a distance, a child's pulling toy with a couple of off-centre wheels. They were taking the long way to the house. This wound a circuitous route through the estate, passing some of its failed or failing business enterprises on the way.

The dog whined and grumbled a little until its master bent down stiffly and let it off its leash, whereupon it gave a gruff yelp of pleasure, lurched forward a couple of paces, and then resumed its hobbling plod, in unison with, but now a good two of yards ahead of, its master. From time to time it glanced back to check that its master was still there, that all was well, and that nothing was going to jump out and bite them.

Moving thus, they slowly rounded a long bend in the drive, the man hunched inside a long dark coat, despite the easy temperature of the evening. After a few minutes they passed on their left the entrance to the zoo that had been such a drain on the estate's limited resources. There were very few animals left in it now: a couple of goats, a chicken, and a capybara, the world's largest rodent. There was also a special guest animal in the zoo at the moment, being housed temporarily while its normal quarters in Chatsfield Zoo were being rebuilt. Desmond—the animal's name was Desmond—had only been in residence for a couple of weeks so far, but his presence had, not surprisingly, caused a bit of a stir in the village of Little Ranting.

As the man and his dog passed the entrance to the zoo, they paused for a moment, and then turned and looked at it again. The low, wooden gate, which should have been secured at this time of night, was standing open. The dog whimpered, and snuffled around on the ground, which seemed to have been scuffed and churned up a little. The man hobbled up to the open gate and peered into the darkness beyond. Among the low huddle of buildings, all was darkness, except for a single dim light that glowed from the hut where Roy Harrison, Desmond's keeper from Chatsfield, was staying. Nothing untoward. No sign of movement. So why was the gate open? It probably meant nothing. Most things, the man would have told you if you had asked him, probably meant nothing. Nevertheless, he summoned his dog with a gruff syllable and limped crossly through the gate, closing it behind them. Slowly, grindingly, they made their way along the gravel path to the single source of light: Roy Harrison's temporary abode.

The place seemed quiet.

The man rapped sharply on the door and listened. No answer. He knocked again. Still, nothing. He opened the door. It wasn't locked, but then, there was probably no reason for it to be. As he pushed his way into the tiny, dark hallway, his nose twitched at an odd smell. Zookeepers' lodgings were exactly where you would expect to find a vast and rich range of odd smells, but not necessarily this particular sweet, cloying one. Hmmph. The dog let out a very, very slight little yelp.

On the right side of the hallway was a door, the source of both the light that could be seen from outside and the fragrance that could be smelt within. Still, all was quiet. Carefully the man pushed the door open.

At first glance he thought that the figure slumped over the kitchen table might be dead, but after a long, drawn-out moment of silence it emitted a light, riffling snore.

The dog whimpered again, and sniffed around the floor nervously. The dog always seemed oddly nervous for its size, and kept on glancing round to its master for reassurance. In fact it was altogether an odd dog, of uncertain breed, or breeds. It was large and black, but its hair was tufty, its body scrawny and clumsy, and its manner edgy, anxious, verging on the completely neurotic. Whenever it came to a halt for a moment or so, the business of starting up again often seemed to cause it trouble, as if it had difficulty in remembering where it had left each of its legs. It looked as if something very nasty had happened to it, or was about to.

The sleeping keeper continued to snore. Next to him was a collection of crumpled beer cans, a half-empty bottle of whiskey, and a couple of glasses. In the ashtray lay the butts of three joints, and scattered around were bits of a ripped-up cigarette packet, a packet of cigarette papers, and a piece of silver foil twisted up in the traditional manner. The source of the smell. Roy had clearly shared a big evening with somebody, and that somebody had clearly then pushed off. The visitor tried gently to shake him by the shoulder, but to no avail. He tried again, but this time the keeper slowly slid sideways and collapsed in an untidy, slobbering heap on the floor. The dog was so startled by this that it leapt wildly for cover behind the sofa. Unfortunately the dog was larger and heavier than the sofa and knocked it backwards as he jumped over it, causing it to topple over on top of him. The dog yelped again, scrabbled briefly at the linoleum, and then leapt for cover once more behind a small coffee table, breaking it. Having run out of places to leap to, the dog cowered back in a corner, quivering with fright.

Its master satisfied himself that Roy was merely in a temporary state of chemical imbalance and not in any actual danger and, coaxing his dog with a few soothing words, left again. Together they followed the path back towards the gate and let themselves back out onto the main driveway, heading on the way they had been going, hobbling towards the main house. There were heavy scuff marks on the driveway.

Desmond suddenly felt bewildered. In an instant everything he had always smelt about the world had gone all swimmy and peculiar on him. There were some lights flashing around him, but he didn't mind that. Lights weren't of any real concern to him. Blink blink. So what? But this was most peculiar. He would have said that he was hallucinating, except that he didn't know the word, or indeed any word. He didn't even know that his name was Desmond, but, again, it wasn't the sort of thing that bothered him. A name was just a sound you heard, and didn't have that rich, heady reek of really being something. A sound didn't well up inside your head and go *woomph* the way a smell did. Smell was real, smell was something you could trust.

At least it had been up till now. But now he felt as if the whole world were tipping backwards over his head, and this, he couldn't help feeling, was a very worrying thing for the world to do.

He took a deep breath to try to steady his huge bulk. He drew billions of rich little molecules over the sensitive membranes of his nostrils. Not that rich, in fact. The smells here were mean little smells—flat, stale, and bitter smells with an acrid undertow of something nasty being burnt. None of the large, generous smells of hot, grassy air and day-old dung that haunted his imagination, but at least these paltry little local smells should steady him and root him on the ground.

They didn't.

Hhrrphraaah! Now he seemed to have two different and completely contradictory worlds in his head. Graaarphhh! What was all this? Where had the horizon gone?

That was it. That was why the world seemed to be tilting up above his head. Where there was usually a perfectly normal horizon, there now wasn't one. There was more world instead. A lot more. It just went on and on and on into a strange and hazy distance. Desmond felt big weird fears welling up inside him. He had a sudden instinct to charge at something, but you couldn't charge at a worrying uncertainty. He nearly stumbled.

He drew in another deep breath. He blinked, slowly.

Haaarh! The new bit of the world had vanished! Where was it? Where had it gone? There it was again! It unfolded itself blotchily into place and he felt as if he were tipping over again, but this time he was able to steady himself more quickly. Stupid little lights. Blink blink blink. This new bit of the world—what was it? He peered forward uncertainly into it, letting his mind's nostril play over it. Those lights were beginning to distract him. He shut his eyes to let him concentrate on his exploration, but when he did, the new world vanished! Again! He wondered for a dizzying moment if there was any connection between these two things, but making logical connections between things was not really one of Desmond's strengths. He let it pass. As he opened his wrinkly little eyes again, the unearthly new world slowly unfurled itself in his mind. Once more he peered into it.

It was a wilder world than the one he was used to, a world of paths and hills. The paths forked, divided, and deepened into valleys, the ridges reared into high hills. The far distance was completely broken up into massive mountain ranges and dizzying canyons shrouded in shifting mists. He was filled with apprehension. Just as making logical connections between things was not one of Desmond's strengths, neither was mountaineering.

The flattest, broadest path lay straight ahead of him, but as he turned his attention to it, worrying things began to become apparent.

Something nasty lay down that path. Something big and nasty. Something even bigger and nastier, Desmond ventured to think, than Desmond himself. For a moment he blinked again, and annoyingly the whole thing vanished once more. When it reassembled itself in his mind's nostril a second or two further on, the sense of impending disaster intensified.

Was that thunder?

Desmond didn't usually mind thunder, scarcely noticed lightning, but this thunder he did mind. There was no uplifting swirl of heavy air dancing, just bad, cracking explosions of blackness. Desmond began to feel very fearful. His enormous bulk began to quake and shudder, and suddenly he began to run. The strange new world shattered and vanished. He ran like a truck. He hurtled through a flurry of small, feeble lights and brought a whole ton of some kind of stuff, he didn't know what, banging down around him. It crashed noisily and flashed a bit, but Desmond ploughed straight through it. He was out of there, fleeing like a locomotive, smashing through a flimsy door, maybe even a wall, it was all the same to him. He hurtled out into the night air, pounding the ground with hammer blows from his enormous feet.

Things around him scattered from him. Things shouted. Distant, plaintive exclamations of alarm and despondency welled up in his wake, but Desmond didn't care. He just wanted some night air in his lungs. Even this night air, stale and acrid as it was, was good. It was cool and rushed over him and into him as he charged. There was hard pavement beneath his feet, then, briefly, bits of fencing around his neck, and then rough, scrubby grass beneath his pounding, churning feet.

He was near the top of a low hill. A real, earthy hill, not some fearsome hallucination rearing up in his mind like the approach of death. Just a hill, surrounded by other low, sloping hills. The sky was clear of clouds, but hazy and murky. Desmond was not interested in stars. You couldn't get a good whiff off a star, but here you could scarcely even see them, either. He didn't care, he was just getting up a good heavy speed going down this hill, waking up some sleepy muscles and getting them going. Braaarrrm! Run! Hurtle! Charge! Crash! Bang! There seemed to be more bits of fencing round his neck again, and suddenly his progress was rather less free than it had been, and he was all encumbered with stuff. He ploughed on

heavily. Suddenly he found himself in a sea of scattering creatures squealing as his huge bulk careered through them. The air
was full of the sound of cries and bellows and little tinkly
crashes. Bewildering odours danced around him—a surge of
burning meat, heady wafts of some kind of woozy-making
stuff, big stabs of viciously sweet musk. He was confused and
tried to fix on things by sight. He didn't trust vision very much,
it didn't tell him very much. He could just about tell when
things were blinking or lurking or running around. He tried to
get a fix on the hollering, scurrying shapes, and then saw a big
hazy rectangle of light. That was something. He heaved himself round and charged at it.

Crash!

And also some nasty, rainy, itchy sensations all over his
flank. He didn't like that. He stumbled as he barged into a large
room and was immediately assaulted with a suffocating splurge
of smell, screamy noises, and splashy lights. He charged into a
huddle of screaming creatures, which roared and screeched and
then went all cracked and squidgy. One of them got stuck on
him and Desmond had to shake his head to dislodge it. Before
him now was another large glinting rectangle, and a little way
beyond it the ground shimmered with a pale blue light.
Desmond lunged forward again. There was another crash, and
another shower of sharp and worrying pain. He hurtled
onwards and out into the open air once more.

The light in the ground was a strange pool of water, with
screaming things in it. He had never seen water glow like that.
And then there were some more blinking lights in front of him.
He didn't pay any attention to the little lights. He didn't even
pay any attention to the banging noises that went with each
blink. Bang bang, so what? But what did catch his attention
was the sudden acrid smell and the flowers of pain that started

to bloom in his body. A flower was planted in his shoulder, and another. His leg began to move oddly. A flower was planted in his flank, which felt very odd and worrying. Another flower was planted in his head, and gradually the whole world started to become more distant and less important. It began to roar. He felt himself tipping forward with enormous slowness, and gradually found himself enveloped in great waves of warm, glowing blueness.

As the world ebbed from him he heard a gabbling, hysterical voice making sounds that made no sense to him, but they sounded like this:

"Get the paramedics! Get the police! Not just Malibu, get the LAPD. Now! Tell them to get a helicopter up here! We've got dead and wounded! And tell them . . . I don't know how they're gonna deal with this, but tell them we've got a dead rhinoceros in the swimming pool."

Chapter 10

THOUGH IT WAS now embarrassingly clear to Dirk that only he and not his actual quarry was aboard the flight, that he had been thrown four thousand miles and a couple of thousand crucial pounds off course by a childishly simple ruse, he nevertheless determined to make one final check. He stationed himself right by the exit as everyone started to disembark at O'Hare Airport. He was watching so intently that he nearly missed hearing his own name being called over the aircraft's PA, directing him to go to the airline's information desk.

"Mr. Gently?" said the woman at the desk, brightly.

"Yes . . ." said Dirk warily.

"May I see your passport, sir?"

He passed it over. He stayed poised on the balls of his feet, expecting trouble.

"Your ticket through to Albuquerque, sir."

"My—?"

"Ticket through to Albuquerque, sir."

"My ticket to—?"

"Albuquerque, sir."

"Albuquerque?"

"Albuquerque, New Mexico, sir."

Dirk looked at the proffered ticket folder as if it were a piece of trick rhubarb. "Where did this come from?" he demanded. He took it and peered at the flight details.

The woman gave him a huge airline smile and a huge airline shrug. "Out of this machine, I guess. Just prints those tickets out."

"What does it say on your computer?"

"Just says prepaid ticket for Mr. Dirk Gently to Albuquerque, New Mexico, to be collected. Were you not expecting to go to Albuquerque today, sir?"

"I was expecting to end up somewhere I didn't expect, I just wasn't expecting it to be Albuquerque, that's all."

"Sounds like it's an excellent destination for you, Mr. Gently. Enjoy your flight."

He did. He sat and ruminated quietly to himself over the events of the last couple of days, arranging them in his mind not in such a way that they made any kind of sense yet, but in suggestive little arrays. A meteor here, half a cat there, the electronic threads of invisible dollars and unexpected airline tickets that connected them. Before touching down in Chicago, his self-confidence had been in tatters, but now he felt a thrilling tingle of excitement. There was something or someone out there that he had engaged with, something that he uniquely had found and that he was being drawn towards. The fact that he still had no idea who or what it was no longer troubled him. It was there, he had found it, and it had found him. He had felt its pulse. Its face and its name would emerge in their proper times.

At Albuquerque airport he stood silently for a while under the high painted beams, surrounded by the dark, staring eyes of the drunk-driving lawyers peering from their billboards. He breathed deeply. He felt calm, he felt good, he felt able to meet with the wild, thrashing improbabilities that lie an atom's depth beneath the dull surface of the narrated world, and to speak their language. He walked unhurriedly to the long escalators, and sailed slowly downwards like an invisible king.

His man was waiting for him.

He could tell him immediately—another still point in the scurrying airport. He was a large, fat, sweaty man with an ill-fitting black suit and a face like a badly laid table. He stood a few feet back from the foot of the escalator, gazing up it with an inert but complicated expression. It was as well that Dirk had been ready to spot him because the sign he held, which read D. JENTTRY, was one he might otherwise easily have missed.

Dirk introduced himself. The man said his name was Joe and that he would go and get the car. And that, rather anticlimactically, Dirk felt, was that.

The car drew up at the curbside, a slightly elderly, black stretch Cadillac, gleaming dully in the airport lighting. Dirk regarded it with satisfaction, climbed into it, and settled into the backseat with a small grunt of pleasure.

"The client said you'd like it," said Joe distantly from his driving coop as he quietly rolled the thing forward and out on to the airport exit road. Dirk looked around him at the scuffed and threadbare velveteen blue upholstery and the tinted plastic film peeling from the windows. The TV, when Dirk tried it, was tuned to nothing but noise, and the asthmatic air conditioning wheezed out a musty wind that was in no way preferable to the warm evening desert air through which they were moving.

The client was dead right.

"The client," said Dirk, as the great rattling thing cruised out onto the dimly lit freeway through the city. "Who exactly is the client?"

"An Australian gentleman, he sounded like," said Joe. His voice was rather high and whiny.

"Australian?" said Dirk, in surprise.

"Yes sir, Australian. Like you."

Dirk frowned. "I'm from England," he said.

"But Australian, right?"

"Why Australian, exactly?"

"Australian accent."

"Well, not really."

"Well, where's that place?"

"What place?" asked Dirk.

"New Zealand," said Joe. "Australia's in New Zealand, right?"

"Well, not precisely, but I can see what you're . . . well, I was going to say I can see what you're getting at, but I'm not sure I can."

"What part of New Zealand you from, then?"

"Well, more sort of England, in fact."

"Is that in New Zealand?"

"Only up to a point," said Dirk.

The car headed north on the freeway in the direction of Santa Fe. Moonlight lay magically on the high desert. The evening air was crisp.

"You been to Santa Fe before?" Joe nasaled.

"No," said Dirk. He had abandoned trying to engage him

in any kind of intelligible conversation and began to wonder if he had been deliberately chosen for his shortcomings in this area. Dirk was trying hard to stay sunk in thought, but Joe kept yanking him back to the surface.

"Beautiful place," said Joe. "Beautiful. If it doesn't get ruined by all the Californians moving in. Californication they call it. Hur-hur. You know what they call it?"

"Californication?" hazarded Dirk.

"Fanta Se," said Joe. "All the Hollywood types moving in from California. Ruining it. Especially since the earthquake. You heard about the earthquake?"

"Well, I did, as a matter of fact," said Dirk. "It was on the news. Rather a lot."

"Yeah, it was a big earthquake. And now all the Californians are moving out here instead. To Santa Fe. Ruining it. Californians. You know what they call it?"

Dirk could feel the whole conversation wheeling round and coming at him again. He tried to deflect it.

"Have you always lived in Santa Fe, then?" he said feebly.

"Oh yeah," said Joe. "Well, nearly always. Over a year now. Feels like always."

"So where did you live before?"

"California," said Joe. "Moved out after my sister was hit in a drive-by shooting. You have drive-by shootings in New Zealand?"

"No," said Dirk. "Not in New Zealand so far as I know. Nor even yet in London, which is where I live. Look, I'm sorry about your sister."

"Yeah. Standing on a streetcorner down on Melrose, couple of guys drive by in a Mercedes, one of those new ones, you know, with the double glazing, and pow, they blew her away—

500 SEL, I think it was. Midnight blue. Real smart. They musta jacked it. You have carjacking back in old England?"

"Carjacking?"

"People walk up to you, steal your car."

"No, but thanks for asking. We have people who clean your windscreen against your will, but, er . . ."

Joe barked with contempt.

"The thing is," explained Dirk, "in London you could certainly walk up to someone and steal their car, but you wouldn't be able to drive it away."

"Some kinda fancy device?"

"No, just traffic," said Dirk. "But, er . . . your sister," he asked nervously. 'Was she okay?'

"Okay?" shouted Joe. "You shoot someone with a Kalashnikov and they're okay, you're gonna want your money back. Hur-hur."

Dirk tried to make sympathetic noises, but they wouldn't form properly in his throat. The car was slowing down, so he lowered the peeling window to look at the desert night.

A passing road sign flared briefly in the car's headlights.

"Stop the car!" shouted Dirk suddenly.

He leant out of the car window, straining to look back as the car gradually wallowed to a halt. In the distance the dim shape of a road sign was silhouetted in the moonlight.

"Can you reverse back down the road?" said Dirk urgently.

"It's a freeway," protested Joe.

"Yes, yes," said Dirk. "There's no one behind us. The road's empty. Only a few hundred yards."

Grumbling to himself, Joe put the big barge into reverse, and slowly they weaved their way back down the freeway.

"This is what they do in New Zealand, isn't it?" he whined.

"What?"

"Drive backwards."

"No," said Dirk. "But I know what you're thinking of. Just like us British, they do drive on the other side of the road."

"Suppose it's safer that way," said Joe, "if everyone's driving backwards."

"Yes," said Dirk. "Much safer." He leaped out of the car as soon as it drew to a halt.

Highlighted in the pool of the car's lights, five thousand miles from Dirk's ramshackle office in Clerkenwell, was a square yellow road sign that said, in large letters, GUSTY WINDS, and, in smaller letters underneath it, MAY EXIST. The moon hung high in the sky above it.

"Joe!" shouted Dirk to the driver. "Who put this here?"

"What?" said Joe.

"This sign!" said Dirk.

"You mean this sign?" said Joe.

"Yes!" shouted Dirk. " 'Gusty Winds May Exist.' "

"Well, I suppose," said Joe, "the State Highway Authority."

"What?" said Dirk, bewildered again.

"The State Highway Authority," said Joe, a bit flummoxed. "You see 'em all over."

" 'Gusty Winds May Exist'?" said Dirk. "You mean this is just a regular road sign?"

"Well, yeah," said Joe. "Just means it's a bit windy here. You know, wind comes across the desert. Can blow you around a bit. Especially in one of these."

Dirk blinked. He suddenly felt rather foolish. He had been imagining, a little wildly, that someone had specially painted the name of a bisected cat on a signpost on a New Mexican road especially for his benefit. This was absurd. The cat in question had obviously been named after a perfectly common-place American road sign. Paranoia, he reminded himself, was one of the normal by-products of jet lag and whisky.

Chastened, he walked back toward the car. Then he paused and thought for a second. He went up to Joe's window and peered in.

"Joe," he said. "You slowed the car down just as we were approaching the sign. Was that deliberately so that I would see it?" He hoped it wasn't just the whisky and the jet lag talking.

"Oh no," said Joe. "I was slowing down for the rhinoceros."

Chapter 11

"PROBABLY THE JET LAG," Dirk said. "I thought for a moment you said a rhinoceros."

"Yeah," said Joe, disgustedly. "Got held up by it earlier. As it was leaving the airport."

Dirk tried to think this through before he said anything that might expose him to ridicule. Presumably there must be a local football team or rock band called the Rhinoceroses. Must be. Coming from the airport? Driving to Santa Fe? He was going to have to ask.

"What exact type of rhinoceros are we discussing here?" he said.

"Dunno. I'm not as good at breeds of rhinoceros," said Joe, "as I am at accents. If it was an accent, I could tell you what exact type it was, but since it's a rhinoceros I can only tell you that it's one of the big grey type, you know, with the horn. From Irkutsk or one of those kinda places. You know, Portugal or somewhere."

"You mean Africa?"

"Could be Africa."

"And you say it's up there on the road ahead of us?"

"Yup."

"Then let's get after it," said Dirk. "Quickly."

He climbed back into the car, and Joe eased it out onto the highway once more. Dirk hunched himself up at the front of the passenger compartment and peered over Joe's shoulder as they sped on through the desert. In a few minutes the shape of a large truck loomed up ahead in the Cadillac's headlights. It was a green low-loader with a large, slatted crate roped down on to it.

"So. You're pretty interested in rhinoceroses, then," said Joe conversationally.

"Not especially," said Dirk. "Not till I read my horoscope this morning."

"That right? Don't believe in them myself. You know what mine said this morning? It said that I should think long and hard about my personal and financial prospects. Pretty much what it said yesterday. 'Course, that's pretty much what I do every day, just driving around. So I suppose that means something, then. What did yours say?"

"That I would meet a three-ton rhinoceros called Desmond."

"I guess you can see a different bunch of stars from New Zealand," said Joe.

"It's a replacement. That's what I heard," volunteered Joe.

"A replacement?"

"Yup."

"A replacement for what?"

"Previous rhinoceros."

"Well, I suppose it would hardly be a replacement for a lightbulb?" said Dirk. "Tell me—what happened to the, er, previous rhinoceros?"

"Died."

"What a tragedy. Where? At the zoo?"

"At a party."

"A party?"

"Yup."

Dirk sucked his lip thoughtfully. There was a principle he liked to adhere to when he remembered, which was never to ask a question unless he was fairly certain he would like the answer. He sucked his other lip.

"I think I'll go and take a look myself," he said, and climbed out of the car.

The large, dark green truck was pulled onto the side of the road. The sides of the truck were about four feet high, and a heavy tarpaulin was roped down over an enormous crate. The driver was leaning against the door of the cab, smoking a cigarette. He clearly thought that being in charge of a three-ton rhinoceros meant that no one would argue with him about this, but he was wrong. The most astonishing amount of abuse was being hurled at him by the drivers negotiating their way one by one past his truck.

"Bastards!" muttered the driver to himself as Dirk wandered up to him in a nonchalant kind of way and lit a companionable cigarette himself. He was trying to give it up, but usually kept a pack in his pocket for tactical purposes.

"You know what I hate?" said Dirk to the truckdriver. "Those signs in cabs that say 'Thank You for Not Smoking.' I don't mind if they say 'Please Don't Smoke,' or even just a straightforward 'No Smoking.' But I hate those prim 'Thank You for Not Smoking' signs. Make you want to light up immediately and say, 'No need to thank me, I wasn't going to not smoke.'"

The driver laughed.

"Taking this old bugger far?" asked Dirk, with the air of one seasoned rhinoceros delivery driver comparing notes with another. He gave the truck an appraising glance.

"Just out to Malibu," said the driver. "Way up Topanga Canyon."

Dirk gave a knowing cluck as if to say, "Don't talk to me about Topanga Canyon, I once had to take a whole herd of wildebeest to Cardiff in a minibus. You want trouble? That was trouble." He sucked deeply on his cigarette.

"Must have been some party," he remarked.

"Party?" said the driver.

"I've always found that a rhinoceros makes a pretty poor kind of party guest," said Dirk. "Try it if you must, but brace yourself." It was Dirk's view that asking direct questions made people wary. It was more effective to talk complete nonsense and let people correct him.

"What do you mean, 'party'?" said the driver.

"The party the other rhinoceros was attending," said Dirk, tapping the side of his nose, "when it died."

"Attending?" said the driver with a frown. "I wouldn't say that it was actually attending the party."

Dirk raised an encouraging eyebrow.

"It charged down out of the hills, smashed through the perimeter fence, crashed through the plate-glass windows into the house, took a couple of turns around the main room injuring about seventeen people, hurtled back out into the garden where somebody shot it, whereupon it toppled slowly into a swimming pool full of mostly naked screenwriters, taking half a hundredweight of avocado dip and some kind of Polynesian fruit melange with it."

Dirk took a moment or two to digest this information. Then, "Whose house was this?" he said.

"Just some movie people. Apparently they'd had Bruce Willis round only the previous week. Now this."

"Seems a bit rough on the old rhino as well," said Dirk. "And now here's another one."

Excerpts from an Interview with the Daily Nexus, April 5, 2000

How does Douglas Adams arrive for coffee? If he were like the Montecitans stopping by Pierre Lafond's, he would show up in an SUV, a luxury car, or a luxury SUV. The basic cup of coffee at Pierre Lafond's costs $1.25 and is called "organic French roast." It tastes exactly like McDonald's coffee or organic crankcase fluid, not that the drivers of SUVs seem to care.

I expected more from Adams than an SUV. I wanted to see him skip out of a spaceship, materialize, or even just walk. This is a guy who wrote *The Hitchhiker's Guide to the Galaxy* and has managed to make life, the universe and everything much more entertaining. So, I wondered, how would he arrive?

Black Mercedes.

Adams is six feet five inches tall, with intensely round eyes. He hadn't had a good day. His daughter was sick, and the croissant he was eating at 5:00 P.M. was lunch. Life hasn't been bad for the forty-nine-year-old Adams, though. He travels the world, his nine books have sold over 15 million copies, and the oft-delayed *Hitchhiker's* movie is now being produced by Disney and has the director of *Austin Powers* signed on.

"The perennial movie, which has been about to be made for about twenty years and is even more about to be made now," Adams said. "But we shall see. I wish I had never thought of doing it as a movie. I'd have about ten years of my life back.

For the first time in over a decade, Adams is working on a book.

"There was a point where I just got massively fed up with it. My books tend to use up ideas at a ferocious rate," he said. "I never intended to be a novelist to begin with. So I decided to go and do a whole bunch of other things. . . . The consequence of that is I have a huge backlog of story ideas, and now the sort of panic is, 'Can I do them all in the rest of my career, given the speed at which they're arriving at the moment?' The other panic, of course, is the perennial writer's problem of application. I think I have more fear of writing than most writers."

The new book is not a *Hitchhiker's* book—there are already five of those—or a Dirk Gently book, but "it will be recognizable in style to anyone who knows those books.

"Since then, I've now got lots and lots of different story lines waiting for me to turn them into books. One of them I shall apply the title *Salmon of Doubt* to, but I don't know which one yet."

In 1990, Adams, with zoologist Mark Carwardine, wrote *Last Chance to See*. It's one of his hardest books to find, and his favorite. When Adams—who has lived in Santa Barbara for the last two years—speaks today at UCSB, it's the book he'll talk about.

"I do talks around most of the rest of the country," Adams said. "So I was very keen to do one here, just to sort of say, 'Hi, here I am.'"

Adams gives a lot of speeches, usually about high technology to large companies.

"I actually much prefer doing this particular one, which I only ever usually get to do at colleges because it's funny, but big corporations don't particularly like to hear about protecting endangered wildlife," he said. "You lose a lot of money to endangered wildlife."

Last Chance to See started as a magazine article for the World Wildlife Fund. The group sent Adams to Madagascar, where he met Carwardine. Adams wrote about the aye-aye, an endangered species of nocturnal lemur that looks like a cross between a bat, a monkey, and a very surprised infant.

"At the time, it was thought that there were only about fifteen. They've found a few more so it's not quite so endangered, just very, very, very endangered," Adams said. "The whole thing was completely magical."

So magical that Adams and Carwardine spent the next year traveling the world and seeing endangered animals, like flightless kakapo parrots in New Zealand and baiji river dolphins in China. The last twenty dolphins will become extinct when the Chinese government completes the Three Gorges Dam and destroys the dolphins' habitat.

"It's a desperate thing, not only because another species is lost and the tragedy of that, but because I don't know why we keep building these fucking dams," Adams said in a surprisingly forceful British whisper. "Not only do they cause environmental and social disasters, they, with very few exceptions, all fail to do what they were supposed to do in the first place. Look at the Amazon, where they've all silted up. What is the reaction to that? They're going to build another eighty of them. It's just balmy. We must have beaver genes or something. . . . There's just this kind of sensational desire to build dams, and maybe that should be looked at and excised from human nature. Maybe the Human Genome Project can locate the beaver/dam-building gene and cut that out."

In *The Hitchhiker's Guide to the Galaxy,* intergalactic bulldozers destroyed the Earth and humanity. A very different sort of bulldozer destroyed the most successful species the planet had ever known. Sixty-five million years ago, a six-mile-wide asteroid slammed into the Yucatán peninsula, created a one-hundred-mile crater, and sent a cloud of searing vapor and dust into the air. That was pretty much it for the dinosaurs.

"I'm rather obsessed with the idea of that comet coming down and it being the single event to which we owe our very existence," Adams said. "It is arguably the single most dramatic thing to have ever occurred in the world and certainly the one that was the most dramatic event in our lives, in that it paved the way for our existence, and no one was there to see it."

Dinosaur-killing rocks are classic physics. The newer physics is a little too outlandish for Adams, a man who wrote that the answer to Life, the Universe and Everything is 42. A computer came up with that answer, and Adams said computers will change everything.

"Now that we've built computers, first we made them room-size, then desk-size and in briefcases and in pockets, soon they'll be as plentiful as dust—you can sprinkle computers all over the place. Gradually, the whole environment will become something far more responsive and smart, and we'll be living in a way that's very hard for people living on the planet just now to understand," Adams said. "I guess my six-year-old daughter will get a much better handle on it."

Adams has done a bit of everything, from radio to television to designing computer games. Not all of them worked out.

"These are life's little learning experiences," he said. "You know what a learning experience is? A learning experience is one of those things that says, 'You know that thing you just did? Don't do that.'

"At the end of all this being-determined-to-be-a-jack-of-all-trades, I think I'm better off just sitting down and putting a hundred thousand words in a cunning order."

Adams writes "slowly and painfully."

"People assume you sit in a room, looking pensive and writing great thoughts," he said. "But you mostly sit in a room looking panic-stricken and hoping they haven't put a guard on the door yet."

Adams will probably be writing for the next few years, before his daughter grows up.

"I think what I'll do, because there has been talk about me doing a big TV documentary series, is that I'll wait until her hormones kick in, and then I shall go off like a shot," he said. "I think when she's about thirteen I'll go off and do a big documentary series and come back when she's become civilized."

The interview ended when Adams's cell phone rang from inside his pocket. In the other pocket there was a little bit of padded cotton, red trimmed with a giraffe on it. It looked like it belonged to his daughter. His wife and daughter were supposed to have flown to London that night, but his daughter came down with an ear infection. "A serious one, actually."

It was time for Adams to climb into his black Mercedes to go home and see her.

And so he did.

Interview conducted by Brendan Buhler,
Artsweek

Epilogue

A LAMENT FOR Douglas Adams, best known as author of *The Hitchhiker's Guide to the Galaxy*, who died on Saturday, aged forty-nine, from a heart attack.

This is not an obituary; there'll be time enough for them. It is not a tribute, not a considered assessment of a brilliant life, not a eulogy. It is a keening lament, written too soon to be balanced, too soon to be carefully thought through. Douglas, you cannot be dead.

A sunny Friday morning in May, ten past seven, shuffle out of bed, log in to e-mail as usual. The usual blue bold headings drop into place, mostly junk, some expected, and my gaze absently follows them down the page. The name Douglas Adams catches my eye and I smile. That one, at least, will be good for a laugh. Then I do the classic double-take, back up the screen.

What did that heading actually say? Douglas Adams died of a heart attack a few hours ago. Then that other cliché, the words swelling before my eyes.

It must be part of the joke. It must be some other Douglas Adams. This is too ridiculous to be true. I must still be asleep. I open the message, from a well-known German software designer. It is no joke, I am fully awake. And it is the right—or rather the wrong—Douglas Adams. A sudden heart attack, in the gym in Santa Barbara. "Man, man, man, man oh man," the message concludes. Man indeed, what a man. A giant of a man, surely nearer seven foot than six, broad-shouldered, and he did

* 289 *

not stoop like some very tall men who feel uncomfortable with their height. But nor did he swagger with the macho assertiveness that can be intimidating in a big man. He neither apologised for his height, nor flaunted it. It was part of the joke against himself.

One of the great wits of our age, his sophisticated humour was founded in a deep, amalgamated knowledge of literature and science, two of my great loves. And he introduced me to my wife—at his fortieth birthday party.

He was exactly her age, they had worked together on *Dr. Who*. Should I tell her now, or let her sleep a bit longer before shattering her day? He initiated our togetherness and was a recurrently important part of it. I must tell her now.

Douglas and I met because I sent him an unsolicited fan letter—I think it is the only time I have ever written one. I had adored *The Hitchhiker's Guide to the Galaxy*. Then I read *Dirk Gently's Holistic Detective Agency*.

As soon as I finished it, I turned back to page one and read it straight through again—the only time I have ever done that, and I wrote to tell him so. He replied that he was a fan of my books, and he invited me to his house in London. I have seldom met a more congenial spirit. Obviously I knew he would be funny. What I didn't know was how deeply read he was in science. I should have guessed, for you can't understand many of the jokes in *Hitchhiker* if you don't know a lot of advanced science. And in modern electronic technology he was a real expert. We talked science a lot, in private, and even in public at literary festivals and on the wireless or television. And he became my guru on all technical problems. Rather than struggle with some ill-written and incomprehensible manual in Pacific Rim English, I would fire off an e-mail to Douglas. He would reply, often within minutes, whether in London or Santa Barbara, or some hotel room anywhere in the world. Unlike most staff of professional helplines, Douglas understood exactly my problem, knew exactly why it was troubling me, and always had the solution ready, lucidly and amusingly explained. Our frequent e-mail exchanges brimmed with literary and scientific jokes and affectionately sardonic little asides. His technophilia shone through, but so did his rich sense of the absurd. The whole world was one big Monty Python sketch, and the follies of humanity were as comic in the world's silicon valleys as anywhere else.

He laughed at himself with equal good humour. At, for example, his epic bouts of writer's block ("I love deadlines. I love the whooshing noise they make as they go by") when, according to legend, his publisher and book agent would lock him in a hotel room, with no telephone and nothing to do but write, releasing him only for supervised walks. If his enthusiasm ran away with him and he advanced a biological theory too eccentric for my professional scepticism to let pass, his mien at my dismissal of it would always be more humorously self-mocking than genuinely crestfallen. And he would have another go.

He laughed at his own jokes, which good comedians are supposed not to, but he did it with such charm that the jokes became even funnier. He was gently able to poke fun without wounding, and it would be aimed not at individuals but at their absurd ideas. To illustrate the vain conceit that the universe must be somehow preordained for us, because we are so well suited to live in it, he mimed a wonderfully funny imitation of a puddle of water, fitting itself snugly into a depression in the ground, the depression uncannily being exactly the same shape as the puddle. Or there's this parable, which he told with huge enjoyment, whose moral leaps out with no further explanation. A man didn't understand how televisions work, and was convinced that there must be lots of little men inside the box, manipulating images at high speed. An engineer explained about high-frequency modulations of the electromagnetic spectrum, transmitters and receivers, amplifiers and cathode ray tubes, scan lines moving across and down a phosphorescent screen. The man listened to the engineer with careful attention, nodding his head at every step of the argument. At the end he pronounced himself satisfied. He really did now understand how televisions work. "But I expect there are just a few little men in there, aren't there?"

Science has lost a friend, literature has lost a luminary, the mountain gorilla and the black rhino have lost a gallant defender (he once climbed Kilimanjaro in a rhino suit to raise money to fight the cretinous trade in rhino horn), Apple Computers has lost its most eloquent apologist. And I have lost an irreplaceable intellectual companion and one of the kindest and funniest men I ever met. The day Douglas died, I officially received a happy piece of news, which would have delighted him. I wasn't allowed to tell anyone during the weeks I have secretly known about it, and now that I am allowed to, it is too late.

The sun is shining, life must go on, seize the day and all those clichés.

We shall plant a tree this very day: a Douglas fir, tall, upright, evergreen. It is the wrong time of year, but we'll give it our best shot.

Off to the arboretum.

Richard Dawkins, in *The Guardian,*
MAY 14, 2001
(Richard Dawkins is Charles Simonyi
Professor of the Public Understanding
of Science at Oxford University.)

Douglas Noel Adams
1952–2001

The Order of Service for His Memorial

Schübler Chorales—J. S. Bach

Shepherd's Farewell, from *The Childhood of Christ*
—Hector Berlioz

Welcome to the Church by Reverend Antony Hurst,
on behalf of St. Martin-in-the-Fields

Introduction and opening prayer by Stephen Coles

JONNY BROCK

Three Kings from Persian Lands—Peter Cornelius

ED VICTOR

Mine eyes have seen the glory of the coming of the Lord—
Traditional American melody & words by Julia Ward Howe

MARK CARWARDINE

Gone Dancing—Robbie McIntosh

Te Fovemus—The Chameleon Arts Chorus (by P. Wickens)

JAMES THRIFT, SUE ADAMS, JANE GARNIER

Rockstar—Margo Buchanan

Prayers of Thanksgiving by Stephen Coles

Holding On—Gary Brooker

Wish You Were Here—David Gilmour

RICHARD DAWKINS

For the beauty of the earth—Music by Conrad Kocher &
words by Folliott S. Pierpoint

ROBBIE STAMP

Vergnügte Ruh, beliebte Seelenlust from *Cantata No 170*
—J. S. Bach

Aria

Contented rest, beloved heart's desire,
You are not found in the sins of hell,
But only in heavenly concord;
You alone fortify the feeble heart.
Contented rest, beloved heart's desire,
Therefore none but the gifts of virtue
Shall have their abode in my heart.

SIMON JONES

For all the Saints who from their labours rest—
Music by R. Vaughan Williams & words by William W. How

BLESSING BY REVEREND ANTONY HURST

Organ Music by J. S. Bach:

Fantasia in G

Prelude and Fugue in C

Italian Concerto

Editor's Acknowledgments

To Douglas, without whom all of us would not be sharing the bounteous pleasures of these pages; I miss you;

To Jane Belson, Douglas's beloved wife; her belief in and support for this book provide the foundation on which it rests;

To Ed Victor, Douglas's long-time agent and trusted friend, whose commitment to this undertaking cleared away every obstacle;

To Sophie Astin, Douglas's invaluable assistant, whose intelligence, devotion, and first-hand contribution to these pages proved essential;

To Chris Ogle, Douglas's close friend, whose computer skills and knowledge of Douglas's thought processes, passwords, and what could very kindly be called Douglas's filing system, enabled Chris to assemble a master disk of all Douglas's work, without which this book would not exist;

To Robbie Stamp, Douglas's good friend and business colleague, who reminded me that Douglas had already created the structure for this book;

To Shaye Areheart and Linda Loewenthal of Harmony Books, who first brought me into this project, and to Bruce Harris,

Chip Gibson, Andrew Martin, Hilary Bass, and Tina Constable, who published and loved Douglas; to Peter Strauss and Nicky Hursell in the UK, for their valuable editorial suggestions;

To Mike J. Simpson, former president of ZZ9, Douglas Adams's official fan club, whose generosity and encyclopedic knowledge of Douglas's life and work was an invaluable resource;

To Patrick Hunnicutt, who assisted my efforts in Chapel Hill, North Carolina, and to Lizzy Kremer, Maggie Philips, and Linda Van in Ed Victor's office;

To the various publications, writers, and friends of Douglas who so generously gave access and permission to use their work as it related to his;

To Isabel, my partner in life;

To my sons, Sam and William, who, as new generations tend to do, devoured Douglas's books;

To all of Douglas's readers: as you know, the love went (and still goes) both ways.

For more information on Douglas Adams and his creations, please visit www.douglasadams.com, the official website.

You may wish to join ZZ9 Plural Z Alpha, the official *Hitchhiker's Guide to the Galaxy* Appreciation Society, founded in 1980. For details of this fan-run club, visit www.zz9.org.

Douglas Adams was a patron of the following two charities: Dian Fossey Gorilla Fund (www.gorillas.org), and Save the Rhino International (www.savetherhino.org).

And don't miss

WISH YOU WERE HERE

The Official Biography of Douglas Adams

BY NICK WEBB

Douglas Adams made the universe a much funnier place to inhabit and forever changed the way we think about towels, extraterrestrial poetry, and especially the number 42 in The Hitchhiker's Guide to the Galaxy series. And then, too soon, he was gone.

Just who was this impossibly tall Englishman? Written by a longtime friend of the author, this official biography is a revealing, cosmic ride through the unique and winsome world of Douglas Adams.

Includes 16 pages of exclusive photos.

"Webb's tale brims with affection and humour; every page is a delight."
—*The Daily Mail* (U.K.)

Published by Ballantine Books
Available wherever books are sold
www.ballantinebooks.com